TWISTED
SECRETS

BASTARDS OF BOULDER COVE: *BOOK THREE*

USA TODAY BESTSELLING AUTHOR
RACHEL LEIGH

"The best way of keeping a secret is to pretend there isn't one."
- Margaret Atwood

TWISTED SECRETS IS THE THIRD, AND FINAL, BOOK IN THE BASTARDS OF BOULDER COVE SERIES. IT IS HIGHLY RECOMMENDED TO READ SAVAGE GAMES & VICIOUS LIES FIRST.

THIS IS A WHY-CHOOSE ROMANCE WHERE THE MAIN CHARACTER GAINS MULTIPLE LOVE INTERESTS OVER THE COURSE OF THREE BOOKS. PLEASE ADVISE THIS IS A DARK ROMANCE WITH BULLY ELEMENTS.

ISBN: 978-1-956764-20-8

For permissions contact: rachelleighauthor@gmail.com

Cover Design by The Pretty Little Design Co.

Editing by Fairest Reviews and Editing Services

Proofreading by Rumi Khan

www.rachelleighauthor.com

PLAYLIST

LISTEN ON SPOTIFY

SECRETS BY ONE REPUBLIC

VOODOO BY TWISTED INSANE

FINGERS CROSSED BY LAUREN SPENCER SMITH

THE SPACE BETWEEN BY DAVE MATTHEWS BAND

KEEP YOUR HEAD UP PRINCESS BY ANSON SEABRA

MY OWN PRISON BY CREED

FOR YOU BY STAIND

THE RED BY CHENILLE

DRIFT AND DIE BY PUDDLE OF MUD

FINE AGAIN BY SEETHER

KEEP AWAY BY GODSMACK

MUDSHOVEL BY STAIND

EPIPHANY BY STAIND

FALL TO PIECES BY VELVET REVOLVER

DRIVEN UNDER BY SEETHER

RIGHT HERE BY STAIND

SEND THE PAIN BELOW BY CHENILLE

EASY ON ME BY ADELE

STUPID FACE BY ABE PARKER

STUCK IN MY HEAD BY BLU EYES

DROPS OF JUPITER BY TRAIN

What Other People Say by Sam Fischer, Demi Lovato
Bother by Stone Sour
Neurotic by Three Days Grace
Broken by Lifehouse
Bittersweet by Fuel
Forever by Papa Roach
CHECK OUT THE PINTEREST BOARD

.

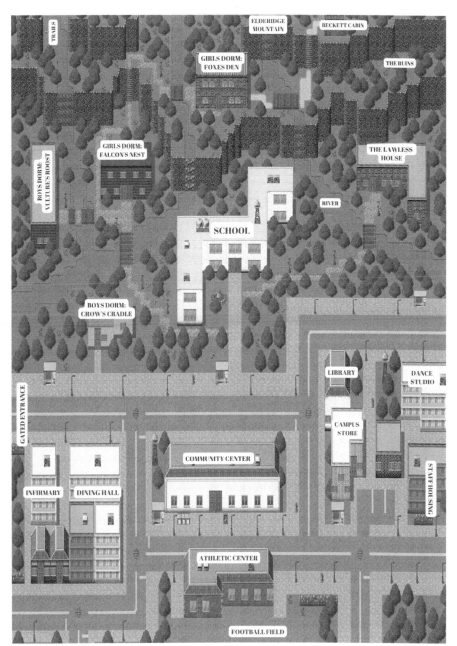

Bastards of Boulder Cove Glossary

BCA: Boulder Cove Academy

BCU: Boulder Cove University

Chapters: Groups within The Blue Bloods Secret Society

The Gathering: Student gathering to inform, promote ranks, and celebrate achievements

Ceremony: An occasion held where ranks are promoted, or demoted

The Ruins: Area of the BCA Property where social events are held

The Tunnels: An underground passage that runs beneath BCA property

Eldridge Mountain: Highest point in Boulder Cove

The Elders: Members of age who have advanced knowledge of The Society, typically the predecessors of current BCA students

The President: Oversee The Society as a whole

The Chairman: Oversee an individual chapter

The Lawless: Oversee the students at BCA

Ladder of Hierarchy: A system in which students are ranked according to their level of authority.

Rook: Lowest rank in the ladder of hierarchy

Punk: Middle rank in the ladder of hierarchy

Ace: Top rank in the ladder of hierarchy

The Ladder Games: Games to achieve rank

The Lawless House: Where The Lawless members live

The Square: Small gathering area in front of the academy's main buildings

Foxes Den: Girl's dormitory

Falcon's Nest: Girl's dormitory

Vulture's Roost: Boy's dormitory

Crow's Cradle: Boy's dormitory

The Guardian: Watchman and protector of society members

Initiation: An act of admittance as a leading member that takes place after graduating BCA, after which secrets of The Society are then revealed

PROLOGUE
NEO

Twelve Years Old

"Quit it, you jerk!" Scar bellows as I tighten my grip on her ponytail.

Crew and Jagger ignore the commotion, too caught up in their game of Minecraft.

"Leave her alone," Maddie hisses, grabbing my arm and trying to break my hold on Scar's hair.

"I told her to never come in my room again. So why'd you bring her in here?"

"Because she's my best friend and so are you, so will you please stop being so mean?"

"Choose, Maddie." I tip my chin. "Me or her? Choose now."

I don't let go of Scar's hair as I wait for an answer. She twists her head to the side, attempting to pry my fingers from her ponytail.

"I'm not choosing!"

"Then I'm not letting go. Me or her?" I'm dead serious. I

1

want Scar to hear Maddie say that she chooses me. Maybe then she'll leave and never come to this house, or my room, again.

"Her. I choose her because, right now, you're being a bully and I don't like bullies."

Her words are like a knife straight into my back. Maddie and I have always been really close. We do everything together, but lately, she's been bringing *this girl* around more and more. Scar never used to come over this much. We'd only see her, and occasionally play with her, at meetings. Now she's here all the time, and I hate it.

"You're lying."

Maddie steps closer to where I'm still holding Scar's ponytail. She grabs my hand, assisting Scar in untangling my fingers. She grabs my middle finger and bends it back. "Am I?" Her eyes hold a sinister glow to them. Something evil I've never seen before.

Finally, I let go. Not because Maddie was hurting me or because I was worried she'd break my finger, but because I've never seen her so serious before. Maybe she wasn't lying. She would choose Scar, and I can never allow that to happen.

"What in the world is going on here?" Mom asks as she enters my bedroom.

I look at Maddie, wondering if she'll rat me out.

"Neo won't let us come in and play video games, and he pulled Scar's hair."

"*Neopolo Saint!*" Mom crosses her arms over the chest of her white-knitted sweater. "You better not have pulled this sweet girl's hair."

Maddie continues to fuel the fire while smirking at me.

"He did. And then he made me choose between him and her."

What has Scar done to my sister?

The next thing I know, Dad's walking in, all stern and serious like he always is. *Great. A family reunion.*

"What happened?" he asks, staring at my mom like she did something wrong.

"Your son pulled Scarlett's hair."

"Wow. Thanks, Mom."

Everyone in this stupid family is turning on me today.

"Why?" he deadpans, now looking at me.

"'Cause she's in my room and I don't want her in here."

My dad looks at my mom, then Scar. "It's his room. If he doesn't want you in here, then leave."

Scar's eyes widen and I swear she's gonna cry. I hope she does. It would be funny as hell.

"Sebastian," Mom bellows. "Be nice."

Dad's shoulders shrug. "Neo doesn't need girls in his room when he's hanging out with his friends. They're not toddlers anymore. We can't force them to play together."

"Thanks, Dad."

"Don't thank me." He looks at Maddie. "You and your friend go play somewhere else."

It's so weird to me that he doesn't often call Scar by her actual name. It's always, *that girl* or *your friend*.

Not that I care, she is just *that girl*.

Maddie and Scar go out, leaving me with my mom and dad, while Crew and Jagger shut us all out and continue playing their game of Minecraft.

"Fun's over. You need to do your schoolwork." My dad crosses my room, positioning himself directly in front of the television.

I look at Crew and Jagger, who have paused their video game.

"That's not fair, Dad. Maddie has her friend here."

"Your sister isn't my problem. She's your mom's."

I look at Mom, hoping this time she'll be the one to jump to my defense. Instead, she hangs her head low, like she's embarrassed or doesn't want to speak up. Probably worried he'll yell at her or something. He's always yelling at everyone.

"You are my son," he continues, "and you will do what I say." He points his finger over my shoulder. "Get to your desk and I better see schoolbooks open when I come back to check on you."

The guys and I share a look before they quietly set their controllers down on the floor in front of them. "See ya at school tomorrow," Crew clips, before he and Jagger both stand up and head for the door.

"This isn't fair, Dad."

"Life isn't fair."

"Just because Maddie's a girl, she gets to have all the fun."

"You and Maddie are headed down two different paths. You did the right thing kicking that girl outta here. The more luxuries we give her, the more comfortable she'll be. But don't fucking pull her hair again, understood?"

For some reason, my dad doesn't like Scar. He's always made that clear to her. Yet, she continues to come around. She's stubborn and tough. Except when I get a good hold on her hair. That's her weak spot, and I use it to my advantage.

"Yes, sir," I tell him, before going to my desk to get started on my schoolwork like he demanded.

Dad leaves and Mom walks over to where I'm sitting.

Her hand rests on my shoulder and she keeps her tone low. "It's okay to make Scarlett feel comfortable, Neopolo." Mom's the only one who can call me by my given name and get away with it. Oddly enough, I sort of like it when she does—but only her. No one else can call me that.

"But Dad said—"

"Your father says a lot of things. If you want to be nice to her, be nice to her. She's your twin sister's best friend and I think it would make Maddie really happy if you two got along."

I spin around in my chair, and Mom drops her hand from my shoulder. "That's the thing, Mom. I don't want to be nice to her. Dad told me some really bad things about the Sunders and I don't think anyone should be nice to her."

"He did, did he?"

I nod.

"Well," she leans closer, "I think your dad just wants the best for you, but the only one who knows what that is, is you."

"I think it's best if she just disappears."

Mom tilts her head to the side and her eyebrows bunch together. "Why is that?"

"Because she's a snake and snakes bite."

Her hand lands back on my shoulder. "Only the bad ones bite, and I promise you, Neopolo, Scar's not one of the bad ones." She squeezes my shoulder gently, before leaning down and kissing my cheek.

Doesn't matter—a snake is still a snake.

Before standing back up, Mom whispers, "Ya know. Sometimes when a boy is mean to a girl, it means he has a crush on her."

I cringe, pulling away. "Ew, Mom. I could never have a crush on Scar."

"Maybe not now. But someday, you might realize you did all along."

CHAPTER
ONE
SCAR

"Dead!" My head shakes in rapid movements, making me feel dizzy. "This can't be!" Everyone speaks at once, but I don't process the words hitting my ears. My knees knock as I shiver under the dim lamppost.

Riley holds up the paper, her eyes wide with terror. "Someone please explain this to me, and fast." She laughs, but the sound is completely void of any humor. "Elias Stanton is expecting me to return to the dance any minute, so I need to know how the fuck I'm holding his death certificate, from two decades ago, in my hand."

I hold on to Crew's arm, trying to stop my body from shaking, but I'm unable to mask the crack in my voice. "Riley and I trusted that guy. Who the hell is he?"

"My guess," Neo pipes up, his hands stuffed in the front pockets of his black denim jeans. "That's Jeremy Beckett and Kenna Mitchell's son." He looks Riley dead in the eye. "You've been fucking Jude Beckett."

Constant shivers skate down my spine, as goosebumps

prick every inch of my skin. When my eyes lift to Crew's, I follow his gaze over my shoulder.

He curls his lip in a snarl, his fists clenched at his sides. "Think fast, fuckers. Ready or not. Here he comes."

"Play it cool," Jagger says, patting Crew on the shoulder and stepping through our circle. He passes by me and walks straight for Elias—or whoever the fuck he is.

Riley whispers, "I don't think I can." I pull her close until our sides are connected, and my arm is wrapped around her shoulders.

"Thought we made it clear you're to stay away from our girl," Jagger sneers at Elias.

"Just coming for my date," Elias retorts, his eyes on Riley. She doesn't look at him, just curls under my arm, while fighting back tears.

"It's okay, babe," I tell her. "This fucking sucks, but it's the beginning of the end. Now we know."

All the tears she was holding back spill out violently. I wrap both arms around her, shielding her face from Elias. Her sobbing breaths are warm and damp as she cries into the sleeve of my dress.

"She's sad her final cheer season is over." I raise my voice to Elias. "Just needs some time."

Crew walks past us, joining Jagger, who's now spitting venomous words at Elias. He slaps a hand on Elias's shoulder, steering him back toward the building. "Riley and Scar need a minute alone. She'll find you when she's ready to see you."

Elias sputters and shuffles his feet, but he eventually leaves, like he's been told to do by two of the three Lawless members. Lifting my eyes, I catch Neo's, who's still standing here for reasons unbeknownst to me. He doesn't say anything, just stands with stiff arms and his hands in his pockets. His expression is blank and his olive eyes appear dark and focused as they rest on mine.

"You can go," I tell him, hoping he accepts the invitation to leave.

He bites on his bottom lip, eyebrows knitted together. "Can't leave you alone, so until you two finish this dramatic crying sesh, I'll be right here watching. Just wish I had some popcorn for the show."

It's just like him to downplay the situation. Riley and I just found out a guy we trusted isn't who he says he is. Not only that, he's potentially dangerous and likely unhinged. Yet, Neo is treating this information like it's no big deal—just another day at the Academy in his eyes.

"Fuck off," I grumble, combing my fingers through Riley's hair. I'm not usually the consoling type. Don't really do well when it comes to other people's emotions, or my own, but Riley is sensitive and trusting and her heart was just broken. For her, I'm sucking it up, and I'll let her cry as long as she needs to, even with Neo watching and tapping the toe of his shoe impatiently on the concrete sidewalk.

"Wish I could, Scar. Wish I could. But rules are rules and now more than ever, we need to abide by them."

It's true that one of the rules for me moving into the Lawless house under the guy's protection is that I'm not out alone, but Crew made that rule to keep me close. Jagger abided by it because he also wanted to keep me close. But, Neo? He'd love nothing more than to stay as far away from me as possible, so he's not making a lick of sense right now.

"Since when do you give a damn about rules? Especially ones that you didn't make?"

He pulls one hand from his pocket, a piece of gum

pinched between his fingers. His eyes narrow as he pulls out his other hand and slowly unravels the wrapper. "Since things just got interesting." He pops the gum in his mouth and balls the wrapper until it's almost nonexistent.

Riley lets go, her cheeks stained with tears that have streaked her heavy foundation. Her eyes are painted with smears of mascara, and one look shows that her black tears have made a wet circle on my dress.

I glower back at Neo, who raises his hand with the balled-up wrapper. He flicks it away, grinning. "Are we done here?"

Growling, I roll my eyes, take Riley's hand, and walk back to the dance. "What are we gonna do about this?" I ask Riley, leaving our next move up to the Guardian of this place.

"Girls' bathroom. Stat."

I'm thankful for that response because she needs a mirror and a napkin before she faces the crowd.

The annoying sound of Neo's boots smacking against the pavement rings in my ears, and when it comes closer and even closer, I know he's hot on our trail.

It's no surprise when he follows us down the hall in the opposite direction of the dance. Riley and I enter the girls' bathroom, and Neo follows. I stop in the doorway while Riley continues inside. My hands brace on either side of the open frame, pressing firmly against the white-painted brick. "You can't come in here."

Neo slaps my arm down and steps past me. "Try and stop me."

"Neo!" I shout, unsure why I'm even bothering. Neo does whatever the fuck he wants.

I round the corner and spot Riley with her hands pressed

to the freestanding porcelain sink. Her head is hung low and her blonde curls cascade around her face. "Ry," I say, placing a hand on her shoulder, while ignoring Neo's unwanted presence behind me. I lift my eyes, looking into the mirror, and see him with his foot kicked up on the wall. He's wearing a shit-eating grin that says, *knew you couldn't stop me.* In my defense, I didn't even try, so I glower back at him. This is all a game to him. He pushes my buttons for a reaction, and I'm slowly learning not to give him one—though sometimes he makes it impossible not to react to his bullshit.

I squint my eyes, my brow furrowed. *Quit staring at me.*

Neo returns my look, tilting his head slightly toward his left shoulder.

He's challenging me! God! What are we, children? Regardless, I won't lose. I won't look away first.

I curl my lip, refusing to blink. Neo is stubborn, but I am, too.

With a lift of his chin, he bites the corner of his bottom lip, and my breath shakes. The perk of this staring contest with Neo: he's fucking beautiful. Like a piece of art you pass by in a museum and can't help but backtrack to it, just to steal another glance. And once you do, you're lost in it. It's grungy with torn corners and splatters of nothing—but everything at the same time. Alluring and dark. You can't make out the story of the piece, but you know it's been to hell and back. The only difference is, Neo's been to hell, but I'm not sure he'll ever get out. He enjoys living in misery. He's comfortable there.

Riley lifts her head and my heart jumps into my throat. My cheeks flush red and it's a strange feeling. Like I've been caught doing something I shouldn't. Three solid minutes of staring right into the eyes of my adversary and for some strange reason, I want to look again.

Neo drops his foot from the wall and takes three spacious steps toward us. My chest quivers when his eyes come back to mine. Still watching me, he swoops an arm around Riley's shoulder, which is odd, considering Neo hates everyone, including Riley. "Come on, girl. Let's get you out on the dance floor."

Sniffling, Riley peers up at him. "You wanna dance?" She looks at me, as bewildered as I am.

"Fuck no," Neo chortles. "But if I have to watch the waterworks, then everyone else should be forced to watch this shitshow, too."

Riley dips out from under his arm, and before he can move, I shove my hands to his chest, pushing him to the wall he was just perched on. "You're an asshole!"

His head drops back and he stares at the ceiling in boredom. "Put me out of my misery already. If I see one more fucking tear, so help me—"

In one swift motion, I slap him hard across the face. I didn't plan to and the sting in my open palm has me wishing I hadn't.

Neo rolls his neck, jaw clenched. "Bitch!" he seethes. His fingers spiderweb and he grabs my wrist, squeezing so tight that I fear he'll snap my bone. It's not often Neo scares me, but his hold on me, paired with the wrathful look in his eyes, has my breath hitching.

How did we go from a lustful staredown to this in only a matter of minutes? *Hormones.* Those fucking bitches are always rationalizing Neo's behavior and forcing me to fall under the spell of his toxicity. As long as I think with my head, I hate him. I despise him. I fucking *loathe* him.

My heart races as Neo's fingernails claw into my skin. One glance at his face displays proof of my slap. Widespread fingers and a palm print on the left cheek. After the way he's been manhandling me, I'm not even sorry. "Let me go, jerk!" I tug my arm, trying to free it to no avail.

"You fucking slapped me, whore!"

"I'm not a whore! Dickhead!"

"You're fucking my two best friends at the same time. I think whore is the appropriate title."

"My god," Riley bellows, "would you two just fuck already and get it over with?" She storms out of the bathroom and I quickly jerk my arm from Neo's clutch.

Grazing the sore spot with my other hand, I shoot him a look of pure hate. "I'd die first." Then I leave to catch up with Riley.

As soon as I'm out of the bathroom, I hear Neo holler, "That can be arranged."

Anger ripples through me. It's moments like this that I want to slap the shit out of myself for ever entertaining thoughts of Neo being anything but my enemy.

I cup my hands around my mouth and shout to Riley, who's walking steadfastly down the hall in front of me. "Ry! Wait up."

Her head shakes rapidly, and it's my first cue that Neo pissed her off, and she's annoyed with me. As she should be. Minutes ago, we found out her boyfriend is potentially the BCA Stalker and all I did was fight with Neo when I should have been consoling her.

I pick up my pace, until I'm sprinting down the hall in my black high-top Chucks. The music blaring from the gym is so loud that I don't hear when someone jumps through the doorway, stopping me in my tracks. My body crashes into his and I steady myself by grabbing his shoulders. It takes a second for the mask to register, but once it does, I curse him. "Jesus, Crew!"

He laughs while I pull myself together. I take a deep breath in, then slap his shoulder on the exhale. "You scared the shit out of me."

"I can see that." He grabs my hand and quickly leads me down the hall. "But pull yourself together. We've got shit to do."

I follow his lead, barely able to keep up, considering my legs are on the verge of giving out. I have no idea when I became such a pussy, but I don't like this version of myself. Not even a little bit. "Where are we going?" I manage to choke out while still catching my breath.

"We have to catch Riley before she does something to raise suspicion with Elias. Jagger and I just sent Elias on a wild-goose chase until we can get Riley's emotions under control. We can't let him know we're on to him."

"What kind of wild-goose chase?"

His lips twitch with humor as we continue walking hastily down the hall. "Let's just say, Melody and her friend, the stalker, are about to be reunited."

"*What* did you do, Crew?"

"Told Melody to go fetch a keg from the Falcons' Nest and bring it to The Gathering room, and made Elias go help her."

"Wait a damn minute." I pull on his hand, halting him. We both stop walking momentarily, and I ask in a serious tone, "You still plan on having the party tonight?"

"Fuck yeah, we're having the party. It's All Hallows' Eve, and the night of the dance."

"Crew!" I say his name with emphasis. "We just found

out that a student here is pretending to be a former student who's dead! Are you insane?"

"Probably. But the party's still a go. Come on." He tugs my hand and we're walking again. "There's something we have to do first."

A heavy breath escapes me. "Do I even want to know?"

"Probably not." He picks up his pace, so I do the same. A couple of girls come out of the other doors to the gym, one dressed as a pink Power Ranger and the other as a slutty nurse. Their giggles overpower the sound of the music, and when they see us, they immediately go quiet. It's Crew's presence that silences them, not mine.

"Riley," Crew shouts, but she's still walking briskly in front of us. "Stop walking now or I'll tackle your ass!"

Finally, she slows her steps. When we catch up to her, I can see that she's on the verge of a complete meltdown. I put an arm around her, pulling her close. "I'm sorry if I was insensitive."

"Apology not accepted." She pouts with a scowl on her face. "What the hell am I supposed to do, Scar? I have no one to help me. You're too busy fighting with Neo, while Crew and Jagger are crawling up your ass. Who do I have?"

"You have me." I pull her closer, hoping she believes it. Riley is the closest thing to a best friend I've got here.

"Do I, though? Do I really?"

"Of course you do. Look," I spin her around until she's standing directly in front of me, "we're going to figure this out. I promise."

Crew taps my shoulder, cutting in. "I hate to break up this moment, but we need to go. Now."

"Go where?" Riley asks.

He nods toward the exit at the end of the hall. "Just come with us."

I'm surprised when she starts walking toward the door. Figured she'd ask more questions, but we all know answers don't come easily when it comes to the Lawless.

Crew and I are walking, hand in hand, when he asks, "So, what the fuck did Neo do to you this time?"

"Just being an ass, as usual." I shrug casually. "The guy has the sensitivity of a pencil. I'll never understand how someone can be so cold toward another human being."

"Well, when you're raised by a wolf, you behave like one."

He's referencing Neo's dad—a wolf, indeed. Sebastian is the epitome of cold and insensitive. Over the years, I've watched his demeanor, and I can't recall a single instance where I saw the man smile. It wasn't even his wife's death that detached his emotions, he's been that way for as long as I can remember. His emotional and physical abuse of his family—even if it was just a slap on the back of the head—was, no doubt, traumatizing. Especially for Neo, considering he got the majority of his father's wrath.

Crew uses his free hand to push open one of the double doors, while still holding tightly to mine. We step outside and a shiver slides down my back. "Brr. The temp feels like it's dropped ten degrees since I was out here."

"Probably has. We've got a killer snowstorm rolling in tonight."

"Please tell me that means the party will be held indoors?"

Crew quirks a brow. "Damn straight. You think I'd let my baby freeze out here?"

I curl my body closer to his, holding on to his bicep. "I'm

not sure what I'd do without you. You're always looking out for me."

He really is. I truly don't know what I'd do without Jagger or Crew. Doubt I'd even be here still, after everything that's happened. I'll never understand how I got so lucky to have these two amazing men open up their hearts and their home to me, but it still feels like a dream. A dream inside of a nightmare, but still a dream.

We all stop right in front of Crew's sled, and he turns my full body toward him. With his thumb and forefinger, he lifts my chin. "You never have to find out." His lips press to mine, warmth rushing through my body. Suddenly, I forget how cold it is outside. I forget that we're on the hunt for a crazed psycho. I forget there's a gymnasium full of students dancing in the building next to us. I forget everything else because everything I need in this moment is standing right in front of me.

"Can we go?" Riley chimes in. "It's really cold out here."

Before either of us can respond, Jagger's voice hits my ears from behind me. "Ready?"

I step out of Crew's tight hold. It's not that I don't want Jagger to see me kissing Crew or being held by him— Jagger's aware of what's going on—but I try not to flaunt my relationship with either of them in front of the other, and I think they attempt to do the same. Unless they're heated and going at it. In that case, they use me as a weapon.

"Yeah," Crew tells him, "we're ready. Where's Neo?"

I walk over to Crew's sled while Jagger comes toward us. "Said he'll meet us there." Jagger lifts a smile. "I think he's waiting for the handprint on his face to disappear before he makes an appearance."

Crew gives me a questioning look, and I bite back a smile. "He had it coming for a while."

Passing by me, Jagger presses a kiss to my cheek and grabs a handful of my ass. "That's my girl." He swings one leg over his seat and drops down, helmet in hand, extending his spare helmet toward Riley. "Ready?"

She sighs heavily, before grabbing it from him and getting on. Seconds later, they're taking off.

I look at Crew, who's handing me my helmet. "Plan on telling me where we're going?"

He gets on the sled, leaving room for me in the front. "The school. We've got some digging to do."

CHAPTER
TWO
NEO

Fᴜᴄᴋ ʜᴇʀ. Fuck them. Fuck everyone.

And fuck me for letting that girl get close enough to slap me—or touch me at all for that matter. Her touch is like fire burning into my skin, leaving invisible scars. At this rate, I'm bound to be covered in them.

I rub aggressively at my cheek's blemished skin, trying to blend the mark. It's not that I care who sees it, except her. She doesn't deserve the satisfaction of knowing she marked me in any sort of way. I should've slapped her back, but the one and only pertinent thing my father taught me is not to hit a woman. Scar's all about pushing boundaries, though, so maybe it's time I push some of my own.

They're all waiting for me to go to the school, but I have no problem making them wait a little longer.

The sound of footsteps drudge into the bathroom, and I snap my eyes to the perpetrator. "Leave," I deadpan, giving some kid—I think he's a junior. No fucking clue what his name is—a look of warning.

His Adam's apple bobs as he swallows and he pushes up

the metal-framed glasses that have slid down his nose. Avoiding eye contact, he nods and leaves.

That was too easy. Everything here is too easy. Where the fuck is the challenge?

Her. She's the challenge. My conquest. One I've been watching and waiting to destroy. There are a few times I let my walls down. Moments of weakness, if you will. But all it takes is the remembrance of why I despise her and the walls go back up and the challenge resumes.

I will break her. Show her why she's never belonged and in the end, she'll cower and leave. With any luck, the whole Sunder family will be abolished, never to show their faces in front of a Blue Blood again.

It's bittersweet, really. On one hand, I'll miss fucking with her; on the other, I won't have to anymore.

Slapping the faucet on, I let the cold water run into my cupped palms. I lean down over the sink and splash water on my face, blinking away the droplets that form on my eyelashes. Without even lifting my head, I reach over and grab a sheet of paper towel hanging, and it immediately spits out more. Eyes closed, I lift my head and dry my face, then chuck the crumpled paper into the open trash bin.

A deep breath in and I chase away any lingering thoughts of her, only allowing them to return when I have a solid plan. Right now, we need to bring down Jude Beckett for what he's done. This is all for Maddie. Everything I do is for her—even exposing her so-called best friend for what she really is—a fraud.

WITH MY SLED PARKED at the back entrance of the school, I use my master key to open the back door that leads into the kitchen of the cafeteria. I haven't heard from the guys at all and I really didn't expect to. Ever since Scar tangled them up in her web, I've been left out of everything. I'm not angry about it, though, because, in due time, I'll have my boys back and Scar will be nothing more than a bad memory.

Snow drops in mounds from my boots as I walk across the marbled floors, taking care not to slip because they've got a fresh coat of wax on them. It's an accident waiting to happen if you ask me.

One push on the shiny doors and I step into the open cafeteria. It's quiet. So quiet that the thoughts in my head are screaming.

When Riley's dad, Samson Cross, passed on the information about Elias Stanton to my father, I snatched it off his desk and came straight here. Never even told my father I knew or that I was leaving. I've got no doubt in my mind my father had every intention of pushing all the information aside because he's too busy with the upcoming elections to worry himself with such a mundane task. Because that's what Maddie's disappearance is to him—a tiny inconvenience that he wants kept out of the public eye. Same shit happened with my mom when she died and the same shit will happen with every instance that involves me or Maddie in the future. He doesn't give a damn about us and it's that cold, hard truth that keeps me moving forward in life. Maddie needs me, and she's also all I've got, so in that sense, I need her, too.

Which brings me here, to the school, because we need to dig up everything we can on Elias—starting with his school records.

Reaching into my pocket, I pull out my phone to check the dozen missed calls I've had from my father. He's set up search parties for Maddie, all the while keeping it on the down-low.

There's also a few missed calls and messages from the guys, but I already know what they were calling for. *Where the hell are you? Hurry your ass up!*

I stuff my phone back in my pocket, and as I walk down the long stretch of hallway, my fingers trail across the row of senior lockers, stopping at one in particular. I'm in no hurry, so I decide to check and see what our girl's been up to. Spinning the lock, I enter her combination and give the lever a lift, popping the door open. Every once in a while, I go through her shit—at school and at home—just to make sure she's not trying to pull a fast one on us. For a while, I suspected she was, but the evidence pointed elsewhere, so I let go of that suspicion, but we can never be too sure. For all I know, she's playing from the same hand as Jude Beckett. After all, she did befriend him when no one else did, so I have to ask myself, why? Has she known the truth this whole time?

Every time I do this shit, I get a feeling of elation. Like, I'm on the verge of uncovering another secret I could use against her. Although, lately, I've come up empty-handed. Doesn't matter, though. I've got everything I need to blow up her whole world, and her family's, too.

Crouching down, I shuffle through a few papers just thrown inside as boredom takes hold. There's not a damn thing in here. Scar's pretty good at keeping her secrets hidden, so I shouldn't be shocked. I'm also not surprised at the lack of decor. Most of the girls here have their lockers decked in frilly pink shit—not Scar. In fact, she has no decorations at all. So basic, yet so intricate. The mystery surrounding her is alluring and has me wanting to know everything I might not already know.

"What the hell are you doing?" Her voice hits my ears before I see her.

A smirk draws across my face as I peer inside her open locker. "Hasn't anyone ever told you that organizing your things is the first step in organizing your life?"

I'm caught off guard when she shoves me aside, the smell of her vanilla body spray, or maybe it's lotion. No, I'm pretty sure it's body spray. Saw a bottle sitting on her dresser one day. Anyway, it floods my senses as I tip over to the right, catching the floor with my hand.

"My life is plenty organized without you trying to do it for me." Her gravelly tone tells me she's pissed, as she should be—as I like her to be.

Dusting off my hands, I stand up and close the space between us, drawing in a deep breath of her intoxicating scent. I don't like the girl, but I can't deny that she looks and smells like a wet dream.

When she curls her lip, I don't say anything. I just stand with my face inches from hers. "What are you doing in my locker, Neo?"

I raise a shoulder, letting it fall slowly. "Just making sure your skeletons aren't hiding in there."

Her brows hit her forehead, nostrils flared as she shoves me back a few steps. "Oh yeah? Is that where you hide yours?" Her voice rises to a near shout. "In your fucking school locker?" She shoves me again, walking me back a few more steps while a rumble of laughter climbs up my throat. "You must think I'm stupid."

I throw my hands up in defense. "You said it, not me."

"Ugh! I hate you so much! Just when I think you're starting to show a little bit of humanity, you start acting like this again!"

"I guess you really are stupid, because you'd be a fool to mistake any humane gesture for kindness on my part." Not that I'm sure what instance she's referring to. As far as I remember, I've been nothing but imperious to the girl.

She taps her head mockingly. "You're right. What the fuck was I thinking?"

"Glad we're on the same page." I step past her, slamming her locker door shut and continuing down the hall. "If I remember right, we have a mystery to solve with the rest of the Scooby squad."

Her footsteps pad heavily behind me until she's walking at my side. My eyes roll, not even granting her a glance.

"Oh, did you suddenly decide to help us?" She careens toward me and does a curtsey while continuing to walk at my side. "Thank you, almighty Mr. Saint, for sparing us a second of your time to aid us in finding your fucking sister!"

She's such a pain in the ass.

"If we're being totally honest, I don't need your help or Crew's or Jagger's. As far as I'm concerned, none of you have done a damn thing to help Maddie. If anything, all you're doing is making shit worse. "

She stops walking and I steal a look from my periphery. Her expression suddenly grows despondent. Eyebrows stoic, lips flat. "Jesus Christ, Scar. Don't be so dramatic." When her feet stay planted to the tile beneath her, my posture goes slack. I spin around to face her, head down, eyes on hers. "We're all doing a shit job. Now, can we go? Please?"

Something about what I said brings life back into her.

Her eyes soften and she bites back a smile. "Did you just say please?"

Fuck. Did I?

"No."

She's full-on smiling at this point, and for some reason, the proof of her happiness twists my stomach in knots.

"Yeah, you did. You said, and I quote, *'can we go, please?'*"

"So what if I did? Who fucking cares if I said please?"

Her shoulders dance, the glee on her face never faltering. "I care, because that's exactly what I was talking about. This is one of those moments I was talking about where you show a bit of humanity."

I sweep the air with my hand and keep walking toward the records room. "You're insane."

She jogs back up to me, warranting a sigh. "And you're not as dead inside as you want everyone to think you are."

We're walking in step when I ask, "Have you not heard anything I've said to you in the past five minutes?"

"I've heard. I'm stupid. I'm a bitch. I'm basically ruining your life. Oh, and you said the word please." Her hands clasp together and that shit-eating grin on her face returns.

She's fucking loving this. One moment where a simple word slips out of my mouth and she will hold it against me until the end of time. It wasn't even a nice *please*. It was more of a *right-fucking-now please*. But whatever. If she wants to think warm blood runs through my veins from time to time, so be it. I know the truth. I'm the one who shivers at my own fucked-up thoughts. The one who fights like hell to wake up from his nightmares, only to find out I was never asleep.

Rounding the corner to the administration offices, our shoulders brush, and you'd think I just lit her arm on fire.

Scar jolts, taking a few steps to the right and away from me. It's laughable how much she pretends to despise me. I say pretend because, deep down, I don't think she really hates me at all. Which is exactly why I have to up my game. I want her to loathe my existence. Only then will I be certain she won't try and get too close because, if she does, I'm afraid I might have another moment of weakness and let her. If that happens, I'll be just as despicable as she is. One touch, and we're both going straight to hell.

CHAPTER
THREE
SCAR

"WHAT EXACTLY ARE WE LOOKING FOR?" I ask Riley, as she picks through a stack of folders she placed on a large desk.

"Elias Stanton's school records. The dates just aren't adding up." She glances over her shoulder. "I'm not finding anything here. Are we sure he was in the class of 2001?"

Jagger is the first to respond. "He was born in 1984. Had to be either 2001 or 2002."

"That would be the year most of our parents graduated." I say the fact out loud.

"All but mine," Riley says. "My mom and dad were two years ahead of yours." Leaving the stack on the desk, she pulls open a large drawer on the opposite side of the one she was just in. She closes it then opens another, repeating the process until she finds what she's looking for. Bunching together at least a dozen folders, she pulls them out and plops them down on the desk beside the others. I watch intently, feeling like I'm not offering much help, but I don't really know what I can do.

With the lights off, the only way we can see is with the

screens on the open computers and the flashlight that's on top of Riley's head, which is attached to some sort of headband. She truly looks like a Guardian in all her glory.

Neo is sitting in the desk chair, staring somberly at a wall—more than likely figuring out how many bodies can fit in a six-foot hole. Crew's in another room, where he got himself logged into the headmaster's account, and I'm almost certain he's changing his American Lit grade because he failed the last test. Jagger is in here on his own laptop, doing some research on the Beckett family. And, of course, Riley is searching for Elias's paper trail.

"Got it," Riley blurts out, her hand in the air holding the folder. Everyone stops what they're doing and hurries over to where she and I are standing in front of the desk.

With Riley's flashlight shining down on the open folder, she reads some random facts out loud. "He came to the Academy his junior year in 2001. Set to graduate in 2002." She flips a few pages. "He entered as a Rook. Climbed up pretty quickly to an Ace." She turns a few more pages, but before she can read further, Neo snatches the folder off the table.

"Gimme that." Using his phone, he turns on the flashlight and shines it down on the folder.

"You're such an asshole," I huff, shaking my head in disbelief at this guy.

Riley draws in a deep breath, holding her composure, while Jagger and I share a look, him just as annoyed with Neo's outburst as I am.

"He went missing…" Neo lifts his eyes to mine momentarily before shifting his gaze to Jagger. "Halloween night of 2001. His body was found days later, floating face down in the river with a knife in his back. Case closed." He slams his hand down on the stack of papers aggressively. "As they always are with any Blue Blood member."

The hairs on the back of my neck stand tall as I say, "Tomorrow, it'll be exactly twenty years since he went missing."

Jagger peers over at the page Neo was just looking at. "It's also the same way we found that dummy in the river last week."

Neo shuts the folder and drops it on the desk. "Think it means anything?"

"Probably not," Jagger says, "but all these coincidences are fucking puzzling."

I'm reminded of the fact that Elias wasn't in any of our classes. It has me wondering if he ever really attended at all, or if he just took the name to trick us, without being registered as a student. "Is there any record of him attending classes this year?"

A minute of shuffling through some other papers, and Riley quips, "Nope."

"Doesn't matter," Neo says. "We know Elias is dead. We know he was murdered. And we know that the guy pretending to be him is, without a doubt, the one wreaking havoc on our Academy."

The door flies open and Crew enters, beaming with his Halloween mask in his hand. "You're now looking at a straight-A student." The wide grin spread across his face makes it obvious he's missed out on what's going on. When he catches our perplexed looks, his expression quickly drops. "Tough crowd. Who died?"

"Elias died," I remind him, "twenty years ago, to be exact."

He crosses the room, joining us in front of the desk. "Shit. He would be like...old as dirt."

"He'd be our parents' age. Probably would have had a kid our age who would have been a student here had he not been murdered."

Crew's eyes widen. "Murdered?"

"Knife straight to the back," Neo says. "Probably one of the Becketts."

"Or," Jagger cuts in, "a student. A Blue Blood. A Lawless member. Could have been anyone. The question is, why?"

"Does it really fucking matter why he was murdered?" Neo folds up the paper with the details of Elias's death and sticks it in the inside pocket of his leather jacket. "People fucking die. Everyone dies and one day we all will too."

"Geez," Riley gripes, "someone's feeling morbid."

I'm watching Neo intently when his disposition shifts. I can hear the pain in his words—see it in his eyes. He's not just talking about Elias, but his mother, too. Is he scared of death? Is he living each day like he's simply waiting to die, as well?

"My point is," Neo continues, "it doesn't matter how or why he died. What matters is why the hell someone is pretending to be him."

I'm still watching him—trying to figure him out—when his eyebrows pull together and he scowls at me, as if I'm doing something atrocious by simply looking at him. "What?" he huffs.

And I say, "Nothing."

He glances away momentarily, before looking at me again, this time, his shoulders taut and his back straight, trying to appear unaffected, but he knows I'm reading him. And I'm making him nervous. "Stop fucking looking at me!"

But I don't. Even when everyone catches me staring into his eyes.

Why haven't I noticed before?

Neo isn't dead inside. The tragedies he's dealt with just make him feel like he is.

"Babe," Crew says, sliding an arm around my waist, "everything okay?"

I lick my lips, finally peeling my eyes off Neo as my chest rises and falls rapidly. Whatever I'm feeling, it's strange. Butterflies in my stomach mixed with a stabbing pain in my heart.

"Yeah," I finally say, suddenly embarrassed that they all saw me trapped in my own thoughts. But I'm not sorry Neo saw me because I think I just broke down one of his walls and I also think he knows it.

With heavy steps, Neo stalks past all of us and walks straight out the door.

Jagger draws his neck back. "What was that all about?"

"Yes. Do tell," Riley says.

"I...I don't know. But I feel like you guys should check in on Neo. With Maddie missing, and all, he might not be okay."

Crew chuckles. "Is Neo ever okay?"

"No. I guess not."

But who does he have when he's not okay, and why the hell do I even care?

"Voodoo" by Twisted Insane is blasting through the speakers coming from The Gathering room, overpowering the sound of students carrying on and having a good time. Caution tape extends from the top of the tunnel to the ground, making an X in hopes that students won't cross it into the tunnels. If anyone else finds that room, we'll all have a lot of explaining to do.

The Punks, who are in the middle of the hierarchy ladder, did a stellar job getting the party ready, and I'm sure the decorations are thanks to the cheerleaders. It's dark inside the room, aside from the neon orange disco balls and the purple lasers shooting down from the ceiling, all moving with the beat of the music. There's a guy on the same stage the Lawless use during meetings, and he's spinning a disc with one hand while waving the other in the air.

My shoulders dance as we enter and Jagger places a hand on the small of my back, keeping me close while Crew stands on the other side, holding my hand. "This is fun," I tell them, hoping it lasts. We could all use a night to let loose and pretend everything is okay.

Who am I kidding? Pretending isn't an option. Not when Maddie is missing and we have so many unanswered questions. Guilt stirs inside me. We shouldn't even be here.

"Don't leave me, 'kay?" Riley says with fear in her eyes. She's terrified of the wannabe Elias, rightfully so, and there's no doubt he's going to attach himself to her tonight. After all, as far as he knows, they're still a couple.

We step farther into the room, Neo already disappearing on his own. At least that's what I thought. One glance to my left shows him sipping on a drink with his Darth Vader mask on the top of his head, while a girl grinds her ass against him to the beat of "Neurotic" by Three Days Grace. She looks like a trashy slut in a football jersey tied just below her breasts with knee-high socks and a pair of boy shorts. Smears of black paint are underneath her eyes. If she's trying to pull off a football player costume, she failed miserably.

Crew leans down and whispers in my ear, "Want a drink?"

"Sure. Make it a strong one."

"Stay with Riley. Jagger and I will be right over there." He tips his chin at the beverage table that holds spiked punch bowls and cups. Two kegs sit on either side and both are surrounded by people.

Once the guys are a few feet away, I lock my arm around Riley's. "Who is that girl?" I ask, nodding toward the slut rubbing her ass on Neo.

"I think her name is Carrie. Why?"

"No reason."

"Does this have anything to do with your little moment with Neo in the records room earlier?"

"Little moment?" I laugh. "There was no moment."

"Umm. Yes, there was. We all saw it. The stare between you and Neo almost caught the room on fire, and I'm pretty sure we were all holding our breaths."

"Whatever. There was no moment, and there was no stare. I was just...challenging him, I guess."

"Then I'd have to say you're an idiot because no one challenges Neo and wins."

My shoulders rise, then fall sluggishly. "We'll see about that."

Riley slithers out of my hold and stands directly in front of me. "No fucking way! You're falling for him, too?"

"Oh my god, Riley. No! Absolutely not. That's insane. Gross. Impossible. I can't stand the guy."

She crosses her arms over her chest and pops a hip

beneath her skimpy red dress, while curling her matching lips.

"What?" I huff. "I am not falling for him! Did you miss the part where I said I can't stand him?"

"Oh, I heard you. I've heard it multiple times, but I don't believe it." With two fingers, she points at her eyes then mine. "I'm watching you, girl."

I shake my head, hoping she realizes how ridiculous she sounds. "As you should be. You're my Guardian." There's a nip of sarcasm to my tone that she picks up on right away.

"I'm not talking as a Guardian. I'm talking as your friend."

Jagger and Crew return with drinks, giving one to Riley and the other to me. "Thank you," I say to them. The first sip is heaven. "Mmm. This is good." I lick the excess liquid of the fruity beverage from my lips. "What is it?"

"Strawberry lemonade with, I think, vodka."

I nod, liking the sound of that, and take another drink. This time, a big one. It goes down so smooth and I can hardly taste the liquor, which makes it that much more quenching.

Riley sips on her drink leisurely, and after a few minutes have passed, mine's gone and hers is still full.

"Be right back," I say to her and the guys, who are standing around observing as if they're waiting for something to happen. "I need a refill."

"I'll go with you," Jagger says, resting his hand on my lower back. "You really shouldn't be alone."

I chuckle. "I'll be fine. There are a hundred other people here."

"Exactly my point. A hundred people and we can't trust a single one of them."

My eyes land on his. "I trust you."

He tips a smile and curls his arm around my shoulder, so I lean into him. Jagger has a way of making all the bad things disappear. Being with him feels like home. It's comfortable and it's safe and it's exactly where I want to be.

"I'm glad we got to that point. Ya know? Where you can trust me."

I return his smile, feeling it in my soul. "Me, too."

The farther we step into the crowd, the louder it gets, so I'm unable to say everything on my mind. If he could hear me, though, I'd say: *I'm not sure there was ever a time I didn't trust you. I know hurting me was never your goal, even if it was Neo's. And that no amount of heat from the outside world, or anyone, for that matter, will ever make me choose because you and Crew are the best things in my life.*

I'm actually glad I don't have the opportunity to say all that because it sounds cheesy as hell. I'm not sure what happened to me, but these guys have brought out emotions inside me I didn't know I was capable of feeling.

"Aww, isn't this cute." Neo bumps my side, causing me to knock Jagger into a group of girls, which sends liquid sloshing from their cups.

They all apologize in unison, as if they're the ones who did something wrong.

"As you should be. Don't let it happen again," Jagger barks at them, before looking at me with a smile that drops quickly when he glances at Neo. "Thanks a lot, asshole."

"For what? Getting you the attention of some other chicks? If Scar can sleep with other people, why can't you?"

"Fuck off," I grumble at him. Once again, wondering how there are times I see this jerk in a different light. The effects of my quick consumption of alcohol are starting to kick in and it hits me that Jagger didn't give him a similar response. I squeeze his hip that I'm holding, grabbing his attention as we approach the beverage table. He looks down at me and I ask, "Do you wanna sleep with other girls?" As soon as the words leave my mouth, I realize how ridiculous they sound, but it's something we've never talked about. Mainly because I've never thought about it, but has he? I'm sleeping with Crew, too—does he have any desire to sleep with other girls? Is what we have exclusive?

"Hell no," he responds almost immediately, glaring at Neo. "Quit putting shit in her head."

But it is in my head, and suddenly, I feel the need to talk it out with both him and Crew. What are we doing? Where are these relationships going?

"I'm just saying, man. It hardly seems fair that you have to share but she doesn't."

It is unfair, isn't it?

Jagger maneuvers us through the group gathered around the table and grabs me another fruity drink and a beer for himself while I hang back with Neo. Normally I'd have a lot to say, but right now, my thoughts are taking over. I've never cared what anyone else thought of me, but I do care about Jagger and Crew. Do they feel like they're both being played by me? Because that's not what this is at all. I genuinely care about each of them, more than I can ever put into words, unless it's three. I love them. I really do. The thought of losing either of them is something I can't fathom. But how long can we go on like this? In the end, will all three of us lose?

"You're thinking about it, aren't you?" Neo says, his words like nails on a chalkboard.

36

I scowl, eyes on Jagger, so I don't lose him in the madness. "Yeah, thanks to you."

"Come on, Scar. You can't really think you'll be the last pussy my boys tap for the rest of their lives. Whatever you three have going on, it's temporary. A few months and we'll be headed to BCU, where you'll all eventually lose interest in this little fling you've got going on."

His words, which usually only graze the surface, cut deep. Someone starts chanting, "Keg stand. Keg stand. Keg stand." And the whole crowd joins in.

My nerves are at an all-time high and my emotions are getting the best of me so I decide to try and numb the pain I'm feeling. Shoving Neo out of my way, I slip through the bodies circling the keg and I raise my hand. "I'll do one."

Neo balls the back of my dress in his fist and pulls me toward him, my back crashing into his chest. "The fuck you will."

I lunge forward, slipping out of his grip. At this point, the entire crowd is watching us, waiting to see if I'll disobey Neo and do what I want. They're all in for a surprise, because damn straight I am.

"Let's do this," I tell Victor, who's holding the keg nozzle.

He looks at Neo, seeking approval, so I snatch it away from him and shove it at another guy. "Do it."

Both hands grip the sides of the keg and when my legs go up, a sinister grin spreads across my face. *Take that, Neo fucking Saint.*

The nozzle slips between my lips and beer immediately begins streaming from it. I swallow it down fast. Swallow after swallow, trying to last as long as I can. The cold liquid ices over my esophagus to the point it feels numb. I've guzzled down at least two beers at this point, so I jerk my head away. The nozzle keeps spraying before the guy holding it realizes I'm no longer drinking. When it stops, my leg handlers set me down.

There's hoots and hollers. Guys all chanting on my behalf. So that's what being the center of attention feels like. I could dig this.

Wiping the back of my hand across my mouth, I smirk at Neo while walking toward him.

"The fuck I am." I mock his words with a swagger to my steps.

"Yeah. Well done, Scar. You just put your ass on display for the entire student body."

Fuck. Eyes wide, my cheeks heat up instantly. I knew I felt a cold breeze on my ass. I completely forgot I was wearing a dress. I tug my dress down, gripping both sides tightly. "Oh my god. Did everyone see?"

"Everyone who was watching. Next time you wanna be defiant...don't." He stammers the word, *don't,* as if he's angry with me. The thing is, I'm not sure if it's because of what I did, or because of what everyone else saw.

CHAPTER

FOUR

CREW

"WHAT DO you think is taking them so long?" Riley asks, her eyes dancing around the room nervously.

I've been wondering the same thing. A glance at my Apple Watch shows it's been fifteen minutes since Jagger and Scar left for drinks. Crunching the plastic cup, I say, "No idea. We should probably go see."

"Actually," Riley says, "I think I might leave. I just don't feel safe here."

I quirk a brow, wondering if she truly believes she'd be safe on her own. Because she's not. No one is. "And you think you'd be safer alone, at the dorms?"

"He's here, Crew." She hugs her arms tightly to her chest, fingers grazing the goosebumps on her arms. "I think he knows. I can feel him watching me."

I swing an arm around her shoulders, surprising myself because I'm not kind to many people. But this is Scar's closest friend and she's worked her ass off as a Guardian. She deserves some respect and appreciation. *Jesus Christ. Who the hell am I?*

Regardless of my momentary identity crisis, I lead her through the crowd in search of Jagger and Scar.

"I doubt he's even here," I tell her, voice raised, so she can hear me. "If he is who we think he is, he's probably in his lair doing his dirty work."

Or, tending to Maddie, who he likely has locked up somewhere. The question is, where? She could be here on BCA property, for all we know. She could be anywhere. There's also a good chance this guy isn't working alone. One person can't possibly do everything he's done over the last few weeks.

"I think I wanna go home," Riley spits out. "Like, *home* home."

I stop walking and she does the same. My arm drops from around her shoulders. "Seriously?" Her response is a subtle nod. "You wanna just throw in the towel and give up? Let this guy win?"

"He won't win. I've got no doubt you all will catch him and give him what he deserves. I just... I'm not cut out for this. I'm no Guardian. I'm weak, and I'm really fucking scared."

"You're still in training. I'm sure all the Guardians are scared at first. It'll get easier. "

"I hope you're right."

"*Almost* always am."

"Almost." Riley cracks a smile. "Ya know, I never liked you guys. Still can't stand Neo. But, you and Jagger are good for Scar. I can see how happy she is now. It's like you've breathed life back into her."

"She's done the same for me. Can't imagine doing any of this without her."

I spot Neo coming toward us with no hurry in his steps.

With an open palm, he shoves a guy out of his path, then another, weaving through the crowd like he owns the damn place.

"What a prick," Riley clips, referring to Neo.

With a red plastic cup in one hand, he takes a sip. "Spicy," he says with a click of his tongue.

"Whatcha drinking?"

"Straight scotch, but I wasn't talking about the contents in my cup. I was referring to your girl's ass that she just bared for all to see. Might wanna get her under control."

"She what?" The words fly out of my mouth before I can even comprehend what he actually said. I shake my head in disbelief. "No. Scar wouldn't do that."

"Scar would do it and if you or Jagger don't stop her now, she's about to do it again."

I follow his gaze to the sound of the chanting, and sure as shit, Scar is pumping her fist in the air near the keg. Without another word, I push through the crowd and head straight for her. "Outta the way, fucker." I shove bodies left and right. Not because I can, but because I have to. Scar will curse us all tomorrow if we don't stop her right fucking now.

A minute later, I'm grabbing her by the arm, only to feel resistance that's not coming from her. My eyes land on Jagger, who's got her other arm. "Dude. What the hell?"

"Lighten up, man. Let her have some fun."

I'm all for a good time and I know better than anyone that Scar deserves it, but not tonight. Not when all this shit is going on.

"Scar," I grit my teeth, mouth ghosting her ear, "you're gonna regret this."

"Nah," she singsongs, "I'm just having some fun. You should try it."

"Nice. I turn my back for one fucking minute and you let her get fucking drunk."

Scar laughs hysterically, and as I'm trying to figure out why, she says, "I'm so lame. It took me one minute to get drunk. I really need to do this more so I have a higher tolerance."

Jagger is no longer tugging her in his direction; instead, he's holding her while everyone watches me silently, waiting to see if I'll give in. It's a rarity when I do, but fuck, she's making it hard to say no.

"Baby, please." She begs with pleading eyes. "We can all use a night where we just let loose. Let this be my night."

Shoulders slumped in defeat, I slide my hand to hers. "Fine. Do your thing. But don't be pissed at me tomorrow for not stopping you. I tried."

Pushing herself on her tiptoes, she presses her lips to mine. The bitter taste of beer coats my lips and I dart my tongue out, tasting hers. "I'm not leaving your side, though. You're already a handful when you're sober."

She smiles against my mouth before giving me one last *thank-you* peck. "I'll be fine," she says, before turning around and chanting again, bringing the crowd back to life. "Keg stand. Keg stand. Keg stand."

Jagger joins my side, grinning, and I can tell he's headed down the same intoxicated path as Scar.

Out of nowhere, Neo sweeps through the crowd, bumping into me, then Jagger. "The fuck you are," he gnashes at Scar, before grabbing her by the waist from behind. He pulls her back, spins her around, then tosses her over his shoulder, pulling her dress over her ass and holding it in place, so no one gets a show. With his eyes locked straight in front of him, he carries her away, parting the crowd as he moves.

Jagger and I share a look of dumbfoundedness before I say, "What the hell was that?"

"Hell if I know." Jagger shrugs his shoulders. "At least she's laughing."

"Yeah. For now. I'm not even sure she knows who's got her." I follow Neo's trail, picking up my pace to try and catch up. I can't be certain, but I'm sure Jagger is following me. With my neck stretched, I try not to lose sight of them, but he's moving quickly.

"Hey, Crew," Melody says, walking in step with me. She's also heavily intoxicated, and I'm wondering how the fuck everyone got so inebriated already when the party literally just started.

"Go away, Melody."

Does she listen? Of course not. It's Melody, an aching thorn in everyone's side.

"I would, but I can't. You see, I just saw Elias escort a sobbing Riley out the door, and when she caught my glance, I'm almost positive she mouthed the words *get Crew*. Either that, or she was telling me to get screwed, but I'm going with the former, just in case. The last thing I want—"

"Shut up," I spit out, no longer walking, but instead, listening intently. "Riley left with Elias?"

Tipping to the left, she stumbles, causing her drink to slosh out of the full cup. "Pretty sure that's what I just said."

I snatch the cup from her hand and tip it upside down, dumping the entire contents before dropping it to the floor and stomping on it with my boot. "You're cut off." That's one less drunken idiot I have to deal with tonight. "Go follow Riley and Elias and tell him he's been mandated to stay here at the party until cleanup, then walk Riley back to her dorm and stay with her until further notice."

"Whaaaat?" she bellows. "That's not fucking fair, Crew. Why do I have to do that shit?"

"Because I told you to. That's why. Do it now or you'll be cleaning up after the party all by yourself."

She stomps her silver heel to the floor in a fit. "You're such a dick."

Time is of the essence right now, so I ignore anything else she has to say. Melody will do what I asked because she knows there will be consequences if she doesn't. We need to get Elias away from Riley before she completely breaks down and he realizes she knows something. But right now, I have to find Scar before Neo goes too far and I have to knock the shit out of him.

Stepping through the sticky mess of Melody's drink, I continue walking to try and find them, but it's pointless. They're gone.

FIVE

SCAR

"WHERE ARE WE GOING?" I scratch my head, digging my nails into my scalp. This damn hairspray is foreign to my hair and it's really fucking sticky.

Neo doesn't respond. He just keeps walking through the tunnels like they're as familiar to him as his own backyard.

"I'm not scared of you," I tell him. "I should be. But I'm not. You've had every opportunity to physically hurt me, but all you want to do is destroy me emotionally. I can handle that. I'm strong enough."

He still doesn't say anything and his silence is really grating on my nerves.

"Ugh. Why did I drink that much?" My arms hang limply down, hands touching his ass. Each step has his cheeks alternating. They rise and they fall. I'm tempted to squeeze them, just out of curiosity. Are they firm? Mushy? Does Neo have a mushy tushy? I start laughing at myself and the sound of my own laughter only makes me do it more.

"What the hell is so funny?"

His gravelly voice hits my ears and my hysterics come to a dead stop. "And he speaks…"

"You were laughing just so I'd talk? What are you, a damn child?"

"Actually, I am. Only eighteen, Neo. Eighteen and a life, you know. Eighteen and a life—"

"If you start singing, so help me, I will toss you into Elias's lair and leave you."

"Chill out. I'm not gonna sing. Not for you anyways."

I'm finally relaxed, hanging over Neo's shoulder and feeling like I could potentially fall asleep, when he sets me down. My feet catch my fall, but the shift of the blood that was pooling in my head sets me off-balance. Two hands land on my hips, steadying me. "You could have just let me fall," I tell him. "I wouldn't have held it against you."

"Sure you wouldn't. You'd hold it against me until graduation, no doubt."

"No," I shake my head, smacking my dry lips together, "I've got bigger things to hold against you. For starters, you just carried me down a tunnel, when there's a raging party going on. Ya know, I got the go-ahead to have fun tonight. Not that I needed permission from anyone. But either way, you ruined it." I tilt my head slightly, quizzically reading him. "Why?"

"Because Jagger wants a drinking buddy for the night and Crew is too fucking obsessed with you to tell you no."

A heavy breath of laughter climbs up my vocal cords. "Obsessed? That's an odd choice of words coming from someone whose life mission is to punish me for a crime I didn't commit." I poke a sharp finger to his chest. "That someone being you."

"Don't touch me." He slaps my hand away. Not aggressively, but enough for me to drop it.

I poke him again, conscious of the saying, *don't poke the bear*. But tonight, I'm feeling brave. I'm feeling free. And I'm feeling like it's high time someone puts Neo Saint in his place. "Oh yeah? What are you gonna do about it? Kill me?"

In a swift motion, he grabs my wrist, squeezing with tenacity. "Don't tempt me, Scar."

His expression is desensitized and the smoldering glare he has pinned on me is chilling. "You want me dead, Neo?"

"Not gonna lie. It'd make things easier."

"Easier for who? Maddie? Crew? Jagger—"

He squeezes harder, cutting off the blood flow in my hand. "For me."

I cut a glance at his hand, suddenly not feeling like this is a joke. The seriousness in Neo's tone is bringing me a few steps down to reality. My head is still spinning and my stomach is pooling with warmth from the alcohol, yet chills are dancing across my skin. "Why do you care if I drink tonight? If I remember right, you don't give a damn about me."

"That's true. I don't. What I do care about is finding and avenging my sister, and all you are is a distraction. Jagger and Crew need to stay focused and you're in the way."

"Oh," I chuckle, my eyes sweeping the walls surrounding us, "and this is your way of getting me *out* of the way?"

"It's a start." He jerks my arm, walking with me at his side.

I follow along, since he's not giving me a choice in the matter. "Where are you taking me?"

"Elias is with Riley, so I know he's not down here—"

I gasp. "Riley is with Elias? No! She's probably terrified."

"And I give a fuck, why?"

"Obviously you don't because all you give a fuck about is yourself, but Riley could blow this whole thing out of the water. She'll cave. I know she will."

"Wow. You sure do have a lot of faith in your friend, the Guardian."

Of course I have faith in Riley. However, I also know she's easily intimidated, insanely awkward, and speaks without thinking. "This has nothing to do with believing in her skills and everything to do with the fact that she's alone with a psychopath."

"Riley's fine."

"How can you be so sure?"

He quirks a brow with a swift glance at me. "Do I dare say, trust me?"

"Absolutely not."

"As I was saying before you interrupted me, Riley is with Elias, so I know he's not down here, so we're gonna do a little digging."

"And you need me, why?"

"Because you're less trouble when I've got my eyes on you. So you're coming with me."

I jerk my arm back, grabbing his attention, but he doesn't let go. "Please don't tell me we're going to his lair." My head shakes in utter disapproval. "Last time Jagger and I got locked in. I can't go back. What if someone locks us in again?"

"I can guarantee I won't be locked in. As for you, we could only be so lucky."

The vacancy in his tone is unsettling. I don't think for a second Neo would try and save me if I got locked in.

"Why do you still hate me so much? You know I didn't push your sister. You know I'm not the stalker. So, why?"

When his response is a malevolent laugh, I jerk my arm again, this time harder. My voice rises to a blaring shout. "Dammit! Tell me why!"

Finally, I free my arm, but not without repercussions. With his arms draped at his sides, chin tipped, he walks into me, chest bumping mine, and with a thud, my back crashes into the rock wall. My heart gallops in my chest when he cages me in with his hands pressed on either side of my body against the wall.

"You wanna know why I hate you so much? Why I will *always* hate you?"

Swallowing hard, I nod, knowing all the while I'm truly not ready for his reasoning.

His teeth grind, brows knitted together tightly, and his expression alone tells me I don't need to hear the reason, because whatever it is, it's more than enough for him.

"I do hate you, Scar. For years, I've loathed your existence. Wanted you gone. Out of our lives. And you wanna know why? Because I have to. I have to hate you."

It takes me a second to process his words, but once I do, I'm more confused than ever. *He hates me because he has to?*

Through dried vocal cords, I choke out, "You have to hate me?"

Pursing his lips, he nods, his villainous stance never faltering.

After years of being on the receiving end of his hatred, I see light at the end of the tunnel—figuratively speaking. My hand rises to his arm. "You don't have to hate me if you don't want to."

In an instant, he slaps my hand away. "Don't fucking touch me." He spins around, fisting his hair, as if his mind is tortured. "Don't ever fucking touch me."

"But—"

He comes at me full force, putting me back in my place. Our noses brush as he grinds out, "I. Will. Never. Not. Hate. You, Scar. Do you understand me?" I inhale his hot breath, my limbs quivering. "Nothing you do or say will ever change the sheer agony I feel in your presence. I despise you. Your touch repulses me. Your existence makes me sick. You are toxic. A poison I refuse to ingest. Crew and Jagger can drink it up, but not me. I'd die first."

My heart caves in before slowly sinking down into my stomach. It hurts. It really fucking hurts. His words are repulsive. As repulsive as he claims I am. But I needed to hear them, because now, I can give up.

I lift a shoulder, my expression apathetic. "It's a shame, really. I'd love nothing more than to watch you suffer a slow, agonizing death while my venom eats away at your dejected soul."

He calls me toxic—a poison he refuses to ingest—but he's already dead inside, so what's it matter? Nothing I say at this point will have any bearing on the way Neo feels about me, and right now, I don't fucking care.

Tears pool in my eyes, but they stem from anger, rather than hurt.

With a balled fist, I bring it down on his arm, causing it to drop from the wall. Then I step around him. Instead of taking the route we were heading down, I leave in the direction we came, back toward the party.

One glance over my shoulder shows Neo with his hands back on the wall and his head hung low. His eyes lift slowly to meet mine, but he doesn't say anything, just looks at me with a scornful expression.

If he wants to stop me, he can try, but I'll fight back this time.

CHAPTER
SIX
NEO

SHE HAD ONE THING RIGHT—MY soul is dejected. I'm already dead inside. The blood in my veins runs cold, has done for years. Even the heat Scar radiates around her cannot thaw the glacial mass inside my chest. What she doesn't know, and never will, is that my biggest fear is never feeling alive again.

When you've been programmed since adolescence to view the world a certain way, it's the only way you know. I can't change who I am. No matter how hard I try, I'm unable to feel some of the most basic human emotions—empathy, love, fear. At least, when it pertains to her.

Loneliness is a fucking bitch, but I refuse to let myself get swept into her chaos for a momentary bout of happiness. Not that she could make me happy. Not that anyone can.

I'm doing the right thing.

Pushing her away while keeping her close. It has to be this way. I've always known this to be true. So why is it getting harder? Why do I look at her with Crew and Jagger and want nothing more than to decapitate my own friends, just so they can't look at her or taste her ever again? Why does the thought of any guy looking at her and undressing her with their eyes make me want to put her in a cage and keep her as my own little pet? I hate her. Everything about her repulses me. So why do I want her so fucking bad?

I shake away the thoughts, knowing it's my pride filling my head with this shit. It's simple. I want her because I can't have her. Because I can *never* have her. She could be the last girl on Earth, and as long as I'm a Blue Blood, she can never be mine. Not to mention, she's already spoken for.

Walking in the direction I was headed, I keep the plan I had, just without Scar. I need to prep Jude's room for him. It won't be long and we'll be able to force out the answers we need.

I really didn't need Scar's help, but it was a good opportunity to get her away from the booze I knew she'd keep drinking. They'd all end up shit-faced, probably have a threesome, and I'd have to listen to them all night. Now, she'll probably go back and flaunt her ass in front of the entire school while doing juvenile keg stands.

It's best this way. One more minute with her and I'm sure I'd forget why I have to hate her so much, and I can never let that happen.

So far everything is adding up. I'm almost positive I know Jude's motive. Now I just have to figure out his means. How has one person been behind all of this shit? A seventeen-year-old kid has preyed upon students here and he's been right under our noses this entire time? He has to have someone helping him, and I don't just mean Melody as his henchman. But, who? Did he recruit another student?

I've searched that room from top to bottom and I've

examined every bit of information. At this point, I probably know more about the Becketts than they know about themselves.

They're trained from birth to hate the Blue Bloods—stemming from the death of Betty Beckett at the hands of Lionel Sunder. Their intentions are to break the blood ties within the Society at whatever costs, even if it means impregnating a member without her consent.

Twisting the combination, I push open the door to the room I've torn apart. I'm not even sure this fucker uses it anymore because he's knows it's been found. How could he not? Papers are now scattered everywhere. The pictures on the wall have been torn down, a few of which have been ripped in half.

I just need some clue that tells me he's not working alone. Anything. I'm just not sure I'll find it here. For all we know, he has a new space he's been occupying while plotting our destruction. Right now, we have an advantage because he doesn't know we've found out who he really is.

An old book lies to my left and I kick it over to the door while holding it open. Letting it shut, it closes until the book stops it. Not long ago, Jagger and Scar were locked down here, and it's a possibility I always keep in the forefront of my mind when I enter. However, they escaped up a pull-down ladder that led to a cabin above—Kol Sunder's cabin. I know this because my dad told me when I was just a kid. He filled me in on all the secrets of the Becketts and Sunders. Some of which I wish I could forget.

Scar's dad bought the cabin and the surrounding property, just a couple months shy of graduating from BCA. He never graduated from the Academy; instead, he finished his senior year out at Evergreen High, when her mom found out she was pregnant. It was only a couple months later, my mom found out she was pregnant with me. A Christmas Eve hookup with my father resulted in her being roped to him for life. Well, her lifetime at least. It pains me every day that her time was cut short before she could ever experience true happiness, or even true love. Her pregnancy forced her into marriage with my father because my grandfather wouldn't have it any other way. For as long as I can remember, I could hear her cry herself to sleep in her separate bedroom. My parents didn't even share a bedroom. What kind of marriage is that?

Doesn't matter. It's not my life and it will never be my life. I'll never get married. Never contribute successors to the Blue Bloods. No matter how much pressure is put on me, it will never happen.

Kicking around a few empty boxes, I keep my eyes on the ground, in search of footprints or really anything that could have been left behind that I've missed.

With my phone's flashlight turned on, I scour the room, every inch of it, unsure how much time has passed. When defeat triumphs, I drop my head back with a heavy sigh.

Of course!

Why the fuck didn't I think of this sooner?

I'm staring up at the carved-out impression in the ceiling, when I remember Jagger saying that Scar found a pendant belonging to Jude. That has to mean he was up there at some point. That's all the information they found that connects him to the cabin, but maybe they missed something.

With the added security guards in place that my father ordered, I have to be careful trekking too far off Academy grounds. The last thing I need is for my meddling to get back to him. It'll result in a lecture about how I need to focus on the Academy and quit digging for information into the Becketts. Sometimes I wonder if it's because he, too, has secrets that could be found. I'm sure I would have found them by now if he had any connection at all to this family, but I have no doubt Sebastian Saint has skeletons hiding somewhere.

Grabbing a stepladder, I drag it beneath the opening and pull down the trapdoor that was already inched open. Once I've got the rope in my hand, I jump down and pull the ladder.

The sound of the door scraping against the concrete ground has my eyes shooting over my shoulder, immediately landing on Crew.

"Again? Really?" he drawls. "This shit is becoming obsessive, man. You need to give it a break."

Ignoring his request, I step onto the ladder, both hands gripping the sides. This isn't the first time Crew's found me down here, and until all answers have revealed themselves, it won't be the last.

"Ever since you returned from your visit home, you've been at it. Three days in a row, Neo. Three fucking days of tearing this place apart, and you're not a single step closer to getting the answers you're searching for."

I don't even look at him as I speak, just stare at the splintered ladder board in front of me. "That was before we knew who he was. Now we know and I'm certain someone is helping him."

"And you think you're going to find proof of it up there?"

"There are so many fucking pieces, Crew." My voice rises to a near shout. "So many fucking pieces that are scattered all over the place and we just need..." I lower my voice, "We just need to put them all together."

He comes closer and I know he's going to do everything in his power to talk me down, as if I'm standing on the ledge of a cliff. Maybe I am. Sure as fuck feels like it sometimes.

"The answers lie within Jude Beckett, and we're gonna get them. Just come down, come back to the party, and have a little fun for once."

"Fun?" I shout, all the while laughing menacingly. "You expect me to have fun?" I turn my head, looking at him where he stands with a flashlight only a couple feet away. "This fucking psycho pushed my sister off a mountain. He's preyed upon Sc, err...all of us for months. Hell, maybe even years. He's been watching and waiting, and for all I know, he's the one who killed..." I don't let myself finish the sentence. I won't allow my mind to go there again. Not right now. Not when I'm here and the answers are under my fingertips.

"Your mom was hit. Likely by a drunk driver, Neo. You can't speculate—"

"You don't know that!" I shout even louder this time. "You don't fucking know. No one knows."

He throws his hands up, then lets them drop back down immediately, smacking the sides of his legs. "Fine. Go. But I'm coming with you."

I shake my head, not understanding why he'd come with me, when all he's been doing is telling me what a mistake this all is. "Why?"

"Because if you need these answers for your own peace of mind, then I'm gonna help you get them."

Right. Of course. "Pacts and oaths?"

He shakes his head. "No, man. Friends. Best fucking friends."

I don't say anything because I'm not sure what to say. I avoid situations like this, where words make me feel a certain way. Instead, I go up, knowing that he'll follow because he is my best friend and that's what best friends do.

We make it to the top, leaving the ladder down, so we can exit the way we came in.

"Well," Crew begins, "what are we looking for?"

"Anything. A jacket. A hoodie. Fingerprints in fucking flour. Hell, I don't know. But you have to admit, Jude doing this alone doesn't sound feasible."

"We know he had Melody's help for a while. I suppose it isn't far-fetched to assume he's likely blackmailed someone else into helping him."

I walk around the dirty kitchen, disgusted at the sight in front of me. "But who?"

Crew shrugs his shoulders, his guess as good as mine. "Hammond, maybe?"

"Nah," I tell him, "I think we've taught ol' boy Victor not to fuck around when it comes to us. He's too much of a pussy anyways."

"So was Melody, but look how tough she got when her secrets were waved in front of her?"

"Something in my gut tells me Victor's not accomplice."

We're searching in silence, Crew in the living room area and me in the kitchen, when he says, "Hey. Did you say something to Scar earlier when you carried her away from the party?"

Shuffling through a stack of old newspapers, I don't lift

my eyes. "Why do you ask?"

"She seemed upset when she came back. Wouldn't tell me why."

"Oh yeah?"

"Yeah. So I'm asking you. What did you say to her?" The shift in his tone is accusatory, and I can tell this conversation is about to take us from friends to enemies real fast. It happens often when Scar is the subject. Fortunately, we always get back to where we should be, but not without some hateful words and a couple punches first. Hopefully that isn't the case this time because I'm really not in the mood to go at it with anyone right now.

I slap my hand on the stack of papers and look at him with stern eyes. "She asked why I hate her so much and I told her the truth. Nothing she didn't already know." My gaze returns to the pile in front of me, but I'm staring humorlessly at it, a prisoner of my own thoughts.

Because I do hate her.

I hate her.

I have to.

Right?

There are times when I feel my humanity trying to break free, but I'm bound by the secrets I know, and because of them, I will never be able to look at the world as anything more than a dark cage full of betrayal.

"It's not fair. Why does Maddie get to go get ice cream with Mom and Mrs. Sunder, but I can't."

Dad licks the tip of his finger and turns the page of the newspaper lying flat on the dining room table. "Life's not fair, son."

"But Maddie gets to—"

His head jerks up in annoyance, eyebrows caved. "Maddie is not in jeopardy of potentially falling in love with the likes of that girl one day. You, my son, are. She's going to grow up to be just as beautiful as her mother, but you mustn't let her looks deceive you. Girls like that will suck you in and spit you out, then stomp on you when you're down."

"Ew. I'm not gonna fall in love with Scarlett. She's gross."

"You say that now, but you wait. One day, you'll see things differently. Which is exactly why you need to listen to me."

Ignoring him, I take another bite of the vanilla ice cream Mom gave me before they left, since Dad said I couldn't go. It's so stupid. I'm never going to fall in love with Scarlett. I don't even think she's that pretty. She's sort of like a boy. Always playing in the dirt and carrying around handfuls of worms. Her knees are always dirty and I'm certain she's the one who broke all the lawn ornaments in Crew's parents' yard a couple days ago.

"Look at me, Neo." When I don't, my father slams his fist down on the table, rattling the china Mom just set out. "I said, look at me, dammit."

I do, but it's still not good enough. He grabs the sides of my head and levels my face with his, while ice cream drips from my spoon onto the table. "Have some respect and look your father in the eye when he's talking to you."

Swallowing hard, I do as I'm told. "Yes, sir."

"There are snakes in the grass, son. Masking themselves, shedding their skin, but you must remember, they will always be snakes. One bite will inject their poison inside you. We must not let them bite." He grips my skull harder, his hands jerky. "Do you hear me?"

I hear his words, so I nod in response, but I don't understand what he means.

"That girl is a snake and she will bite if you let her. Never forget what I told you. It's our secret, but it's the truth. Stay far away from her."

That wasn't the first time my father drilled it into my head that Scar was a snake. All my life, he's made it a point to keep me away from her out of fear that one day I'd fall in love with her. It's fucking ridiculous. Of all the girls in the world, why would he think I'd fall in love with that one?

But that day was just the beginning.

So, yeah. I hate her because I have to.

"Ya know," Crew says, "I was kinda hoping all this shit would open your eyes a little bit. Jagger and I have tried being patient because of all you're going through, but don't you think it's time you quit blaming her for everything?"

"Don't blame her anymore," I retort with a drawn-out exhale. Just as all the air escapes my lungs, my eyes land on a drawing on an old newspaper.

"Then *why* do you dislike her so much?"

I hear his words, but I don't process them as I tug the paper out of the stack, holding it out with two hands. Circled in black marker is an article from 2002—the year my dad graduated from BCA.

Crew keeps talking, but I no longer hear anything he's saying, even as he shouts at me. Instead of listening, I read the headline...

Body Recovered of Eighteen-Year-Old Elias Stanton of Evergreen, Colorado.

After a weeklong search into the disappearance of Elias Stanton, his body has been recovered in an apparent suicide at Eldridge Mountain in Boulder Cove, CO.

Suicide? "What a bunch of shit," I blurt out. I think every member of the Society knows damn well his death was not suicide. The way they cover this shit up baffles me daily.

"What is that?" Crew asks, peering over my shoulder.

"Article on Elias's death." I shove the paper at him, then run my fingers through my hair.

"Jude Beckett likely did his homework before taking over this guy's life."

"No shit. He had to have done a lot of homework to pull it off for this long."

"How were we so fucking blind?"

It infuriates me to no end. All this time, he was right fucking there.

"Whatever," Crew drops the paper back down on the stack, "none of this matters. All we need to worry about right now is letting him lead us to Maddie, and once we've got her—"

"We'll kill him."

Crew nods in response, but I'm not one hundred percent sure he's up for the task. Doesn't matter if he is or isn't. I'll kill that son of a bitch with my own bare hands. It'll be one less Beckett grazing the soil of this earth.

"Oh shit," Crew blurts out, eyes beaming out the window.

As soon as I see the lights shining through it, I crouch down, pulling Crew along with me.

"Who the fuck could that be?" he asks as I shut off the flashlight on my phone and hold my hands under the table to hide the screen light.

"It's gotta be Jude."

"Can't be. He was mandated to stay for party cleanup."

"And you think he'd fucking listen?" I tap on my open text messages to Jagger and shoot him a quick one.

Me: Where is Jude?

"Dude. Dude. Dude," Crew repeats as he scoots beneath the window, pressing his back to the wall. "He's coming closer."

I spot a pair of scissors lying on the floor and snatch them up with my free hand. "Man the fuck up.

His eyes widen, but he doesn't say anything. Gripping the scissors tightly, I watch my phone, waiting for a response.

Whispering, Crew asks, "You think he'll come in here?"

Before I can respond, my phone lights up with a text.

Jagger: Staring straight at the sorry motherfucker while he sips on a beer without a care in the world.

"Fuck," I grumble under my breath.

Crew's eyes light up, still wide in fear. "What?"

"It's not Jude. I fucking knew someone was helping him."

Still whispering, we converse on the matter. "Whoever it is has a sled or wheels."

"Well, there's only one way to find out." He's not gonna like this, but I say, "You ready?"

"No. No, I'm not ready. Now put the damn scissors down. We're not killing anyone tonight."

Suddenly, I'm wondering who this pansy ass is in front of me. Sure as hell isn't the same guy who threw firecrackers through the headmaster's bedroom window last year.

Still crouched down, I say in a low tone, "If this asshole was an accomplice to my sister's fall, then you bet your fucking ass I'll kill him." I stand up, not making any attempt to hide myself. Staring straight into the headlights coming through the window, I curl my lip. "Bring it on, fucker," I grumble under my breath.

The lights are so bright I can't see anything beyond them. I can't even make out what sort of ATV I'm looking at —a four-wheeler, maybe. Whoever it is, they see me.

Holding my stare, I don't flinch a muscle. I don't breathe. I don't blink. I challenge him.

The next thing I know, Crew is standing beside me. "Think he'll make a move?" he asks, joining in on the stare-down with the perp.

"Nah. If he wanted to show his face, he would have done it by now. But now we know, Jude isn't working alone."

In an instant, the engine revs on the ride and the lights whip to the side before the guy takes off, heading down the same snow trail he came in on.

Finally, I exhale, releasing all the pent-up air in my lungs and dropping the scissors to the floor.

"Yep," Crew says, "now we know. Let's get back to the party. There's nothing else to find here."

CREW WENT BACK to the party, but I called it a night and came home. I've got more important shit to deal with than a bunch of drunk idiots making asses of themselves.

With a brown bag in one hand that holds a Gatorade, a ham and cheese sandwich, and an individual bag of Doritos —her favorite—I pull open the basement door and close it behind me, clicking the lock for safety measures. Taking two steps at a time, I go down.

Bypassing the gym equipment, I head straight for the

door that leads to a storage room. With my master key in hand, I insert it in and unlock the door, making sure to lock it again once it's closed.

Then I come up to the next door. So many damn doors, but each one is a necessary level of protection.

With the same key, I unlock the next door—this one leading to the tunnels. It's a long stretch from the tunnels we use often, such as The Gathering room and Beckett's lair beneath the cabin. I'm not even sure Crew and Jagger have entered or exited through this end, which is exactly why I knew it'd be the perfect spot.

I close the next door and walk a few feet down until I'm at the room I've been visiting frequently.

Unlocking the final door, I step inside the small cubic room.

Tossing the bag at her, she rolls her eyes and catches it in the air.

"Well, hello to you, too, sis."

CHAPTER
SEVEN
JAGGER

LAUGHTER ROARS through the trails as we walk back to the dorms, or in our case, our house. Sleds left behind, we make the trek, because Lord knows none of us are in any shape to drive.

Scar tips to the left, crashing into Crew as giggles escape her. I tighten my grip on her waist, holding her up with Crew's help. "One foot in front of the other, baby."

"I'm trying." She chuckles. "I'm trying so damn hard."

When she stumbles again, I crouch in front of her. "Hop on."

"Ahhh," she bellows, with a bounce in her step, as she crashes into my back. With her hands in the air, she squeals. "I can fly."

"Let's not fly," I tell her. "Hold on before you fall."

"I won't fall," she argues. "I'm not even drunk."

Crew and I share a comical look and I'm positive she's further gone than we are. At least I'm able to stay on my feet while carrying the weight of her body.

It's nice hearing her laugh, though, and now that I think

about it, it's been hours since any of us have even mentioned Jude or the threats. Scar said we needed this, and she was right. Even if it's just for one night.

We part ways with the rest of the students, taking a different trail to our house. "Wait," Scar says in a panic, her legs stiff in my arms, "we forgot Riley."

"No, babe. Riley's in her dorm room with Melody," Crew assures her.

"You're sure? Because if that bastard hurts her because I left her, I'll never forgive myself."

"I'm sure," Crew says. "Melody's staying with her. She's fine."

Crew's words seem to appease her because her body goes slack again. With her arms wrapped around me, she rests her head on my shoulder. "I love you guys," she mumbles. "I really do."

"Love you, too," I tell her, while Crew just laughs at her drunkenness.

Her head shoots up and her voice rises. "I have an idea."

"Oh boy. Can't wait to hear it."

"We can all sleep in my bed tonight."

When neither Crew nor I respond, she keeps talking. "Oh, come on. It's not like you guys have never shared a bed with a girl. I've heard all the stories. What's the big deal?"

"No big deal," Crew says. "If that's what you want, then fine. We'll all sleep in your bed."

Once again, she's satisfied with the response, so she puts her head back down.

A couple minutes later, Crew is opening the front door while I walk inside with Scar still on my back.

"Is she sleeping?" I ask Crew as he closes the door.

He takes a peek at her and nods. "She's out cold."

"Damn. I was sort of hoping she'd eat and drink some water before bed. She's gonna feel this one tomorrow."

I walk over to the couch and let her fall back so I can pick her back up with a better hold. If I attempt to walk up the stairs with her on my back, there's a good chance she'll fall backward, taking us both down.

"All right. I'm taking her up," I tell Crew.

"You sleep with her tonight. She won't even notice I'm gone."

"You sure?"

He nods. "Yeah. I'm gonna cook a pizza and probably crash on the couch."

Crew's been sleeping on the living room couch a lot lately. The only reason I can ascertain is that he's playing watchdog and keeping an eye on the door at night. I haven't asked, but if I did, I'm sure that's the reasoning I'd get.

If Scar weren't here, I know he'd give two fucks less, but she is, and for that, he wants to keep her safe. I can't fault him for that. I'm actually pretty impressed with how serious he's taking this. His number one priority right now is keeping her safe, as is mine.

After taking off her shoes, I scoop her up in my arms, cradling her like a baby while I carry her to her room. As I kick open her bedroom door, I look down at her. Eyes closed, mouth parted slightly. *She's perfect.*

"Crew," she grumbles, eyelids fluttering.

Crew? There's a pang in my chest hearing her ask for him.

"No, baby. It's me."

Her eyes open slightly. The stench of liquor rolls off her tongue as she asks, "Where's Crew?"

"He, uh, he'll be up in a minute."

For the first time since Scar and I started dating, I'm jealous. Jealous that she's asking for Crew when I'm standing right here. I'm the one who carried her home and brought her up to her room. I'm here, yet she wants him?

One arm goes around my neck and she curls her head against my chest. "I'm drunk, Jagger."

"Yeah, you are." I lay her down gently on the bed and slide off her damp fishnet tights. She must've fallen in the snow at least a dozen times. Gripping the corner of her comforter, I bring it up to her shoulders.

When I turn to walk away, planning to go get Crew for her, she says, "Don't leave me."

I turn back around, stepping closer to the bed. My fingers run through her hair, pushing it off her forehead. "Okay. I'll stay."

She sits up, pulling her dress over her head then lies back down, wearing only her black satin bra and matching panties.

After shedding myself of my jeans and hoodie, I'm in only my boxers when I climb under the blanket with her. Scar throws an arm around me, burying her head against my shoulder, then flings a leg over mine.

I'm staring at the ceiling, the only light coming from her nightlight plugged in beside the bed. The complete silence leaves me with only the screaming thoughts in my head.

Will she ever want me as much as she wants Crew? They have history. He was her first. From what I hear, they loved each other in secret until Neo blew it all apart with his theories. What would they be, had he never done that? More than likely, a solid couple without me as the baggage in her life.

"Is he coming?" Scar asks, her voice muffled by the pillow pressed between my shoulder and her face.

"Think so," I lie. I could reach down, grab my phone and shoot him a text to get up here, but that sting of jealousy won't let me do it.

Self-doubt isn't something I get often, but when I do, it hits me like a fucking tidal wave. Only one person has ever made me feel less than good enough, and that's my father. If I don't do things exactly the way he wants, I'm a failure in his eyes. I once got a B on a test and he grilled me like a sergeant. Screaming in my face that my future was on the line and these types of grades will get me nowhere in life. A fucking B! Never got one after that, until now. My grades are slipping lately. I'm too hung up on everything else. This stalker case, being a member of the Lawless...Scar. But what good is any of it if I'm not coming in first place? Is there a place with her? Fuck! I'm in my head too goddamn much.

Scar lifts her head, her bloodshot eyes wide. "Do you think something happened to him?"

"He's fine." My words come out harsher than I planned, but damn.

"Hey," she says, tone low, "what's wrong with you?"

"I'm here, Scar. Isn't that enough?" My head shakes in annoyance, and I know I'm being ridiculous, but I don't care either way. I've been told I get reckless and careless when I'm drunk. I tend to take more risks than I would sober and I put my foot in my mouth far too much. I think alcohol just makes you say the things you always want to but aren't brave enough to speak when you're not under the influence. Then again, I don't think I'm even drunk anymore.

Her eyebrows pinch together as her face hovers over mine. "Of course it is. Why are you even asking that?"

"Maybe because he's all you've asked about since I carried you in here."

I can't even look her in the eye because I know I'll see disappointment.

"Jagger! Where is this coming from? I thought you were content with this situation. In fact, you're the one who said you didn't care if I was with Crew as long as you had me, too."

My eyes roll to the left and I stare at the door with stillness. "Forget I said anything. Let's just go to sleep. We've both had too much to drink."

Her palm cups my cheek and she turns my head, forcing me to look at her. "No. We're talking about this now. Are you having second thoughts about us?"

"What? No!" I blurt out. "God, no, Scar. I'd never have doubts about us. I want this. I just... I don't know. I'm overthinking shit."

She exhales a breath of forced laughter. "You're starting to sound like Crew."

I scowl back at her at the mention of his name, again.

"Sorry, I didn't mean it like that. It's just, he questions this whole thing all the time. I never expected it from you. I always assumed you were fine with it all. It's my fault. I should have known you'd need reassurance, too."

"No, baby." I shift onto my side, wrapping her in my arm while propping my head up with my hand. "You didn't do anything wrong. You shouldn't have to reassure either of us."

"I do, though. This isn't an easy situation and I don't want either of you to think for a minute that one relationship is superior to the other. Because it's not. You and Crew each offer me something different, but the intensity of my feelings for you are exactly the same."

I quirk a brow, wondering if this is the alcohol talking, because Scar never talks emotions. "You still drunk?"

She cracks a smile and swats my chest. "Yes. A little, I think. But I mean what I'm saying. Whenever you feel like this, please talk to me about it. I don't want you to ever second-guess what we have."

Leaning down, I press my lips to hers, suddenly feeling like a damn idiot. But I'm also relieved. I needed the reassurance tonight.

"Do you still want me to get Crew?" I ask her, our mouths ghosting. "I don't mind. Really."

Her head shakes while our noses brush. "No. I only want you tonight." I'm certain her words are coming from a place of guilt, but I'm not arguing her decision.

My arm swoops under her side, and I lift, pulling her on top of me. "Oh yeah? Prove it?"

"Plan to." Her mouth meets mine. It's abrasive and rough, but passion sizzles between us. Our teeth clank as our tongues knot in a web of desire. "I'm yours, Jagger."

I believe what she says. She is mine. She might be his, too, but it doesn't take away from the fact that she is still mine. "There's no one else for me, Scar. Never will be." My words have never been truer. No one can satisfy me the way Scar does. She gives me everything I want and need. The sass that puts me in my place. The emotions that drive me fucking crazy. The body that sets my soul on fire. We connect on a level I've never experienced with another person. My heart calls to her and she answers. Always knowing exactly what to say to talk me off the ledge, or what to do to show me how serious she is about us. I was a fool to doubt what we have. Nothing compares.

Lifting up, I grind my erection against her hip bone, showing her what she does to me. Her legs wrap around either side of me and her back curves. Skating my hands up the cups of her bra, I get a firm grasp on her tits.

"Mmm," I hum into her mouth. "Mine." My teeth graze the skin of her lip before sucking it into my mouth. Her heady breaths satisfy my need for oxygen as I inhale each one.

My hands move around her back, fingers grating against her soft skin. With one flick, her bra comes unclasped and falls to her waist. I let it settle there, too focused on what's in front of me to bother moving it.

Lifting my head, I suck the pink bud of her nipple in my mouth while massaging both her breasts. Scar purrs, dropping her head back and flexing her chest outward. I move to the other one, giving it the same attention. My balls ache with a dire need of release. Pins and needles shoot through my body, heat pooling in my stomach. "Fuck, baby. I need you so bad."

Scar lifts up, giving me access to my boxers, and I slide them down just enough to spring my cock free. With an open palm, she grabs a hold of it, eyes locked on mine. Her hand slides up and down, thumb swiping the head. "Suck it, baby." I give her head a gentle push, guiding her downward, and she grins.

As she repositions herself, she slides her thumb across her tongue, licking up the bead of precum she gathered. "So fucking sexy."

Twisting around, she sticks her ass right in my face, her bra falling somewhere in between. "Now this is a sight I like to see." I grab two handfuls of her smooth ass while she takes the shallow end of my dick in her mouth, using her hand to satisfy the bottom half. I give her cheek a slap and she shrieks with a mouth full of cock.

My hands move to her hips and I tug her back an inch so that I'm eye level with her pussy, then I sit her down on my face. Swiping the pad of my tongue between her folds, I press my thumb to her asshole, not going in, but toying with the nerves I know will make her feel good.

Her head bobs up and down as she sucks me off. Every once in a while, she gives her jaw a break and slides her tongue up my length, coating it with saliva, then pumping her hand a few times before taking me back in her mouth. She's mastered the blow job and my only regret is not being able to see her doe eyes peer up at me. I've got the second best view right now, though.

I slide one finger inside her pussy, immediately adding another. Bringing my other hand around her, I use the pad of my fingers to massage her clit.

She howls around my cock, as I push my fingers in deeper. My tongue slides up between her ass cheeks, while I continue pumping my fingers violently inside her. Her back arches and she leans into me, desperate for more.

Sucking deeper and faster, her tongue laps around my shaft, my body fills with an insatiable need. The sweet smell of her juices dripping into my palm floods my senses and it's an aphrodisiac that sends me soaring. "Baby, I'm gonna come."

Instead of stopping, she sucks harder. My cock hits the back of her throat, resting on top of her tongue.

Shrills of ecstasy escape her as her walls clench around my fingers. I bring her closer and just before she comes undone, I pull my fingers out and suck on her clit. Proof of her orgasm spills out and I keep licking, cleaning up the mess she made while my cum shoots down her throat. A heady growl rips through my vocal cords as my chest rises and falls rapidly.

My lower half convulses, cock twitching as she takes me out of her mouth. I give her one last lick before she drops her ass on my chest. Sitting up, she looks over her shoulder, grinning. "Wow," is all she says.

I slap her ass gently, giving it a subtle squeeze. "Wow, is right."

Just as she goes to turn around, her arousal seeping onto my chest, her bedroom door flies open and we're faced with a panic-stricken Crew.

"Shit. I thought something was wrong." He goes to close the door, probably feeling a little humiliated, but Scar stops him just before it latches.

"Wait," she calls out, "don't go."

Turning around, she drops down beside me and pulls a flat sheet up over the both of us. "You said you'd stay with me." She curls the white sheet to her chest, propping herself up on one elbow.

I'm lying flat on my back when I reach down to the floor, fishing for my boxers. When I come up empty-handed, I climb out from under the blanket and sit up, my semi-erect cock on display for all to see. Not that I care. Crew's seen me before. Hell, we've all seen each other. In fact, a couple years ago, we got the ruler out just to see who was bigger. Obviously, I won by a good inch and a half.

Crew steps into the room and I pay him little attention, while I get up in search of my boxers. Once I've found them, I go into Scar's bathroom, leaving the door cracked a tad, to clean up while listening to the conversation being had inside the room.

"I'm glad you came," Scar tells him.

"To be honest, I wasn't going to, but I heard you screaming and...well, now I know you weren't screaming at all."

"Sorry you had to walk in on that."

"Don't be. Doesn't bother me anymore."

"I'm glad." There's a moment of silence and I can only assume she's kissing him.

Hmm. Hope he doesn't mind the taste of my jizz.

I chuckle at the thought. Immediately stopping when I realize it's very possible I've kissed her after she's sucked him off and I wouldn't have even known it.

With one hand pressed to the wall, I spring my dick free and point it down to take a piss while still listening.

"So you'll stay?"

"As long as Jagger's cool with it. Don't wanna step on any toes."

I raise my voice, speaking so they can hear me. "It's fine."

Crew hollers back, "You listening to us, fucker?"

"Yup."

This isn't about me; it's about her, and if she's happy, so am I—as long as I get to be a part of said happiness.

CHAPTER
EIGHT
SCAR

"I'm so glad you decided to stay with us, Ry. I'd hate for you to be alone right now."

Riley rolls over on her side, facing me in my large king-size bed. "Me too. If you wouldn't have invited me to stay here, honestly, I think I would have dropped out of BCA and gone home."

"Don't talk like that. You're not dropping out and you're not giving up on your training. We've got this. Each day we get one step closer."

"We don't *got this,* Scar. Whoever is in charge has this, and right now, they have us all under their thumb."

"You're being a pessimist again."

"How can I not be? My boyfriend is pretending to be a dead guy and the sick thing is, I have to keep being his girlfriend."

"It won't be much longer. As soon as the guys figure out who's working with him, they'll take action."

After the Halloween party two nights ago, Melody spent the night with Riley at her dorm, so she wouldn't be alone.

Elias, or Jude rather, spent the entire night at The Gathering room on cleanup duty, so we knew she was safe. But now, I've insisted she stay here with us because I really don't feel like she should be alone.

A subtle knock at my door has my head twisting. "Come in," I say loudly.

She tsks. "Still too trusting, Scar. Still too trusting."

I pull my pillow out from under me and chuck it at her. "I knew it was either Crew or Jagger."

"Right," she drawls. "Because Neo doesn't knock." Her tone drops to a mumble. "Prick that he is."

Crew enters the room, walking slowly, shoulders slouched.

"What's wrong?" I ask him.

He rubs his shoulder as he comes closer. "Boxing in the basement with Jagger and Neo. Neo got me good."

"Boys," Riley murmurs, shaking her head while getting out of bed. "I'm gonna go get ready in the spare bathroom downstairs. You two should start getting ready, too."

Once Riley's gone, Crew takes a seat on the edge of the bed and I draw in a deep breath of his cologne. "You smell good. Must've showered after your little boxing event?"

"Before. I didn't last long boxing. Neo's a fucking psycho. I swear the guy actually wants to kill both Jagger and me."

I laugh, believing every word of it, but I'm still unsure why anyone would want to harm their best friends. "Why?" I tug the blanket up over my shoulders, not wanting to leave this bed. "Did you two piss him off again?"

"Seems like that's all we're doing lately. The thing is, Jagger and I were just having a conversation about you. Nothing that even pertained to him. Neo was pressing on the bench, while we were blocking harmless shots. I was checking in with Jagger to make sure there were no hard feelings with me crashing with you and him the other night after the Halloween party, and the next thing I know, Neo's sliding on his gloves. Didn't even speak a single word. Just started throwing shots."

"Hmm. That is weird."

"He'll never admit it, but I think he hates that we're with you."

I sigh. "Yeah. Because he hates me. Of course he doesn't want his friends hanging out with me. Let alone dating me."

"No," he shakes his head in disagreement, "it's more than that."

Stretching my hand out of the blanket, I rest it on his leg, and he curls his fingers around mine. "You're overthinking things."

"Don't think so. Deep down, I think he really wants you. And I think he wants you all for himself."

That warrants a heavy breath of laughter. I shoot up in bed, tossing the blanket off me, ready to end this conversation. "You're insane."

"Babe. I'm dead serious. I know Neo, and I've never in my entire life seen him so wrapped up in a single person like he is with you."

I spin around to face him in my cropped tee shirt and underwear, half serious, half not. "No shit, Crew. For two years, the guy thought I tried to kill his sister. Not to mention, he blames me and Jagger for his mom getting hit by a car."

Dammit. I've gone too far. I don't think Crew even knew about all that.

"Wait." He jumps onto his feet. "What?"

I swallow hard, knowing I put my foot in my mouth. "Nothing. Forget it."

Casually going about my business, hoping Crew lets this go, I pull open my dresser drawer in search of black leggings.

His hand lands on my shoulder, and he turns me around to face him. "No way. Tell me what you meant."

Shoulders slack and head hung low, I explain, "The night Neo's mom was hit, Neo found me and Jagger in my treehouse. We used to meet up there occasionally to...talk." I don't tell him it was to make out because I'm almost certain Crew knows Jagger was my first kiss and many more after that. "Well, Neo claims his mom ran some errands to kill time while Neo searched for Jagger. Had Neo not had to search for him, his mom wouldn't have run those errands." Saying it out loud makes me understand Neo's feelings so much better. I honestly don't blame him for thinking that way. I'd probably feel the same. I'm actually really surprised he hasn't beat the shit out of Jagger over it yet—or worse.

Crew rakes his fingers through his hair. "Damn. Why didn't I know this sooner?"

"Would it have mattered?"

His eyes lift to mine, wide and sad. "Yeah. For sure. Neo's kept this shit inside all these years."

"Please don't say anything to him. I don't want him to think I'm butting into his personal life."

"But he told you."

"Yeah. I mean, it wasn't a pleasant conversation. It's not like we were having a friendly chitchat or anything."

"Doesn't matter. Neo doesn't open up to anyone, Scar. *Anyone.*" He emphasizes that last word. "But he did to you.

Even if it was out of anger. He shared something really fucking big with you that he never even shared with us."

I shuffle past him with my leggings in hand. "Over-thinking again."

"I don't think so. And I'm gonna prove it. You make Neo feel shit, babe, and I don't think it's just hate that he feels."

"You're being ridiculous. What other feeling could possibly go alongside hate?"

"Love. After all, that line is thin."

And now I laugh out loud because Crew has lost his damn mind. "Okay. Enough of this. We need to go to school."

I head into my bathroom and get ready, glad that this conversation has ended.

REGARDLESS OF MY disdain for Neo, I'm still forced to sit beside him in American Lit. I find it odd that being so superior, he doesn't request a different seat, considering he hates me so much.

He does hate me, right?

Crew's words have been playing on repeat in my mind, and I could slap him for putting these thoughts in my head.

Love.

It literally makes me laugh out loud, drawing attention to myself from all three guys in my row—Neo, who's to my left, Crew, to my right, and Jagger, who's beside Crew.

"What's so funny?" Crew asks in a whisper.

"Nothing. Just thinking." And while I'm thinking so hard, another thought pops in my head. "Hey. Tell Jagger to switch seats with Neo."

I look over at Neo, who's looking at his phone that he's holding under the table. His brows dip low, but he doesn't lift his eyes.

"Hey." Crew says, nudging Jagger, "Switch seats with Neo."

Jagger looks at Crew, then me, and finally Neo. "He won't. I've tried."

Crew relays the message to me, even though I already heard. "He's tried."

"Why won't you switch seats with Jagger?" I ask Neo, who's definitely not amused with this conversation.

He twists his head a tad, glowering. "Keep your enemies close. Right?"

"Seems a little backward given our situation. You have nothing to gain from being near me. So why not just switch?"

I'm not sure why I'm pressing the issue so much. As ridiculous as it is, I can't help but consider what Crew said, along with what Neo said in the tunnels before the party a couple days ago. He said he hates me because he has to. Among many other vile words about how toxic I am. But his only reasoning was, *because he has to.*

I sink back in my chair, getting comfortable, all the while watching Neo out of the corner of my eye.

What is he thinking about at this very moment?

CHAPTER
NINE
NEO

Stop fucking looking at me!

I wanna scream it at her, but I don't because it means she'll know I notice. How can I not? Her eyes are burning into the side of my head. It feels like her stare is eating away at my skull, while infusing my brain with her poison. Making me think irrational thoughts, such as, how sexy she looks with the top three buttons of her uniform shirt undone. Nonchalantly, I steal a glance, avoiding her eyes. Sure enough, the skin of her cleavage is peeking out, and fuck if it doesn't make my cock jump.

She's the enemy, Neo. Even the devil was once an angel.

My eyes skate up, locking with hers.

Busted.

I snarl in disgust, giving her the idea that I'm appalled by her presence. However, in order for her to believe that fallacy, I'd have to make every attempt to move away from her. Yet I don't because the thought of seeing her sandwiched between Jagger and Crew for an hour every day appalls me more than she does.

Rock and a hard place. I don't like her. Don't want her. But I don't want anyone else to want her either. Especially them.

Maybe it's time I do something about that.

I'm torn away from my thoughts when my phone vibrates on the table. Scar looks at it, followed by the guys. I snatch it off the table quickly when I see that it's Maddie calling.

Scar leans over, being the nosey shit she is. "Who is that?"

"Hasn't anyone ever told you curiosity killed the cat?" I scoot my chair back, not bothering to push it in as I slide behind the row to leave.

What the hell does she want? I told her not to call unless it was an emergency. I get it. She's bored. She expresses that multiple times a day. But right now, she has to stay bored because that boredom will keep her safe.

"What's up?" Jagger asks, but my response is an exaggerated sigh.

Mr. Collins gives me a look, and when I catch his stare, he quickly snaps his attention back to the class. "Attention up here," he says. "Now, who read last night's required passage from Frank Herbert's *Dune*?"

Thank fuck I'm outta here because I sure as hell didn't read that shit.

I dip out of the open door, closing it just as far as it was before I made my exit. With my phone in hand, I tap *Call Back*.

Maddie picks up on the first ring.

"Jesus, Neo. What took you so long?" Her voice is a whisper and she should not need to whisper.

84

"I'm in the middle of class. What the fuck do you think took me so long?"

"Well, it's a good thing you called back. Someone's in the house."

My feet move quickly down the hall as I head straight for the exit. "Maddie," I press. "Tell me how you know this? You better not be outside that room."

"I was bored. So damn bored. I did really well with therapy today and my physical therapist told me I needed to move around more in my wheelchair. These tunnels creep me the hell out, Neo."

"Dammit! I thought I made it clear that you cannot leave that room under no circumstances."

Still whispering, she says, "You're ignoring the fact that I just told you someone is in your house. I'm not playing. Someone is here."

"Get your ass back in that room. I'm on my way."

"I can't. I'm sort of...stuck."

"What do you mean you're stuck? Did you get your wheelchair caught up on something?"

"No. I'm pressed in a corner and this chick is in the bath-room...singing."

Chick? I drop down on my sled and stick my key in the ignition. "For the love of God, Maddie. Are you seeing shit again?"

"No, I'm not seeing shit." The defensiveness in her tone is obvious. "I'm completely of sound mind and body. Have been for days. Someone is definitely in there singing."

"Can you see who it is?"

"One sec," she whispers, even softer this time.

There's a beat of silence before she returns and says,

"Definitely a girl. Curly blonde hair. Dancing around and using a shampoo bottle as her microphone."

"Son of a bitch!" I press my lips together. "It's gotta be Riley. Stay where you're at. I'm coming."

I end the call, immediately shooting a group text to Crew and Jagger.

> Me: Make it clear to your girl that her dumb-ass friend is not welcome to freely roam around our house. I'm heading home to kick her ass out for good. Skipping the rest of the day.

Not waiting for a response, I stuff my phone in the inside pocket of my leather jacket and take off for the house.

In record time, I'm pulling up directly in front of it. I turn off the engine and hop off, leaving my keys in the ignition. I walk quickly to the door, sweeping the fallen snow from my hair. As soon as I'm inside, I shout, "Riley!" But it's not loud enough for her to hear me, if she's still in the basement.

With heavy steps, I stomp through the living room to the basement door, leaving a trail of snow behind me.

"Riley!" I shout again, this time much louder. My feet thud down the stairs as I continue to holler. "Where the fuck are you?"

When I reach the bottom, I make a beeline for the bathroom and see that the door is already wide open. Before stepping inside, I give the basement a lazy sweep, immediately spotting Maddie in the far corner with a stack of boxes surrounding her and her wheelchair.

Riley spins around, still holding a bottle of shampoo in her hand, and her cheerful expression drops. "Neo. Hi. What are you doing home?"

I snatch the bottle of shampoo from her hand before violently tossing it to the floor. The top comes off on impact and clear liquid oozes out. In the same breath, I snatch her phone, that's blasting, "What Other People Say" by Sam Fischer and Demi Lovato, off the vanity and end the song then slam the phone back down, unsure if I cracked the screen, but not caring either way.

"Are you mad? I'm so sorry," she begins with a panic-stricken expression, "I wasn't feeling well, so I left class early and—"

"And what? You thought you'd come to my house and help yourself to my shower?"

"Technically, it's not *your* house. It belongs to the Blue Bloods."

My phone buzzes against my breastbone, so I pull it out and read the text message from the guys, while Riley pleads her case about how Scar said she could stay here, so she assumed it was fine to come back.

> Jagger: Relayed the message and she stormed out of the school to get some fresh air before her next class. Said she wants to be alone. She's pissed.

With my phone clutched in my hand, I return my attention to Riley. "I don't give a flying fuck what Scar said. She's a guest, the same as you. It's high time both of you show a little respect. Now get your fucking shoes on and get the hell out of my house."

Am I being harsh? Yes. Does she deserve it? Hell yes, she does. This isn't a fucking shelter for the lost and needy.

"You're..." she stumbles over her words before finally spitting out, "...really mean."

Classic. Shouldn't expect anything else from Riley. She's far too sweet, and with that demeanor, she'll never make it as a Guardian.

"I am mean and you're about to see just how mean I can get."

"I'm going," she scoffs. "Just give me a darn minute."

My hands press to the vanity and I drop my head, wondering how much longer I have to deal with these idiots. Scar is one thing—I can handle her. In fact, tormenting her is sorta fun. Riley, on the other hand, is not part of the plan and her being here is nothing short of an inconvenience.

The sound of boxes moving around has my eyes shooting to where Maddie is hiding. *If looks could kill.* She's furious. No, she's fucking irate. I shake my head no, and mouth the words, "Not yet."

Thanks to Riley, I have a lot of explaining to do now.

I lift my head slightly, eyes on Riley. "Hurry your ass up."

With an armful of clothes, she pouts. "I have to change." Her eyes wander down to her clothes, and I notice she's wearing pajamas.

Straightening my back, I level with her. "You've got clothes on," I point a stern finger at the door, "now get the fuck out."

Once again, a little too harsh, but necessary. I need her out of here before Maddie overhears more shit I don't need her hearing.

It's just my fucking luck that heavy footsteps fill the air, and the next thing I know, I'm faced with a fuming Scar. "What the hell did you say to her?" She rages, eyes dancing from me to Riley.

Getting some fresh air, my ass.

I need to diffuse this situation quickly or all hell is about to break loose. I walk into Scar, bumping my chest to hers while backing her out the doorway. "Upstairs!"

"No!" She shoves me back a couple steps, forcing me into the bathroom. "I told Riley she could stay here and she stays."

Looking down at her, I narrow my eyes as I try to pull the door shut behind me, so Maddie can't see or hear anything, but Scar has the toe of her boot wedged in it. Doesn't matter anyway, there's no way she missed this. "You're walking in on shit that's not your business so get back to class and let me handle this."

"It's fine," Riley says from behind me. Snatching her phone off the sink with a huff, she shoves the door open and storms out of the bathroom, still speaking. "I'll just go back to my dorm and change there. Don't worry, asshole. You won't see me here again." She steps past us, ramming her shoulder hard against mine, but I'm certain it hurt her more than it did me.

Scar reaches out, grabbing Riley by the arm. "No, Ry. This isn't just Neo's house. Crew and Jagger said it was fine for you to stay. Ignore him." Her eyes are on mine as she grits out the words. "He just hates his life, so he wants us to hate ours, too."

Riley pulls her arm away. "You might be okay with this mess, but I'm not." She stomps up the stairs, and if she knows what's good for her, she'll go straight out the front door.

"What are you waiting for?" I tip my chin. "Go after her."

"You'd love that, wouldn't you? Two birds with one

89

stone?" Steam rolls out of Scar's flared nostrils, her arms crossed tightly over her chest. "I'm not going anywhere until you tell me..." Her voice rises to a screeching howl, her teeth bared. "...why you're such a fucking asshole!"

Damn. I'm not sure I've ever seen her this mad. Of all the things I've done to try and get her to this boiling point, all it took was me being a dick to her friend.

Her hands meet my chest as she shoves me back, farther and farther, and while I should fight back, I don't because I'm kinda turned on right now.

Each word that leaves her mouth is proceeded by another shove backward. "Time and time again..." My back hits the glass shower door. "...you do this shit just to piss me off. We both know this isn't about Riley being here. It's about you wanting to make me miserable."

I'm not sure whether to laugh or fight back at this point.

When my response is nothing but pressed lips and a bitten back smile, she shouts louder, "Say something, dammit!"

She's right. I do need to say something because if I don't act fast, shit will hit the fan. There's no way Maddie didn't hear Scar's voice. They've been best friends for years. She'd know her voice anywhere.

My hands land on Scar's curvy hips. I lean close and I whisper in her ear, while inhaling her floral, yet earthy scent, "You're gonna do exactly what I say, understand?"

An airy laugh escapes her. "Not a chance."

Ghosting her ear with my lips, I repeat myself, "Do. You. Understand?"

Her hands find my chest and she pushes herself off me. One hand remains on her hip, and while I hate what I have to do, it needs to be done. Confused eyes meet mine. "No," she says pointedly.

I keep my voice low, so Maddie doesn't hear me. "Remember that secret I told you I had? Well, it will be exposed to, not only the entire student body, but The Elders, if you don't do exactly what I say."

If Maddie finds out that Scar and Crew are together, she's bound to give up her fight. She's come so far since she's woken up, and I'd hate to see her take steps backward. Not to mention, her heart will be shattered. This is also the perfect opportunity to break apart the trio that has been haunting my house.

Her head shakes rapidly. "No. You're fucking insane. I'm not doing shit for you. Expose my secret. I don't care."

I quirk a brow. "You sure about that?"

"I don't care what you do, Neo. Just leave me the hell alone." She spins on her heels to walk away, but I grab her arm and tug her close.

With my chin resting on her head and her body trembling in my arms, I say, "You're risking abolishment from the Society, Scar. Not just you, but your parents, too."

She tenses. A beat of silence between us. "You're bluffing."

"Try me."

Audible breaths escape her while her chest heaves against me. "What do you want from me?" She chokes on the words, on the verge of tears.

"Nothing. And everything. At the same time."

"Scar." Maddie's voice hits Scar's ears, before they do mine, and I don't even process them until Scar is breaking free from my hold.

I stand back, observing the reunion, and while I should

91

be happy for them, it feels more like a slow suffering. Knew this was coming. The minute I saw Scar's face, I knew Maddie would show hers.

"M-Maddie?" Scar blinks rapidly, regaining her focus and failing to believe what's right in front of her.

They're at least five feet apart. Scar stands directly in front of me and Maddie is sitting in her wheelchair beside my weight bench. They stare at each other for what feels like minutes and I'm certain all the blood has drained from Scar's face. She's as pale as the snow tracks on our living room floor. She takes a couple steps. And a few more, trying to get to Maddie.

I know she's going down before she does, but as she starts to fall, I'm right there, catching her limp body.

"Scar," Maddie gasps, wheeling quickly over to where I'm lowering Scar to the floor. "Is she okay?"

"She'll be fine. She's just in shock."

"What is she even doing here, Neo? You told me she was back in Essex."

Maddie's looking at me now, waiting for a response, so I tell her the truth. "She's here because...she lives here..." Or at least, it started as the truth. "...with me. We're dating now."

You stupid, fucking idiot! Now I'm pretty sure all the blood has completely drained from my face.

Maddie laughs and it's a little disheartening that she doesn't believe Scar and me could be together. "Why is that funny? You think she's too good for me?"

"Umm. Yes. Among other reasons. For instance, you've never liked Scar. So how the hell did this even happen?"

"Things change. People change."

Unlike my ability to get myself into shit I can't get myself out of.

Fuck. What did I just do? Now that my lie is out there, it doesn't feel like it will reap the benefits I'd hoped for. I could have easily said she's with Jagger and all would have been fine. As long as Maddie doesn't know about Scar and Crew, we're good. So why in the fucking world did I just tell her Scar and I are dating. No. This is fine. Scar will be forced to dump Crew and Jagger, and I won't have to see her with them anymore. Instead, I'll have to pretend she's with me. It's wrong on so many levels, but it's not real. This can work. It has to.

Maddie looks back down at Scar, a brush of sadness in her expression. "I can't believe I've missed so much. My best friend and my brother?"

Scar begins stirring, her lashes fluttering, and I need to think fast again. "Go get her a wet washcloth from the bathroom. Top drawer."

"You go get it. I need to be here when she wakes up, so she knows it wasn't a dream."

"Dammit, Maddie. Would you please go? I'm worried about her."

Man, I'm pretty good at this. I almost believe it myself. Truth is, I'd love nothing more than for Scar to stay passed out for the next six months.

"I know how you are, Neo. Be gentle with her."

I huff. "I've changed, Maddie."

She sighs heavily as she wheels around us. "Yeah, right."

Once she's gone, I pat Scar's cheek a couple times. Her eyes flutter open before shooting wide. "Was that really…Maddie?"

"No. You're seeing shit." I fuck with her a little. With any luck, she'll believe it and leave immediately. Not likely, though.

"I know what I saw. Maddie is here."

"Fine. yes. She's here. We'll fill you in soon." I sweep an arm under her head and lift it up slowly. "Can you sit up?"

"I can." She slaps my arm away. "But I don't need your help. Get your dirty hands off me."

This isn't going to be as easy as I thought. Then again, I didn't think at all.

"About that," I begin with a whisper, hoping to get this out quickly before Maddie returns. "Maddie is still in love with Crew and she doesn't know he's here at BCA."

"Oh my god, Neo." She rubs her forehead aggressively. "You haven't told her?"

"Haven't exactly had time, *Scar*," I put an emphasis on her name. "She's only been here for a couple weeks and for half of it, she was in and out of consciousness."

"How?" Her forehead creases more and more with each one-word question. "Why? When? What the hell is going on?"

"I told you I'll fill you in, but right now, you need to know something else. That secret I told you I'd keep. It's not safe until you pretend we're dating. You need to dump Crew and Jagger. It's the only way it'll appear real."

I've seen Scar's eyes go wide. Seen her surprised. Shocked. You name it. But none of that touches the look on her face right now. "Not. A. Chance. In. Hell."

"Then I guess I have no choice—"

Maddie returns with a gleeful smile and a wet wash-cloth. "There you are, Sleeping Beauty."

Scar shakes her head. "I...I don't need that." She pushes herself up, moving slowly. Tears expel from her eyes as she throws herself into Maddie's arms. "I can't believe you're awake. And here."

While they're reuniting and crying like fucking babies, I read my missed text messages from the guys.

> Crew: Have you heard from Scar?

> Jagger: No. I'm heading to lunch. She's probably at the table already.

> Crew: All right. Lemme know.

I decide to chime in and tell them she's here before they send out a search party.

> Me: She's here at the house. She's fine. No need to play knight in shining armor.

The next thing I know, Jagger's calling. Of fucking course.

"She's fine," is the first thing I say.

"Having a hard time believing that. Put her on the phone or Crew and I are coming home."

I'm not sure how much longer I can pull this shit off. Maybe I need to just come clean with everyone. Maddie's bound to get her heart broken eventually. Prolonging it is only going to make the heartbreak that much more painful.

I join Scar and Maddie, interrupting their hug-fest. "Hey, Jagger wants to talk to you." I cover the phone with my free hand. "They can't know, Scar. I'm dead serious. Do not tell a soul she's here." I hand Scar the phone and push Maddie's chair a few feet to the left.

"Why's Jagger calling Scar?" she asks.

"We're...all good friends now. It's a weird situation."

"No kidding. I'm still reeling from you and Scar being together. I was asleep for over a year, but I thought even a friendship between you two would have required a lifetime." She looks back at me, at where I'm holding the handles of her wheelchair, a wide smile on her face. "I'm proud of you, Neo. Finally opening up your heart and letting someone in."

I scratch the back of my head, hating the shit out of myself right now. I don't like lying to Maddie. It's not something I've done often, but I would do it time and time again to protect her.

"About that. I've been sort of thinking about breaking up with her. She's sort of a leech." It's true. I've seen the way she is with Crew and Jagger. All clingy and shit. I sure as fuck don't want that.

"Neo!" Maddie reaches back, trying to slap me, but misses. I chuckle a little, only pissing her off further. "I swear to God if you are leading Scar on or playing some stupid game, I will cut you."

"I don't doubt that for a second." Maddie is a beast and probably the only person in the world who can put me in my place. Now that she's awake and here, I need to prepare myself for that.

"I mean it. I better not find out you're playing with her heart. And who was that girl that was here earlier, dancing around in your kitchen? Please don't tell me this is some ménage à trois thing going on and you've got another girlfriend, too? Or worse," her expression goes solemn, "she's not with Crew, is she?"

"No. Hell no. I told you, Crew isn't seeing anyone. He's been waiting for you. That was Riley. Jagger's fling."

I just keep digging this hole deeper and deeper.

This was almost easier when Maddie was in a coma. Now I'm certain she and Scar will team up against me. And now that they have Riley, too. *I'm screwed.*

Scar returns with my phone, and when I hold my hand out, she slaps it down hard, scowling. Her distaste of the situation is more than apparent.

"Mads," I say to my sister, "Scar and I need a minute."

The two girls share a look before Maddie responds with, "Of course. I'll just go back to my room." She puts all her attention on Scar and says, "Then you and I need to catch up. It seems we have a lot to discuss."

Scar gives Maddie one more hug before they separate, and Maddie wheels back to the tunnel door.

Her shadow hasn't even left when Scar's open palm flies across my face. "You son of a bitch!"

Grinding my teeth, I rub the sore spot. "Jesus! What the hell was that for?"

"What was that for?" she growls. "For keeping Maddie from me. For lying about her whereabouts. Oh, and how about you lying to your sister, who just woke up from an eighteen-month coma. What were you thinking, telling her we're dating? We hate each other! Of all the things you could have said, you said that?"

I really don't know what to say. I'm pissed at myself, too. It's not often I admit I'm wrong, but I'll accept it right now. "You're right. It was a split-second decision, and it sort of just came out."

"Well, you need to fix this." A menacing laugh rips through her vocal cords. "There's no way in hell I'm breaking up with Crew and Jagger and pretending I'm with..." Her hands wave up and down in front of me, her lips curled in disgust. "...you."

I'm a little taken aback by what she's insinuating here. "You're acting as if being with me would be a girl's worst nightmare."

She huffs out a breath. "I'm not agreeing or denying that."

"Wow."

She tsks, taking a seat on my weight bench. "Don't act like the feeling isn't mutual."

I sit down beside her. Not because I want to be near her, but because we need to keep our voices down. "You're right. It is. But this isn't about me, or you. It's about Maddie."

Her head twists, eyes on mine. "You're blackmailing me, Neo. Even if it is for Maddie, this is not okay."

"Maybe so. But if you want your secret safe, you'll keep up with this charade until I come up with a plan."

"How about this for a plan... You tell her the truth. You can't hide Crew from her. He lives here."

I hate it when she's right.

"Not to mention there is no way in hell I'm pretending we're some loved-up couple. I wanna vomit just sitting this close to you."

"Well, now you're just being dramatic. We sit next to each other every day in American Lit."

"Yeah. And I tried to get you to switch seats, but for some reason, you won't. Why is that, Neo?"

"Told ya. Keep your enemies close."

"Bullshit."

"Why is that bullshit?" I chuckle. "Are you suggesting I'm into you?"

She shrugs a shoulder, warranting another laugh. "Not a chance. Pretty sure I've made my feelings for you clear."

Huffing and puffing, she presses her fingers to her temples and rubs aggressively.

Scar should have no reason to assume I feel anything toward her, except extreme loathing. I've never once given her a glimpse at my tortured mind. Sure, my fingers have swam in her pussy, but that wasn't to pleasure her; it was to humiliate her during class. I may have failed, but it was a nice attempt and sure as hell a nice escape from Mr. Collin's lecture. Aside from that, she doesn't know how hard I've trained my mind to dislike her, because a tiny space in my heart says she isn't so bad. But she is. She is that bad. She's a forbidden fruit, and while it might taste sweeter, it's forbidden for a reason—it's a poison that can ruin my life. I refuse to put my fate in her hands.

Scar gets on her feet. Not even looking at me, she says, "Where is Maddie's room? I need to talk to her and tell her the truth. She deserves that much."

I'm still seated on the bench, peering up at her. "You won't be telling Maddie anything. We're going to keep this reunion short and sweet. She and I will fill you in on why she's here and why it needs to remain a secret. Jagger and Crew can't know yet. Do you understand me?" I grit out, so she realizes how serious I am. "Had your idiot friend not helped herself to our home, you wouldn't know either."

"I'm willing to hear you out before I make a decision— for Maddie. But don't think for a second I'm acting like your girlfriend. Stage a breakup if needed, but I will not play like that. Not with the likes of you."

There it is again. That disgusted look. I know I've treated the girl like shit, but she looks at me like I have the face of Michael Myers.

"Why are you looking at me like that?" I finally ask her.

"Like what?"

"With such revulsion. Like I'm the ugliest thing you've ever laid eyes on?"

"If you really have to ask, then you're more of a sociopath than I've given you credit for. Now, where is she?"

I tip my head to the right, gesturing toward the open door. "Just keep going, you'll find her."

With a sour expression, she scoffs. "You've been making her stay in the tunnels?"

I quickly jump to my feet. "The girl's got it fucking made. Her room is immaculate. She's got a private bathroom, kitchenette, and she has a nurse and physical therapist that come in daily during the week while we're at school."

Scar shakes her head in disbelief and I'm feeling pretty judged right now. Keeping Maddie's whereabouts a secret is necessary. Someone tried to kill her, and until we know who and why, her safety is a priority. No one can be trusted.

There's only one thing left to do. Bring in and bring down Jude Beckett. And for my grand finale, I'll expose Scar.

As she walks away, heading to the door, I'm left with a thousand different thoughts in my head. What have I done? What am I going to do? Why the hell does it bother me that she hates me as much as I hate her?

CHAPTER

TEN

SCAR

"THIS IS UNREAL." I wrap my arms around Maddie for the umpteenth time, still not believing my eyes. "How are you here?" I step back, hands on her shoulders. "And out of bed?"

A broad smile spreads across her face, and she lifts a shoulder. "Neo saved me."

"But how? You were in a coma, Mads."

"*Was*, is the operative word." Her shoulders dance, as if this is the most casual thing ever. "He woke me up."

There's a tall stool to the left, so I grab it and take a seat, knowing this conversation is going to take a while. My only hope is that Neo stays out of it. "None of this makes sense. Please, make it make sense to me." I hold my hand out, noticing that it's still shaking. *She's really here.*

"Well," she begins, popping a piece of gum in her mouth and balling the wrapper between her fingers. "I was asleep, obviously, but Neo sent in a new team of doctors and security guards because he was worried someone would hurt me. My memory is still missing from that day and even the weeks prior to the fall, but he said someone pushed me."

"Did he also tell you he thought it was me that pushed you?"

Her head tilts slightly, eyes wide. "Oh no, he did not?"

"Oh yes. He sure did. In fact, he made it a point to make my life hell after your fall. To say it hasn't been easy is an understatement."

"But he knows the truth now and you forgave him? I mean, you two are together?" Her questioning tone leads me to believe she's not buying it. I mean, why would she? She's seen firsthand how much Neo has hated me all these years.

"Actually, there's something you should know—"

"And what you should know is that the past has been laid to rest." Neo comes in the room and my eyes shoot over my shoulder. Stepping behind me, his hands rest on my shoulders and he begins massaging them. *Who the fuck is this guy?* Just a couple days ago, he said I was toxic and he could barely stand being near me, and now, he's rubbing my shoulders?

Maddie smiles, pleased with his response. "I always knew there was something between you two. Ever since I caught Neo watching—"

"Okay, that's enough," Neo spits out, shutting her up, but now I'm curious what she was going to say.

"Oh no, dear." I pat his hand on my shoulder. "Let her finish."

Neo jerks his hand back so quickly, you'd think I just touched him with fire.

"Oh, come on, Neo. Let me tell her. It's not a big deal."

I look over my shoulder, grinning while Neo gives her a

death stare, shaking his head in slow motion. "Don't you dare."

"Okay. Now I have to know. Go on, Mads."

She winks at me, then smirks. "We'll finish this conversation later, when jerkface isn't around."

"Not if I can help it. In fact, I plan to be a third wheel with you two until I'm certain the threat has been extinguished."

"You can't be serious?" My body tenses under the touch of his hand. I'm not even sure he's conscious of its placement.

"I think I've proven how serious my words are, haven't I, *Scarlett*?" The way he enunciates my name sends a sweep of chills down my spine.

"That you have, *Neopolo*."

Maddie tosses us a glance. "Aww. That's cute how you two use each other's given birth names."

"In fact," I push my stool back, hard enough to have Neo grabbing his junk and letting out a squeal, "I think it's time you see how serious I am." Neo is repulsed by me. Says he'd die before ingesting my *poison*—and I believe him. However, two can play his games. If I'm as poisonous as he says I am, he'll make it clear to Maddie by pushing me away and putting this fake relationship to rest.

I grab him by the face, the stubble of his cheeks grating against my palms. It feels masculine and so unlike the Neo I've always viewed as a childish bully. He resists, but not enough to stop what's coming. I pull his mouth to mine, hard and forced. Our lips collide with so much tenacity, my lungs immediately deflate, and I find myself gasping for air yet unwilling to stop what's happening.

Neo growls into my mouth with a whispery, "Stop." But I don't. I pull him closer, forcing my tongue in his mouth. It glides between his teeth and any fear of him clamping down and biting the shit out of me is quickly diminished when the muscle of his tongue stretches out, wrapping around mine.

One hand lands on my hip, and with a swift jerk, he tugs me closer. I immediately feel his erection pressing into my inner thigh and a subtle moan slips through my lips. His other hand slides up my back, stopping on the nape of my neck. He bunches my hair, coercing my mouth harder on his.

Tingles shoot down my body, webbing out and taking hold of every nerve in their path. Moisture pools in my panties, and it's something I'd never admit to a living soul.

When I kiss Crew, it's different from the kisses shared with Jagger, and vice versa, and in the same way, this kiss is different than any I've shared with either of them. I've never felt anything like it. I'm surprised I'm still on my feet because my legs have turned to Jell-O.

The softness of his lips, the flex of his tongue, the feeling of his chest rising and falling against mine. It's all so alluring, but it's nothing compared to the breathless pants he hums into my mouth. It's proof that he doesn't hate this as much as he wants to, or wants me to believe.

My hands glide from his face to the back of his head, fingers locking, and somehow, we managed to move at least three feet away from where we were initially standing and his back is now pressed against the closed door. I'm not sure if it's the push or the pull, but whatever it is, it's enlightening.

"Whoa," Maddie says, snapping me out of the trance I was in. My eyes shoot open and I see Neo staring back at me.

He immediately pulls away, turning his head but keeping his eyes locked on mine. He draws his fingers around his mouth and I watch the motion.

Look away, Scar. Look. Away. But I can't. Not until he stops looking at me. I find myself fighting to breathe, to stand, to think. I can't do anything. What the hell was that?

"I've..." Neo sputters, stumbling over his words, and finally saying, "I've gotta go call Jagger to make sure he's still at school. Be right back."

I crack a smile as I watch him jerk open the door, while adjusting his dick in his pants.

"Okay. That was hot," Maddie says. "But please don't force me to see it again. He's my brother, for God's sake."

"Yeah," I mumble, staring blankly at the open door, where Neo's shadow is slowly fading. "It was...something."

"Earth to Scar." Maddie snaps her fingers in my face. "Where did you go just now?"

"I'm not sure." Blinking rapidly, I peel my eyes from the doorway and look at Maddie. Once I've come back down to reality, I'm hit with the cold, hard truth. I'm here, and Neo still hates me and I still hate him. It was just a kiss. A fake kiss at that. Didn't mean a damn thing. "Sorry." I return to the stool I was sitting on before the kiss. "Tell me what you were going to say when Neo wouldn't let you finish. What did you catch him doing that involved me?"

Maddie steals a glance at the entryway, making sure Neo isn't around before leaning in. Her voice is low and I watch her lips as they move, focusing intently on the words that come out. "A few days before we lost our mom, I caught Neo watching you."

I crane my neck, not believing what she's saying. "No way. Watching me, where?"

"Mmhmm. He was lost in a lustful gaze, watching you while you were tying your shoes. I slapped him *hard* on the shoulder and it still didn't snap him out of it. It wasn't until you turned around and looked at him that he finally did."

"So what?" I chuckle. "He was probably daydreaming and his stare accidentally fell on me."

"Nope." She pops the P, shaking her head, and it's a reminder of how much alike her and Riley are. It's no wonder I gravitated toward Riley after fighting hard not to. "I asked him about it later that night and his face got *beet red*. I'm talking lobster fresh outta the sea. He brushed it off like it was no big deal, but it was. From that day forward, I always knew his acts of hatred were actually him just pushing you away because he was afraid to let you get close."

Not a chance in hell. Maddie has no idea what I've been through this past year. She knows the small childish acts of bullying the guys bestowed upon me throughout the years, but she doesn't know about the sheer torment they put me through while she was asleep.

"Maddie. I'm sorry, but I still can't get over this. How are you even here?"

Wheeling closer, our knees bump, and her expression turns serious. "Wish I could say it was a miracle, but that's not the case. Neo's convinced I was never in a coma at all."

Biting my lip, I search for my words carefully. "Mads," I begin. "Don't let Neo convince you of something that isn't true." I reach out, taking her hand in mine. "I visited you daily in the beginning, and weekly toward the end. You were most definitely in a coma."

Unaffected by my words, Maddie holds her head high

and squeezes my hand. "You saw me sleeping, Scar. It doesn't mean my body needed the rest."

Damn Neo for putting this bullshit in her head. I know I need to be as gentle as possible because I'm sure her mind is still foggy. She said so herself, she doesn't remember the weeks prior to her fall.

"What did your brother say that made you think you weren't in a coma?"

She lets go of my hand and leans back, getting comfy in her chair. "This is all from Neo and I have no recollection of it, but from what he said, he hired a doctor to do daily check-ins on me at the home I was staying in. The doctor noticed something off with the meds that had been getting administered into my IV. After a blood draw, he realized I had been given some medicine that is actually used to induce a coma. After a phone call to Neo with an update, he demanded I be taken out of the home. So, with this new doctor's help, they brought me here. Twenty-four hours later, I started to show signs of life. Another twenty-four hours and I was conscious."

My mouth remains open, as it has been the entire time she's been talking. I'm speechless. No idea what to say. In fact, her story is so plausible that I actually believe it myself. Regardless of the how and the why, she's here, and that's all that matters to me right now.

"I'm...I'm just shocked."

She keeps talking, adding more to the plate, while I'm still processing everything already said. "I was really out of it and don't remember much until last week, but I'm eating on my own now and started to use my legs a little bit more. My therapist is confident that I'll be on my feet in another month or so with a walker."

"This is unbelievable, Maddie." I get up and fall into her again, taking care not to hurt her because I'm not sure how fragile she still is. All those months of seeing her lying in that bed so helpless, and now she's really here.

She hugs me back. She really hugs me, and it's official, I'm not dreaming. *She's really here.*

After we break apart, we talk through everything while laying in her bed, trying to figure out who would want to keep her in a coma. I fill her in on Jude and the whole situation, and we've both concluded it has to be him. It also means he's the one who pushed her. Throughout our entire conversation, I let her believe that Neo and I are actually in a relationship, because when she asks about Crew and her eyes light up, I can't bear to tell her the truth.

"I miss Crew so much and I can't wait to be able to leave this room and live my life again. Has he changed much?"

"Not really. Taller, maybe. A little scruffier, depending on the day."

Staring past me, she smiles. Likely daydreaming of a life with him. It hurts my heart so much because I, too, love Crew. I have no idea what this means for us and I'm so scared I'm going to lose him. And even if I don't, I risk losing Maddie when I've only just found her again.

The door flies open and I'm a little disgusted by Neo's lack of respect. "Sorry to break this up, but Jagger's on his way. He's worried about you. As you both know, we have to keep this under wraps for now."

"But why?" I spit out, climbing out of Maddie's bed. "We know we can trust Jagger. Why can't we tell him?"

Neo glowers at me and I hate that I know exactly what he's thinking. If Jagger knows, Crew will know.

"Oh, right. Because you call all the shots." I scoff at Neo

before giving Maddie one last hug. "I'll come see you again when I get a chance. Or when the master allows it." I peg Neo with a scathing glare as I pass him and walk out the door.

No matter what happens, a heart is going to break, and I'd rather it be mine than Maddie's.

CHAPTER
ELEVEN
CREW

"THERE YOU ARE. What the hell happened?" I cup Scar's face in my palms, relishing in the warmth of her skin. "Are you okay?"

One hand lays over top of mine, stroking it. "I'm fine."

With bent knees, I look into her eyes, searching for any sign she's holding back. "You sure? An afternoon with Neo is enough to make anyone lose their minds."

She smiles, and it's just what I needed. "I'm sure. Neo was Neo, but I survived."

"Glad to hear." I press my lips to hers and her resistance has me questioning the truth when she says she's fine. "Baby," I whisper, "tell me what happened."

Her eyes dart to the left, avoiding contact with mine, and the second red flag is raised. Intently, I watch as her smile fades. "I love you, Crew." Her blue orbs find mine again and the sadness behind them is like a knife to the chest.

"Hey," I fight for her full attention, knowing that her mind is elsewhere, "I love you, too."

I'm not sure what the hell happened, but I have every intention of finding out. Neo did or said something. I swear to all that is holy, if he filled her head with some bullshit that has her doubting us, I'll bury him alive.

Her lips press softly to mine and I can only hope for this brief moment, all the worries of the day have escaped her.

When she pulls out of the kiss, she gives my waist a gentle squeeze and smiles. "Everything is going to be okay, right?"

"Of course it is. We're so close to nailing Jude Beckett on the head. Everything's gonna be fine."

"No. I mean with us. It'll all work out, right? I won't lose you?"

I hate that she's doubting what we have, and shit, I even hate that she's doubting what Jagger and her have. "Where is this coming from? Did Neo say—"

Her head immediately shakes no. "It has nothing to do with Neo. Just tell me we'll be okay when this is all done. No matter what."

"We'll be more than okay. Promise."

Jagger comes jogging down the stairs, already changed from his uniform into a pair of gray joggers and a hoodie. "Oh good. You found her."

I kiss Scar one more time before saying, "I'll let you two talk. Looks like we're all ditching the rest of the day, so I'm gonna go change."

When I hesitate for a second, making sure she's good, she chuckles. "Go." She swats my arm, assuring me that she's fine, but I can't help but wonder if she's really okay.

Regardless, I head up the stairs, taking two at a time. As I'm going up, Scar hollers, so I stop halfway to the top. "Hey, Crew. Could you get in touch with Riley and have her come here after dinner. If she gives you any shit, tell her it's Lawless orders."

Riley. Of course. That's why Scar's so down today. Neo kicked out her best friend. "Yeah. Of course." I continue up, spotting Neo standing at the top of the stairs with his arms crossed over his chest and legs spread about a foot apart. His dominant stance tells me he's pissy and I really don't feel like dealing with his shit right now.

"Riley's out. Don't bring her back to this house."

"Fuck off," I grumble, sailing around him while battling the demons in my head that tell me to shove him down the stairs.

"Quit being a little bitch, Crew."

I step up to him, chest inflated, fists clenched. "Come again."

"You heard me. Quit being a little bitch and doing everything that whore asks of you."

My jaw tics with fury. Rage swims through my veins, and with little thought process behind it, I raise my fist and plant it right on Neo's jaw. His head flies to the left and he crashes into the wall, bracing himself before he falls. I shake my hand, working out the kink in my knuckles. "If you ever call her by anything but her name again, it's your funeral. And I won't be in attendance."

"Oh yeah? Will Scar attend? After all, she did kiss me earlier."

Gritting my teeth, I hiss, "You're fucking lying."

He raises his shoulders in a cocksure shrug. "Am I?"

I don't even give him a second glance as I walk to my room, stretching my fingers, my heart pounding in my chest.

With a whip of my hand, I slam my door shut then smash my fist into the hardwood. It stings, but not as bad as the ache inside my chest. I know when Neo's lying, and what he said wasn't a lie. He's boasting and trying to piss me off, so he told me the truth. Scar kissed him and there isn't a doubt in my mind he kissed her back. Neo likes to walk a fine line when it comes to Scar and I bet this gave him the push he needed right into her arms.

Doing what Scar asked, I page Victor on the walkie-talkie and tell him to bring Riley here after school.

I'm dropping my pants when there's a knock on my bedroom door. "Crew. Can I come in?"

"Yeah," I deadpan, still reeling from what I just heard. I'm not sure if I'm angrier with Neo or Scar. Either way, I need to hear what she has to say, and once again, I'm giving her the chance to come clean first. Hopefully it pans out this time because when she fucked Jagger, it took days for me to get the truth.

She steps inside, closing the door behind her. I kick away my pants and snap the band of my black briefs. "I take it you heard I decked Neo?" Pulling open my drawer, I start shuffling for a tee shirt and end up with a solid black one.

My shirt is hung around my neck when she grabs my hand, fingers grazing my swollen knuckles. "I didn't just hear. I saw. What happened?"

Eyes on our entwined hands, I stand still. I can't even look at her. "He was talking shit, and if he knows what's good for him, he won't do it again."

Her head hangs low, which makes me wonder if she's fighting eye contact because of the guilt inside her. "Talking shit about me?"

"Why?" I lift my eyes, and she does the same. "Is there something he'd need to say about you?"

She nods subtly and I catch a glint of a tear in the corner

of her eye. *Good. She feels bad.* "There's something I need to tell you, Crew."

I don't say anything. Instead, I wait for her to speak.

Seconds later, she looks up at me. "I kissed Neo."

My eyes close momentarily and I wanna bang my fucking head against the wall when the image of them making out pops into my head. When I open them, I seethe. "Why?"

"Because something happened today, Crew. Everything changed. And I need to be honest with you, even if it means slicing myself open in the process."

I roll my neck, exhaling profusely. "What happened, Scar?"

She hesitates, opening her mouth to speak then closing it again. Finally after a few moments of uncertainty, she says with a trembling voice, "I can't be with you anymore."

"Wait. What?" That's not what she was supposed to say. No. She was supposed to tell me about the kiss with Neo. This isn't right.

Tears expel from her eyes. One by one, dropping so loudly that I swear I can hear them hit the skin of our held hands.

"What are you talking about?" I laugh it off, though I'm not feeling any humor in this situation. "Sure you can."

She shakes her head no, and each movement pushes the knife deeper into my chest. "I love you so much, Crew, and this is killing me." Her sobs become more violent and when I pull her close, wrapping my arms around her, she comes undone.

"Stop talking like this. Whatever happened with you and Neo, it's okay. We can all move past it." I squeeze her tighter, relishing in how right her body feels against mine. How perfect she fits in my arms, like it's home for her.

Pulling back an inch, she looks up at me with questioning eyes, arms still wrapped tightly around my lower torso.

"He already told me about the kiss. I'm sure he coerced you into it somehow and I'm not upset." I watch meticulously as she swallows, her throat bobbing. "He did force it, didn't he?"

Her tongue darts out, sweeping up the tears that have fallen. "No. It wasn't forced. I kissed him of my own free will."

I step back, letting go of her. My shoulders fall, willing to take my body down with them. "That's impossible. You despise Neo."

"You're right. I do."

CHAPTER

TWELVE

SCAR

I CAN'T DO THIS. It hurts too much. The look of betrayal on his face. The way he stares back at me like I'm a stranger and not the girl he's loved since he was just a kid.

I can't do this. But I have to. I'm not sure what Neo has hanging over my head, but at any time, he can bring down the veil and suffocate me with the truth. Until I know, I have to do what he's asked and break up with Crew. Not for him, but for my family. And most importantly, for Maddie.

"You're not making any sense, Scar." Crew's voice rises to a shrilling shout. He spins around, unable to look at me, and I get it. I wouldn't want to look at me either. "Explain to me what the hell happened earlier."

"I...I'm not sure how it happened, but Neo and I found ourselves in a compromising position. My heart told me to go for it because of what you said today. You said you don't think it's just hate Neo feels toward me. So I kissed him and it was freeing. After all these years, I knew exactly why Neo treated me the way he did—because deep down, he was in love with me."

Just saying the words makes me sick. My stomach churns, bile rising up my throat.

Crew's hands fly in the air and his face reddens. "I didn't know what the fuck I was saying, Scar. I was pulling shit out of my ass to make you feel better because Neo *does* hate you so much."

"He doesn't, though. He told me so."

"Scar," he screeches, pointing a finger at the door, "ten minutes ago, the guy called you a whore."

Of course he did. More confirmation that Neo does hate me. Which is exactly why I need to do this. His hate will drive him to destruction. If given the chance, he will hurt me and feel nothing.

I need to get out of this room. I can't look at Crew anymore. I'll crumble if I have to see the pain in his eyes a second longer.

"I...I have to go." I turn around, walking quickly to the door. Crew stops me, his hand wrapped around my wrist.

"Don't go. Don't do this. He's blackmailing you, isn't he? I know it. Just tell me. I can help you."

He might be able to help me with Neo, but what about Maddie? What about when she sees him and expects to pick up where they left off? If she ever knew the way Crew and I feel about each other, it would kill her.

"You can't help me, Crew, because I don't need to be saved."

I jerk my arm away and tear open the door, leaving before he can say anything else.

My feet don't stop moving until I'm slamming my bedroom door shut and clicking the lock.

One down. One to go.

With my back to the door, I slide down, gripping the

sides of my head and tugging at my hair so aggressively that strands break loose. Opening my mouth, I scream at the top of my lungs. "Whyyyyyyy?"

Seconds turn to minutes. Minutes to hours as I lie on the floor, crying until my tears have run dry. My throat is on fire, my ribs hurt from the continuous sobs, and the pain of knowing no one has come to check on me makes matters worse.

Crew probably hates me. He must not have told Jagger yet, because I'm sure he'd be in here by now.

A rush of anxiety hits me when there's a knock on the door.

I sit up before getting to my feet. I wipe my hands across my eyes and tuck my tear-soaked hair behind my ears, then pull open the door, hoping it's Crew.

"Oh, Scar," Riley sulks, throwing her arms around me. "Tell me everything."

"I can't talk about it right now. Just stay with me. Please."

Riley nods, before taking my hand in hers and leading me to the bed. "Of course. I'm not going anywhere."

We lie there for almost an hour in complete silence. A couple times Riley has tried to speak, but each time, I give her a look that begs for a few more minutes.

Finally, I break the silence because if I don't get this out, I'm going to combust. "Neo's sister is here."

Riley shoots up in bed, hovering over me. "Maddie?"

I nod. "Yeah. Neo brought her here. She's awake." I sweep my hand in the air, continuing, "It's a long story, but she's good. She's doing really well." Just saying those words makes this all worth it. *Maddie is okay.*

"Is that why Crew bombarded me at the door and told

me you dumped him before kicking up snow on his sled and taking off?"

He did that? Crew left. But where did he go?

I shake away the thoughts. "Yeah. Neo forced me to dump him and Jagger. He knows something, Ry. I have no idea what it is, but he swears it will destroy me and my family."

"Whoa. Hold up. So Neo forced you to dump them so Crew and his sister could get back together? What's that have to do with Jagger?"

My shoulders shrug against the plush pillow. "No clue. I guess for plausibility because I now have to pretend I'm in a relationship with him to appease his sister. Otherwise, she'll wonder why I'm living here. I guess it's too far-fetched that I'd just be friends with these guys." The vein in my neck throbs with ill intent. I've already plotted Neo's murder in my head multiple times, and I've concluded that a slow, tortuous death is fitting.

"What. A. Fucking. Asshole."

"Asshole doesn't begin to describe what Neo Saint really is." I roll to my side, facing where she sits. "I'm pretty sure he's the devil incarnate."

"We can't let him get away with this, Scar. I mean, who the hell does this guy think he is?"

I roll my lips, wishing there was another way. "Until I know what he has on me, I can't make any bold moves." I stir a little, remembering the kiss we shared. "You know what's strange? Neo and I kissed today—"

"You kissed Neo? Why on God's green earth would you ever do that?"

"It was stupid. I did it in hopes that he'd be repulsed by me and shove me away, but he...fell into it. It was almost as if he liked it." I'm staring blankly at the door, thinking hard about that kiss.

It was incredible. Mind-numbing. Soul-tingling. Like nothing I'd ever felt with anyone else. The only thing I have to compare it to is the kiss in the library with Crew, right before we tore into each other like wild animals. Well, I'll be. It seems I enjoy messing around with guys who hate me. I'm such a mess.

With Crew, though, it was different. There were already emotions and that day brought them back to the surface. With Neo, there is no attachment. I quite literally can't stand him.

"Hello. Scar. Are you there?" It isn't until Riley snaps her fingers in my face that I'm pulled out of the memory.

"Yeah. Sorry. Just overthinking. As usual."

"I asked if you liked it."

"Liked kissing Neo? No way."

Her eyes level with mine, and her brows lift as her way of repeating the question.

"No. Absolutely not." *I didn't. Did I?* "Okay. I'll be honest—"

"There it is."

I crinkle my nose at her, then finish my sentence. "The kiss was good. It went beyond casual. I felt it deep in my core. But then I opened my eyes and saw Neo standing there and I was disgusted with myself."

"And you think Neo felt it, too?"

"I mean. He didn't pull back and the look in his eyes told me it took him by surprise."

"It seems you've got your ammo." Her eyebrows dance to their own tune and I have no idea what she's suddenly so chipper about.

"Ammo?"

"If Neo felt what you did, then it means he's questioning the kiss, too. Use it. Fake this relationship to get closer to him. Get under his skin and when you have him right where you want him, pull the trigger and force your secret out of him."

"Are you suggesting I use Neo?"

"That's exactly what I'm suggesting. This is all temporary. Do what you have to do to find out what he knows, so you can get your guys back."

"You're forgetting one thing. Maddie still loves Crew."

"Well, babe. As my mother always says, if you live your life to please everyone else, you'll die a lonely old hag."

I laugh. "Your mother says that?"

"Sure does. She's a very poetic lady. Great with words." Her sarcasm is apparent and only makes me laugh more.

"She sounds lovely."

"Eh. She's all right. A bit of a hardass, unlike my dad."

"Oh. You're dad's pretty chill?"

"Fuck no. My dad's the hardest ass I've ever met. I'm talking drill sergeant status."

"Yikes."

"It is what it is. Anyways," her pitch rises a few octaves, "you gonna do it?"

On paper, it sounds like the perfect plan. Seduce Neo without actually seducing him. Break him in the process and find out what he has on me. In reality, it's a disaster waiting to happen.

"Seems I've got no choice. I have to do something."

Her arms fly around me, wrapping me in one of her tight Riley hugs. "Good. Now go dump Jagger, so you can get him and Crew back."

The nonchalance in her tone is unsettling, and a bit comical.

"Actually," I spit out, pulling back and looking at her as the wheels turn in my head. "What if I don't have to break up with Jagger. What if I tell him the whole truth?"

"And risk Neo finding out. Not worth it. Remember, this open wound is just temporary. It will heal."

God, I hope she's right. Her words alleviate some of the sadness inside me, but it's also a reminder that this is only the beginning. I'm not sure what I'll do about Crew, but I hope someday we find our way back to one another with Maddie's approval. If not, I can only hope they make each other as happy as we were.

"Can we talk?" I ask Jagger, poking my head through his open door.

He closes the textbook on his desk and looks up at me. "Always." Patting his lap, he calls me over.

Don't accept, Scar. It'll only make this harder. "Actually. I prefer to stand."

His neck cranes, eyes quizzical. "Oh. Is everything okay?"

"No," I tell him honestly, "everything's a mess."

With that, he gets up and crosses the room to where I'm standing beside his bed. Just like with Crew, I can't look at him. My heart is still in pieces from seeing Crew's expression when I broke up with him, and now, I have to do it all again.

"I can't do this anymore," I spit out, not wanting to think or make excuses or try to soften the blow.

"This nightmare is almost over. Just a few more days and hopefully—"

"No." I shake my head. "That's not what I mean. This," I wave my hands between us, "I can't do it anymore."

"You mean us?"

Still unable to look at him, I just stare at his feet. White, warm socks. Probably ankle ones that are digging into his skin. They'll likely leave an imprint for a couple hours that will go away when he's sleeping because Jagger hates sleeping with socks on. I know this, because three out of seven nights a week, I sleep with him. He always holds me. All night long. Even when he's sweating and would probably love his space, he holds me tight because he knows it makes me feel safe. I don't even mind the sweat because it's proof of the sacrifices he makes for me. And here I am, not willing to make one for him. I'm breaking his heart to save my own ass.

"Yeah. Us. I already broke up with Crew and now—"

"Broke up with Crew?" He blows out a heavy breath of air. "What are you even talking about, Scar?"

I look up at him. It was an accident, but now that I have, I can't look away. "I broke up with Crew and now I'm breaking up with you."

"The fuck you are." He grabs my hands. Both of them. He massages them with his fingers, his way of saying he's here and he's not going anywhere until I'm ok—until we're okay. "What's going on with you?"

"Nothing. I've just been thinking, and it's best this way. Better to let you both go now before feelings get too strong—"

"Before feelings get too strong? Are you kidding me right now? I fucking love you. What feeling is stronger than that?"

I didn't expect him to be so angry. Crew was hurt, but he kept calm. Jagger is not holding it together as well.

"Well. I don't love you."

Ouch. Holy shit. I didn't think anything could hurt worse than watching my best friend lie lifeless in a hospital bed, but this one did it. I'd rather die than feel a pain like this ever again.

"You're lying."

There it is. More pain. Take me out of my misery, God. I can't do this.

"I'm not lying, Jagger. I don't love you or Crew and I don't want to be with either of you."

I spin around to leave, unable to do this anymore.

I'm not even out the door when the harrowing sound of something crashing to the ground has my eyes shooting over my shoulder. Jagger has tipped his entire dresser over. He glares at me with hard-pressed lips as he kicks it repeatedly.

Holding back my tears, I save them for when I'm in the hall. Once I am, I fall to the floor.

CHAPTER
THIRTEEN
NEO

"How's it make you feel, knowing you inflicted this pain on your best friends?"

Crew and Jagger moved out five days ago after Scar broke up with them. I didn't see it coming, but I can't say I'm disappointed. Now the fear of them finding Maddie is eliminated. She's safe to recover in the comfort of our house. I've moved her from the basement to the spare room, installing countless locks to be certain no one will enter.

Riley's still here. It was a last-minute deal struck with Scar, and I should've fought it harder, but I'm beginning to lose all fight inside me. I pride myself as being indestructible, but those who appear strong are usually the weakest players. I can finally admit to myself, I am weak. And each day that passes, I become weaker to desire.

"To answer your question," I begin, biting hard on the toothpick wedged between my teeth. "Feels good."

"Of course it does. You've hurt people. Isn't that your goal in life?"

"Not my goal, per se, but it doesn't hurt me at all, so why should I care?"

The next thing I know, Scar is shoving her thumb into my swollen cheek. "What the fuck?" I shriek, jerking my head back.

"Hmm. So you do feel things? Weird."

Scar gets up from the opposite end of the couch where she was sitting. Slow steps lead her toward me. "I think you just want everyone else to be as miserable as you are."

I shrug, not agreeing, but also not disagreeing.

She's in front of me now. Crouching down, she places her hands on my thighs and I squirm unintentionally. "What are you doing?"

Her hands move up, trailing along my inner thighs, and I pick one hand up, removing it from me. "Stop touching me."

"This is what you wanted, isn't it? Me. And you?"

"Hell no." I pick the other one up, also moving it until both her hands are resting on the couch cushion on either side of me. "It's for Maddie. I don't fucking want you."

She pushes herself up until her legs are bent and slides on my lap. When she grasps my head with both hands, I turn to the right. "Get the fuck off me, Scar," I grit out, heart hammering inside my chest.

Turning my head, she forces eye contact. "Maybe I do. Maybe I want a taste of something I've never had."

"You've tasted my mouth, so what is it you want? My cock?"

She doesn't respond, just stares lustfully back at me, and I'm done for. "Well. Is it?" I grab her waist, jerking her close while lifting my hips and giving her a feel of my bulging cock. "You wanna suck my cock, Scar?" Her eyes widen in surprise and her hands fall from my head. "That's what I thought."

As quickly as she climbed on, she climbs off. Her head drops as she paces in front of me. "I can't do this."

"Sure you can. It's not forever."

"Are you sure, Neo?" She pins me with a hard glare. "Because it feels like I've lost Crew and Jagger for good, and while I might get Jagger back, I'm not so sure about Crew."

"If you really care about them, you'll let them go."

"Are you insinuating that I don't care about them if I fight for what we had?"

"I guess I am."

"They told me they'd fight for this, too. Even if I begged them not to because that's what you told me to say, they will. Their absence right now doesn't mean they've given up, and I'm not giving up either."

"You're holding them back, Scar. Don't you see that? What kind of future could you possibly offer them when you can't even give your whole heart to either of them?"

"A happy one, full of love. Something you will never experience."

The truth to her statement hits hard. Then again, when I picture my future, it's veiled in darkness. I see nothing. Not the plans my father laid out for me. Not a wife and kids, or a career. It's blank. Like an empty page still waiting to be written.

"I don't need love. All I need is myself."

"You keep telling yourself that, Neo. And one day, when you wake up all alone because the world moved on without you, I hope you keep yourself nice and warm."

Scar leaves and I'm thankful my phone rings immediately because I didn't want to think about the words she just said.

"Yes, sir," I say into the speaker of the phone.

"You've got some fucking nerve leaving this family when your sister is still missing. Get your ass back to Essex and aid in this search or you're dead to me. Do you hear me? *Dead to me.*"

"Pretty sure I already am, so what's the point?"

"Don't you take that tone with me, Neo. Do you have any idea what this mess will do to my career if Maddie isn't found? I've got search parties out everywhere while fighting to keep this out of the tabloids. If anyone catches wind—"

"Your reputation will be in jeopardy and you risk the election. Yeah, Dad. I get it."

"Listen here, you little shithead. You're going to get back here now and help find your sister or I will personally come there and drag your ass back, before kicking it to the curb and cutting you off for good."

The last thing I need is him coming out here and bringing his search parties with him. So I buy myself some time. "Fine. Give me a couple days. Wherever she's at, she's not going anywhere."

"You've got forty-eight hours. Not a minute longer. Oh, and bring my fucking files back that you stole off my desk. We were really close to cracking this case before you stole them."

"Files?"

"Don't play dumb with me. I know exactly what you did, and if I find out you're doing this because that Sunder girl put you up to it—"

"None of this even has anything to do with Scar."

"Good. Keep it that way. If you let that girl sink her teeth into you, I will cut you off from everything. No more money. No more education. You will be out of this family."

"I get it, Dad. You've reminded me every day for the last ten years of my life. She's a snake. Stay away. Don't share our secrets. Don't be her friend, or I lose everything."

Fuck. I don't even care anymore. He can keep his money and his reputation. This conversation has proven that I'll never live up to his expectations, so there's no point in trying.

"Good. Drill it into your head and keep it here." His tone shifts abruptly to an even more serious note. "Some words of wisdom, son. You can't win against someone who loves a challenge." He ends the call and I slam my phone down on the cushion beside me.

No. But I sure as hell can fool him into thinking I'm playing his game.

> Me: Meet me at The Ruins in one hour. I'm bringing him in. Pissed at me or not, we still have the Academy to run and protect, and duties to fulfill.

> Jagger: Fuck off. And keep in mind, if you touch our girl, I'll slit your fucking throat.

> Me: Show me your knife because I already did and she fucking loved it.

> Crew: Scar wouldn't touch you with a ten-foot pole. Get it through your head. She hates you. She'll never care about you. You're not worthy of an ounce of her affection.

> Me: That's not what she said last night before my tongue parted the folds of her pussy.

> Jagger: We're no longer working together. In fact, Crew and I are now working against you. Deal with it yourself.

> Me: Have it your way. And I'll keep having my way with Scar.

WELL. Can't say I didn't try. Looks like we're doing this without them. I never planned for any of this to go this far. If fucking Riley would have just stayed out of our damn house, none of this ever would have happened, and they'd still be living here.

"Are they coming?" Riley asks, stepping into her boots in front of the doorway.

"No. And I'm really doubting your ability to help me out in this situation. You've proven to be the world's worst Guardian in existence."

A hand smacks the back of my head, rattling my brain. It seems Scar is done checking on Maddie. "Don't talk to her like that," she hisses. "Riley is a damn good Guardian and she's just going to get better from here on out."

I ram my chest into hers, walking her back until her ass hits the backside of the couch. "Hit me again. I fucking dare ya."

With a balled fist, she punches me in the shoulder. Not hard, but enough to piss me off. Her eyes dance, brows lifted. "Now what?"

I point a stern finger at the door. "Get out the fucking door now, so we can get this shit done."

"That's what I thought," she mutters, grating on my

nerves. Her voice rises enough to hear her clearly. "You go first. I don't trust you at my back."

I scoff, "Fine."

I lead the way, followed by Riley, and Scar shuts the door behind her, turning the handle to make sure it's locked.

"Enjoy your walk," I tell them, hopping on my sled. Without giving them the chance to argue, I start it up and take off.

Hey. Not my fault. There's barely enough room for two on this thing and I'm not offering it up to them and walking instead. Not to mention, I'm the one who's bringing Jude out there. There's no way in hell I'm engaging in small talk with that fucker during a long walk to The Ruins.

It's only a mile. They'll be fine.

SLAMMING my foot against Jude's dorm door, I bust it open, taking it off a hinge. It felt pretty badass, however, it was unlocked to begin with. Still doesn't take away from my grand entrance.

"Whoa," he throws his arms up from where he's sitting in the desk chair, "what's going on?"

With one hand holding the door open, I angle toward the hall. "Out. Now."

"I don't know what you think—"

"It wasn't a fucking question. Get out in the hall now or I will drag your ass out by your ear."

"Ugh. Okay." He gets up, pushes his glasses higher up his nose, then returns to a surrender position with his hands afloat beside his head. "Can you tell me what this is about?"

It takes everything in me not to knock him upside the head as he passes by me, but...oh hell, fuck it.

Bending my elbow, I ram it into his gut. Immediately, he hunches over and clutches his stomach, grunting through each splintered breath.

"You know? After all the shit you've done, I was really expecting someone who might put up a fight. Instead, I find out it's you. A fucking pussy."

His eyes lift, glasses teetering on the edge of his nose. "I didn't do anything."

My fist lands hard on his cheek, sending him to the ground. "That lie is going to get you in a lot of trouble if you keep it up."

I stomp my foot and he holds his hands up, warding me off. "Yep. Fucking pussy."

"Neo. I swear. It wasn't me. I—"

"Shut up!" I roar. "Shut the hell up. I know it was you, *Jude*."

His eyes grow wide with caution, and he swallows hard, his Adam's apple quivering in his throat. "My name is Elias. Elias Stanton."

This time, it's the toe of my boot that meets his gut. He chokes back his sobs, scooting away from me, until he's crawling like a baby.

His roommate's on his bed, watching in shock, but not daring to say a word, or help. I give him a stern look, warning him that this will be his fate if he dares step in.

"Get up," I tell Jude.

Stumbling a few times, he gets to his feet, coughing repeatedly and spitting out puke that must have risen up his throat. One hand pushes up his glasses, while the other pacifies his stomach.

In a swift motion, I grab his arm, dragging him out the open door.

"I...I think I'm gonna pass out."

"Good. It'll make it easier to get you where you need to be." I punch him again, watching as his body falls to the floor in the hall. A few guys shuffle away before I can see their faces, but I hear, "oh shit," and "we gotta go." I'm glad to see I've maintained my reputation, and right now, I need someone to do my dirty work.

"Get back here," I shout, unsure who I'm shouting to. "I saw you shitheads. Now get over here. I need a hand."

A second later, none other than Victor Hammond is showing his face. "Wonderful. Just the Rook I need. Pick his ass up and carry him outside."

Victor does as he's told without any lip, following behind me as I lead the way to my still running sled.

Once we're there, I lift the seat and pull out the double ropes I brought along, then shut it tightly.

I gesture toward the seat. "Just drop him there."

Again, Hammond obliges, and Jude is now hanging over the seat, his head on the left and his feet dangling on the right. I slap the rope to Victor's chest. "Tie his hands up. And make it a good knot. Not one of those pansy ones a chick could break free from. Then strap it to the seat."

Victor hesitates and shoots me a look like he's staring into the eyes of Satan. I snap, "Fucking do it!"

He starts with Jude's hands, wrapping the rope around his wrists three times, before tying it off in a triple knot.

"He's waking up," Victor tells me, though I can see for myself.

"So knock him back out."

Victor gulps but doesn't knock him out. Instead, he

works faster, tying his ankles the same way he did his hands.

"Now go. And don't you dare say a word about this to anyone."

He nods in response, then jogs through the snow, back up to the dorm entrance.

Crouching down, I look at Jude's face, which is looking down at the ground. "If you're smart, you'll stay very still." His glasses slide down his nose and into the snow, so I stomp on them, shattering the frames.

"What are you planning to do with me?"

"Come on now, Jude." I smirk. "Don't make me ruin the surprise."

I fling my leg over the seat and drop down while Jude rides on his stomach behind me.

It would be really easy to be an ass right now and go fast, sending him flying into a snowbank. But that means more work for me because I need to get him to The Ruins. Instead, I take it slow, ensuring he stays put.

We come up on Riley and Scar, near the end of the trail, and I slow even more. "You girls look cold," I tease, before picking up speed again and passing them.

Taking double the time it would normally take to get there, we finally arrive. At the same time, a shivering Scar and Riley step off the trail, the look on their faces priceless.

Bringing Jude out here right now wasn't the plan. I was really hoping I'd find out who's working with him before I brought him in for interrogation, but after the call from my dad, I knew I needed to hurry things along.

With any luck, he'll tell me everything I need to know.

CHAPTER
FOURTEEN
SCAR

"Such a jackass," I grumble, passing by Neo, who's got Jude thrown over the sled like he's a sack of potatoes.

Snickering, he pulls Jude's feet, dropping his body in the snow. "Someone's bitter."

"No shit, we're bitter. It's freezing out here," I snarl, dragging my eyes up and down Neo's body. "Look at you in just your hoodie and jeans. Oh yeah. You didn't have to trek through snow on foot." The sarcasm in my tone is apparent, and he eats it right up. Neo lives to make others miserable.

"Please don't hurt me," Jude whimpers from where he's lying on the ground.

I slouch down to where he's at, elbows pressed to my knees as I peer over him. "Hurt you?" I chuckle maliciously. "We're gonna do more than that. Once we're through with you, you're gonna wish you were never born a Beckett."

"I'm not...my last name is Stanton."

"Liar," I shout directly in his face. "And such a terrible one at that. Did you really think you wouldn't get caught?"

He's trembling in fear, as he should be. This guy has no

idea what's coming. When we're done with him, we'll know all his secrets.

When Neo tugs Jude's feet, dragging him through the snow, I stand up and dust my legs off.

Out of the corner of my eye, I see Riley. She's facing the trail, chewing haphazardly on her thumbnail. I give Neo one last glance, hoping he can get Jude down the ladder on his own.

"You okay?" I ask Riley, now at her side.

She turns to look at me, her thumb still lodged between her teeth, and she shakes her head no. Finally removing her hand from her mouth, she drops her tense shoulders. "Are we sure it's him? I feel so bad. What if it's not and we're—"

"It's him, Ry. There's no one else it could be." I press my lips into a thin line, hoping she sees that this isn't all for nothing.

Her sad eyes show me the reflection of mine as I look at her. "But what if it's not?"

I put an arm around her shoulder, leading her to the open trap door to the tunnels. "Then I guess we really fucked up."

By the time we get there, Neo has Jude's legs untied and he's following him down the ladder.

I'm looking down when Neo looks up. He stops mid-step. One foot on the step below the other.

"What?" I huff the question, wondering why he's putting his attention on me and not Jude.

"Nothing." He shakes his head and continues his descent.

Neo is so weird sometimes. The word *weird* can have so many different meanings. At least to me, it can. It can mean awkward, confusing, strange, fantastical, creepy, mysterious. My reference to him as weird is most definitely confusing.

He can be a total douchebag—the absolute worst. Then there are moments like this when I look at him and convince myself he's not that bad. I try to justify his actions in my head and it works for a while. That is, until he shows me his true colors again. Black is the one I see most. Which also happens to be my favorite color.

I'm halfway down the ladder, Riley just above me, when Jude takes off running.

I hit the ground and watch. Jude's at least six feet ahead of Neo, glancing over his shoulders, but still frantically running. Neo is chasing him while screaming profanities.

"Should we help?" I ask Riley, eyes still on the guys as they fade into the darkness of the tunnels. Only a glimmer of light shows the way from the sconces on the walls, but they're so far down now, I lose sight of them.

"Nah. He can't go too far. Neo will catch him."

We take our time walking to Jude's lair. It's a good fifteen minutes by the time we get there and find Neo sitting on Jude's back, tapping into his phone.

"'Bout fucking time. I didn't bring the other rope to tie his legs up, so I need one of you to open the door."

I go straight for the door, knowing the combination by memory. Once it's open, Neo lugs Jude inside by his arm.

Riley stands by idly, pointing the flashlight, and while we could use a hand tying him to the chair Neo set up, I know she's not ready to take part in this. The chair is nothing fancy. It's not an electric chair, like he actually deserves. Just an old office chair that was down here with a pile of rope on it and some duct tape.

Neo tosses him down, and when Jude starts begging for

mercy, he grabs the duct tape and pulls a long strip of it out. Using his teeth, he tears it off the roll.

"When we're ready to hear you talk, we'll let you." He slaps the tape over Jude's mouth, who immediately begins sobbing. Tears fall onto the silver tape and my heart splinters. Not because he doesn't deserve this after all he's done, but because I'm still human and carry a large amount of empathy for others.

"Little help here," Neo barks, adjusting the rope behind the chair.

I step beside him and he orders me to hold Jude's hands in place while he knots them up real tight. Next, we tie his legs back up, ensuring he can't run, and when the same rope is bound to the chair, we know he's not going anywhere.

"All right," I say on a clipped exhale, slapping my hands to my sides, "what's next?"

"Now, we get answers." He crouches down in front of Jude and begins his spiel. "We know Elias Stanton died twenty years ago. We also know you're Jude Beckett. So you can drop the act now. What we want to know is why you did it and who's helping you?"

Jude shakes his head no, sputtering behind the tape and fighting to free his hands and feet.

"Take the damn tape off," Riley snaps. "He can't talk with his mouth covered."

Neo rolls his neck to look at her. "Did I ask for your fucking advice?"

And just like that, all the justification for his actions has disappeared, once again.

Riley exhales deeply, spinning around and facing the door.

"Could you try to be human for five fucking minutes?" I

gnash at Neo. Heat flushes through my body as I cater to Riley. "Ignore him."

"It's not him. I'm used to his asshole ways at this point. I just can't help but feel that this is all wrong."

The sound of tape being ripped off Jude's mouth has us both shooting our eyes to where he's bound to the chair.

He vomits words quickly, trying to get them all out while he has a voice. "There has to be another Elias Stanton. You've got the wrong guy. I swear. It wasn't me."

Neo lifts his hand, and with an open palm, he smacks Jude hard across the face. Riley winces, burying her face in my chest. I wrap my arms around her and whisper, "You wanna leave?"

She nods, so I take her out of the room without even telling Neo. He doesn't deserve that courtesy.

Leaving the door open, we start our hike through the tunnels. "This will all be over soon," I reassure Riley, or, attempt to at least.

"No, it won't," she argues. "Sure. Maddie is safe and well, but this is just the beginning." She stops walking, looking at me with red eyes that threaten tears. "What happens once they get the truth? Do they kill him?"

"I don't know," I tell her, truthfully. "I really don't know."

We start walking again, and when we're at the halfway point, we spot Crew and Jagger coming toward us.

My heart skips a thousand beats. Sweat breaks out on my forehead and my knees go weak.

"What do I do?" I whisper to Riley, taking her hand in mine. It makes me feel less alone. Like I have someone in my corner when I'm on the verge of crumbling.

"Hear them out, I guess."

Seeing them now, I want more than anything to run into their arms and tell them I lied. That I do love them and I never want to be apart from them again. I need them to know I have no feelings for Neo and he forced me to do this.

But when they're standing directly in front of me, staring down at me like I'm an outlier, I go around them, taking Riley with me.

"I can't do it," I say in a hushed tone, choking back my tears. "I can't look them in the eyes and lie again."

"Scar," Crew calls out. "Wait."

I stop walking, close my eyes, and draw in a deep breath.

I can't do it.

His footsteps behind me carry the weight of a horse. Each step is deafening as he draws closer and closer to me.

"Can we talk?"

I open my eyes, a tear breaking free and sliding down my cheek as I say, "No."

I just can't.

CHAPTER
FIFTEEN
JAGGER

"At least we know they're safe since Neo has Jude. Still. I don't get why she's being so damn cold."

"I told ya. She doesn't give a damn," I tell Crew, who's walking by my side.

"No. He did something. I fucking know it. I don't know about you, but I know what I had with her was real."

My feet stop moving, rage coursing through my veins. "Are you implying what I had with her wasn't real? You think she was just a quick fling?"

"Didn't say that. But if you're so sure she'd turn on you this quickly then you must not have had what I did with her."

"It was fucking real! It was the realest thing I've ever felt in my goddamn life, so don't act like your relationship with her sat above mine."

"Calm down, man. I wasn't implying anything. Look. We're both angry right now. Both fucking hurt. But if we wanna get her back, we have to give her the space she needs while fighting for her behind the scenes."

He's right. I've been a mess lately, and Crew's the only punching bag I've got right now, so I've been taking all my aggression out on him. Fuck. I can't eat. I can't sleep. I've gone to the house twice, just to try and steal a glance at her, because I miss her face so damn much. Both times, I failed. Neo changed the fucking locks on the doors and all the curtains have been drawn shut.

Hell, maybe Crew and I should tie that fucker to a chair right beside Jude, and we can really put this shit to rest.

We come up to the door, right away noticing that it's open.

Crew scoffs. "He's pretty brave, leaving the door open for anyone to see what's in there."

"It's Neo. He doesn't fucking care."

My phone buzzes in my pocket, so I reach inside. When I pull my it out, I see that it's Scar's mom. "Fuck. Mrs. Sunder's calling me."

"Don't answer it. Just send her to voicemail."

I tap the Decline button and put my phone back in my pocket. *Wonder what she wants?*

As soon as we step inside the room, my eyes are shooting wide open.

"What the fuck, Neo!" I hurry over to where Jude's strapped to the chair, all bug-eyed and bloody. "Have you lost your damn mind?"

"We want answers and he won't give them, so we're doing this the hard way." He continues to choke Jude, not allowing him a single breath.

"And how the fuck are you gonna get answers when he's dead?" Crew grabs Neo's arm, tugging and pulling to no avail. In fact, I'm certain Neo just tightened his grip.

No thought process behind it, I cock my fist and land it right on the side of Neo's head, forcing him to let go.

Neo stumbles to the right, catching his own fall. "What the fuck!" he screams, while at the same time lunging at me. I step to the side, and he misses, falling straight to the ground. "He almost killed my fucking sister!" he screams even louder. "So what if he dies?"

Crew and I watch as he gets back on his feet, his bloodied fists balled at his sides, teeth bared.

"That's not the way to pay him back for what he did. You break his face and he can't speak. You kill him and we get nothing."

"You're right," Jude mutters, but it's loud enough for us to hear him. We all silence ourselves, not making a single sound. With his chin to his chest, he chokes and sputters, but manages to say, "Elias Stanton is dead."

Chills shimmy down my spine at his admission. We knew this to be true, but hearing him say it out loud makes all the hell we've been through worth it.

"See," Neo quips, "that's why I did what I did. And that's why I'll continue to do what I'm doing until the truth climbs out of his wretched throat. From one beating to the next."

Neo walks over to Jude with a slow and steady swag, chest inflated, fists still locked. "Why'd you try to kill my sister?"

Jude lifts his head, blinking rapidly. "Your sister?"

Neo howls, getting right in his face. "Don't play dumb with me, kid."

"I...I swear. I didn't do anything to Maddie."

Crew and I share some unspoken words, but I know he's thinking the same thing I am, so I ask, "Then how do you know her name?"

"I know who she is. I know who all of you are. I've memorized everything there is to know about the Blue Bloods. But I didn't hurt her. Never wanted to hurt anyone. I just...wanted to be one of you."

Neo sputters a laugh. "One of us? You did all this shit because you want to be one of us?" His voice rises with each word that leaves his mouth. "You will never be one of us. You're an inbred. A half-breed. The worst kind of Beckett because you were created as a pawn in this war waged on the Blue Bloods years ago."

Everything Neo is saying is true. In Betty Beckett's diary, she pleaded with her predecessors to do whatever it takes to bring down the Blue Bloods, even if it means impregnating female members to taint the bloodlines. That's exactly what Jeremy Beckett did to Kenna Mitchell. Jude was born to destroy us and he's been trying to do just that all school year.

Jude sobs some more, snot and tears mixing together and running down his mouth. "I didn't want anyone to get hurt. I swear."

Neo straightens his back before punching him, sending Jude's head thrashing to the right. "Yet, someone did." Flexing his fingers, he turns around and heads for the door. He stops in the doorway, hands pressed on either side of the frame as he looks out into the tunnels. "See if you guys can get anything out of him. Otherwise, tape his mouth and we'll try again tomorrow." Then he leaves.

Crew starts interrogating Jude, much less aggressively than Neo did. While he's working on him, I pull out my phone and listen to the voicemail Scar's mom left.

"Uh. Yeah. Jagger." Her voice is low, panicked even. "It's Luna Sunder. I'm trying to reach Scarlett. It's imperative that she call me immediately. I just heard about poor Maddie Saint and I'm beside myself. My husband informed me she's been kidnapped. If Scarlett doesn't return my call within the next hour, I'll be forced to come there to pick her up, so I know she's safe."

I end the call and immediately blurt out, "Fuck!"

Crew's eyes shoot over his shoulder. "What?"

"We've gotta go. Tape his mouth. Make sure the ropes are secure."

"Dude." He throws his hands up. "Tell me what the fuck happened."

"Scar's mom called. If Scar doesn't return her call within," I glance at the timestamp of the call on my phone, "twenty minutes. She's coming here."

Dammit. I knew I should have just answered the call. There's no other reason Mrs. Sunder would be calling my phone unless it was important. Word about Maddie's disappearance seems to have leaked, which can only mean one thing, Sebastian Saint is going to lose his shit. He'd offer up his children before letting the public see him in a negative light.

CHAPTER
SIXTEEN
SCAR

"You have to do it, Scar. Just seduce him and force the truth out."

The straw sticking out of my glass of iced tea dangles between my teeth. "Easier said than done."

I hear what Riley is saying, but she doesn't understand how hard it is to pretend with Neo. I tried. I climbed on his lap and gave it my best shot, and as soon as he opened his mouth, letting his venomous words fall out, I retracted. I forfeited. I quit. Because I knew there was no way in hell I could keep up that charade. The thought alone makes me feel dirty. *It's Neo, for fuck's sake.*

"Well, you have to do something because this nightmare needs to end. I'm ready to wake up and enjoy the rest of my senior year. Tie him to his bed if you need to. Leave him there until he spills all his secrets.

Now she's talking. I might not be able to seduce Neo, but I can torture the hell out of him. I won't hurt him physically, but I can sure as hell fuck with him emotionally. This could work.

She keeps talking, while the wheels in my head turn. "Once you know, you can get your guys back and send Jude away unscathed, so we never have to see him again."

I let the straw break free from my mouth and set my glass down on my nightstand. "This could actually work."

"Sending Jude away unscathed?"

"No. That'll never work. The guys would never go for it. But I *could* tie Neo up and force it out of him."

Riley grows quiet again. I know she's worried about Jude. I'm fighting hard to understand why, since she knows everything he's done. I chalk it up to her not believing it's him and I chalk that up to her hoping that somewhere in there is the guy she started to fall for. Maybe he is, but it doesn't change everything he's done. Pushing Maddie and keeping her in a coma, stealing the identity of a dead guy, and terrorizing me. She might have it in her heart to forgive him, but I sure as hell don't. In fact, now that I know I'm safe out there, there's a big part of me that wants to go back to where he's tied up and force the truth out of him.

But first, I need to collect my secret that Neo claims to have.

I look down at my outfit, or lack thereof. Technically, it's not mine—it's Riley's—but she lent it to me for the night. A baby pink satin nightie with a lacy, low-dipped V-neckline. I wanna vomit just looking at this color on myself, but I won't deny that my body looks fucking amazing. "You really think he'll go for this?"

"Girl, you are a bombshell. If he doesn't, I'm sure every other guy at this Academy would."

"Not exactly what I'm going for, Ry. I need Neo to do the groveling." *Ugh.* Neo and the word 'grovel' do not go well together.

"Neo's a slut. Of course he'll go for it. Get him in the bed, cuff his wrists with these," she holds up two pairs of hand-cuffs—I don't even bother asking why she has them, "then his ankles, and start your interrogation."

"And what happens when he doesn't tell me anything? I let him go, so he can return the favor and cuff me to the bed?"

"Nope. You leave him there. No matter how long it takes."

"You do have a ruthless bone in there, don't you?"

She smirks. "Only for those I don't like, and Neo is at the top of that list."

I nod repeatedly, my thoughts getting the best of me. *This'll be easy. I've got this.* "Okay," I blurt out. "I'm going in."

Her eyebrows do a little waggle as she says, "Good luck."

With my shoulders back, and my chest puffed out, I give my cleavage a little boost with my hands before jerking my bedroom door open.

Before I step out, a thud on the window has me turning back around. "What was that?"

Riley springs from the bed, and I shut the door.

"No idea, but I think something hit the window."

We both hurry over to it. Before pulling back the curtains, it's hit again. Riley and I share a fretful look. "Someone's out there," I tell her.

Riley peels back a small corner of the curtain and looks out. When she exhales a sigh of relief, I breathe a little better. "It's Crew and Jagger," she says, sending my heart back into my throat.

"Shit." I gasp. "What do you think they want?"

"You. Of course. And if you don't go out, they might try to come in."

I lick my dry lips, tucking my hair behind my ears. "You're right. I should go out there?" It's a question, more than a statement, because I need her to tell me what to do. I hate the position I'm in and I can't think rationally.

Riley draws the curtains back, and I snap, "What are you doing?"

"They obviously see us. There's only one way to find out why they're here."

She pushes the windowsill up a couple inches and bends down, stuffing her mouth into the opening. "What do you want?" she shouts, and my eyes bolt to the door out of fear Neo will hear her.

"Tell Scar to come out or we're coming in." That's Jagger's voice.

She lifts her head. "Told ya."

"And make it quick. It's fucking cold out here." This time it's Crew.

"Okay." I nod. "I'll just go out there."

Riley crosses the room to my bed and grabs her plush bubblegum pink robe that matches the nightie I'm wearing. "Put this on."

"Right. I don't need them seeing me in this and thinking I really am sleeping with Neo."

"Well, that's sort of what they're supposed to think, so..."

"True, but I'd rather not shove it down their throats.

Keep an eye out. Make sure Neo doesn't find out I'm out there with them."

She nods in response, and I thank her.

Once I've got the robe tied tightly around my waist, I hurry out of the room before I change my mind and let them come into the house. Maybe that would be easier; let them find out the truth about what's been going on all on their own.

Neo couldn't blame me for that. Wouldn't be my fault if they walked in and found Maddie.

I'm walking down the hall, Riley right behind me, when we hear the sound of Neo's bedroom door opening. "Where are you two going?" Neo asks.

Riley and I share a look before she says, "Maddie needs some water. Scar's going down to get it and I'm going into her room to wait with her. Is that a problem?"

I love Riley's snarky side. I don't see it often, but every time I do, I'm reminded that she does have some fight inside her.

"Is she okay?"

"Maddie?" I ask, before answering my own question. "Yeah, she's fine. Just thirsty. That's all."

Neo walks toward us slowly, clad in a pair of black gym shorts. There's a suspicious look in his eyes that tells me he knows we're up to something.

"Maybe I should check on her. Make sure she's okay."

"Why?" I huff. "She's fine, Neo. We're having some girl time. Go back to your room and leave us alone."

He keeps coming, his eyes deadlocked on mine, even as he passes by us. It isn't until he reaches the door to the room Maddie's in that he finally breaks the hard stare.

"Go!" I tell Riley in a whisper-yell.

Riley scurries to where Neo's opening Maddie's door, and I hurry past them and go downstairs.

I hope Riley thinks fast and doesn't blow this.

My feet don't stop until they're stepping into my snow boots. Glancing over my shoulder, watching for Neo, I slowly pull open the door, trying not to make a sound. This house is ancient and the door is known to squeak loudly. Somehow, I do a fine job of making sure it doesn't.

Before my feet even hit the ground, I'm met by the guys. "Why'd Neo change the locks?" Jagger asks, his expression fueled by anger.

Because he's hiding his missing sister inside and doesn't want either of you to find her.

Obviously, I can't say that, so I go with a partial truth. "I...don't know why Neo does anything he does, to be honest."

"Your mom called. You need to call her back ASAP or she's threatening to come here."

My eyes widen. I wasn't expecting that. "Did she say what she wanted?"

Jagger shakes his head as he stares at the blanket of snow at his feet. He reaches into his pocket, pulls out his phone, and hands it to me. *He hates me. He can't even look at me.* "Hit Play."

I do as he says and put the phone to my ear, listening to the voicemail my mom left on Jagger's phone. Each passing second has my heart beating faster. Once I'm finished listening, I tap her number in and call her back. While it rings, I tell the guys, "She can't come here. She'll make me leave and there's no way I can go right now."

"Weird how things change. Just a couple weeks ago, you were begging to get out of here. What's keeping you?"

I roll my eyes at Jagger's words because I know what he's insinuating—that Neo is the one keeping me here. As in, our nonexistent relationship.

"Scarlett! Thank God! Are you okay?"

"I'm fine, Mom. There's no need to come here."

My gaze dances between Crew and Jagger, and when I notice Crew trying to get a peek at the V-neck of my robe, I hold the phone between my cheek and shoulder and tighten the tie.

"Since when does she wear pink?" Crew asks Jagger, not taking his eyes off me.

Trying to ignore them, I listen to my mom ramble on about Maddie being kidnapped, which I'm well aware of.

"I heard, Mom. And I also know Mr. Saint is doing everything he can to get her back."

"Leave it to that son of a bitch and the poor girl will never be found. That's why your father and I, along with the Vance and Cole families, are organizing a search party."

"You can't do that," I spit out, wishing I'd thought before I spoke. "I mean, let Sebastian handle it. It's his daughter."

"Do you know where Sebastian Saint is right now, Scarlett? He's at the state capitol for his campaign. The elections are next week. There's no way in hell he's doing anything to help his daughter."

I hear the words and I know she's absolutely right. Had I not known Maddie was safe, I'd encourage the search. But she is safe, and until we finish what we started, we can't let them find her.

"Okay. Then let me help." I look at Crew and Jagger. "There is no need for you all to come here. Let us search this area and you all focus on the surrounding areas back home. We have the Guardian..."

My words trail off when I realize what I just said. I mentioned the Guardian—Riley. Who I'm not supposed to know about. Crew and Jagger both shake their heads in annoyance.

"End the call," Crew grits out.

"What did you just say?" Mom asks, seriousness in her tone.

"I...um...I meant to say we have *Guardians of the Galaxy* playing at the community center right now, so I have to go before I miss the ending."

"What have those Lawless boys been telling you, Scarlett?"

I hate it when she says my name like that. Like I'm a child.

"Nothing, Mom. They're just my friends now." I change the subject quickly, so she doesn't press me any further on my mishap. "Let me and my friends coordinate a search here, okay? There's no need to worry. Maddie will be found."

"That she will. Once the local newspaper catches wind, and it's gone public, she will be found."

"But that won't happen, right? The Blue Bloods will handle this?"

"Not if I can help it."

My heart drops down to my stomach. "Okay. I've gotta go, Mom. I'll call you if we find anything, and you do the same."

I end the call before she can say anything else. As of right now, it doesn't sound like we're in jeopardy of our parents showing up here.

When I hand the phone back to Jagger, he squeezes my hand back, the phone pressed between both our palms.

"Why don't you want anyone searching for Maddie here? She's your best friend. Don't you want her found?"

"Of course, I do." I snort. "But she's not here. And if they come to the Academy, we risk them finding Jude."

Crew steps up to me, hands stuffed in his jean pockets. "What are you hiding, Scar?" He pulls one hand out of his pocket and reaches out, untying my robe. "And what the hell are you wearing?"

In short, jerky movements, I tie the robe back up. *I'm going to seduce your best friend into his bed, then cuff him to it and find out what he knows that could destroy my family.* Once again, I can't say that, so I go with, "None of your business."

Jagger looks at me with disgust, his lip curled. "Who the hell are you?"

"Someone you don't know anymore." I turn around and head up the stairs, but in true Crew fashion, he grabs my arm, halting me.

"You don't have to do this."

I swallow down the lump in my throat and say, "Yes, I do." Then I jerk my arm away and hurry in the house, slamming the door shut behind me.

Yes, I do.

CHAPTER
SEVENTEEN
SCAR

"HERE YOU GO," I tell Maddie, handing her a glass of water as she pins me with a baffled expression.

"Where were you?" she asks, taking the water and bringing the rim to her lips, holding it there.

"Went to get you your water." With taut brows, I subtly tip my head toward Neo. "You were thirsty, right?"

"Yeah. Very much so." She takes a sip of her water, still confused. I was hoping Riley would have taken care of this already, but it seems they've all been in here, having a chummy time.

I'm taken aback by the tranquility in the room. There's no tension. No foul words coming from Neo's mouth. All three look relaxed and content. Riley's sitting in Maddie's wheelchair beside the bed, her arms resting on the arms of the chair. Neo is on his side at the foot of the bed, holding his head up with his hand. And Maddie's lying down, guzzling the shit out of her water.

She finishes every last drop then hands the glass back to me. "Yep. I was thirsty all right."

I take the glass, cupping it in both of my hands, and mouth the words *thank you*, while Neo watches Maddie like she's this fragile object in need of care. She is fragile, but Neo has always babied the shit out of her. It's almost sickening.

Neo grabs Maddie's foot through the blanket, giving it a squeeze, though her lack of response tells me she didn't feel it. "Get some rest. I'm gonna do the same. Back to school tomorrow." He rolls off the bed and positions himself right in front of me. "I need to talk to you."

"I'm hanging out with my—"

"Now."

I sigh. "Gimme ten."

He presses his lips to my cheek in a chaste kiss. "Not a minute longer." Faking a smile, he looks at Maddie. "Night, sis."

Angrily, I wipe the smidge of dampness from my cheek. *How dare he?*

"All right, ladies," Riley says as she gets to her feet, "I'm going to bed, too. Morning is going to come much too soon."

"I'll be there soon."

Her response is a wink and the words, "Hopefully not too soon." Her eyes drag up and down my body, noting her robe that's covering her nightie I'm still wearing. I almost forgot what I'm supposed to do tonight, and now that I remember, I wish I could forget again.

Once Riley leaves, closing the door behind her, I sit down on the edge of the bed beside Maddie. "How are you doing?" I ask her.

"Good, actually. In fact, with my therapist's help today, I was able to get on my feet."

I grab her hand, giving it a squeeze. "I'm so proud of you, Mads. Your strength has always been so admirable."

When I say that to her, I don't just mean her physical strength. Maddie is mentally strong. She's been through so much in her short eighteen years of life. The loss of her mom, dealing with a workaholic father, who's been absent for years, and now this—her fall and her recovery.

"Me?" She chuckles. "You're the strong one. Look at all the hell those guys have put you through, yet here you are, stronger than ever and dating one of them."

Ugh. Don't remind me.

"Speaking of the guys," she continues, "have any of you heard from Crew?"

I roll my lips, unsure of what to say. Not wanting to overthink it, I just lie. "No."

"Good."

My surprise in her response is shown with my drawn-back shoulders and creased forehead. "Good?"

Her voice drops a few octaves. "Can I tell you a secret?"

"Of course you can. Remember when we used to call each other our human diaries? That still stands."

Maddie swallows and looks down slightly as she speaks. "The truth is, I think some of my feelings for Crew left with my memories, Scar. And it scares me."

"I don't understand. Are you saying...you don't love Crew anymore?"

"No," she blurts. "I mean, yes. Or no. I don't know. Of course I love him. But I'm not sure what that love means anymore."

I should be happy to hear this. I should be overjoyed, but instead, I feel sad. Sad for my friend, who has already lost so much. I hate seeing her lose any more.

"Give it time, Mads. I'm sure it'll all come back."

She lifts her head, forcing a smile. "You're right. I'm just being silly."

"No, you're not," I assure her. "And anytime you want to talk, I'm here. I'm no good at giving advice, but I'll always listen."

"Thank you." She wipes a tear from her cheek with our clenched hands. "Now go to bed. You've got school tomorrow."

"Yes, Mom." I snort.

As soon as I leave her room, I feel the weight of a thousand bricks on my chest.

It's cool. I can totally walk in Neo's room and seduce him with my body, just so I can tie him up.

I'm Scarlett Sunder, and when I want something, I get it. And right now, I want to know this secret, so I can keep it, if need be.

After a quick stop in my bedroom, tiptoeing so I don't stir Riley, I drop the handcuffs into the pocket of my robe and head to Neo's room.

Once I'm there, I knock softly on the door. "Neo," I say, my tone low.

When he doesn't answer, I knock again. This time louder.

The door flies open, and I'm face to face with a soaked Adonis. Dripping from head to toe, with only a towel wrapped around his lower torso.

"Jesus, Scar. I was in the middle of a shower."

Don't look down. Don't do it, Scar.

Instead, I pin my eyes to his, where they're nice and safe. "And I should be sorry for interrupting you? You're the one who told me to come talk to you, so why were you even taking a shower?"

"I said ten minutes, and it's been fifteen." He turns around, leaving the door open for me.

I step inside, closing it behind me before stuffing my hands in my pockets, accidentally rattling the handcuffs. I grip them tightly, so they don't make another sound. "What did you wanna talk about?"

He shuffles through some shirts in his drawer, before retrieving a solid white one. "Why did you have snow on your robe when you came to Maddie's room?"

"I didn't."

"You did. So either you went outside to melt snow for Maddie's water, or you were out there doing something else. Which is it?"

"You caught me." I beam with sarcasm. "I wanted her water extra cold, so that's exactly what I did."

He walks into his bathroom and I use this opportunity to quickly hide the handcuffs under his bed. "Are you mocking me?" he asks when he returns.

"Does it sound like I am?"

For the love of all that is holy, I cannot be anything but bitter with this guy. Even when he's standing there...

Oh. My. Fucking. God. He did not just remove his towel. Three feet in front of me, he's standing butt-ass naked, drying his hair with the towel that should be covering his junk.

I hold my breath, moving my eyes to the ceiling. "What are you doing?"

"Drying my hair. That a problem?"

"No. It's..." I stutter, at a loss for words, "not."

In fact, this is the perfect opportunity to dive right into my plan.

My eyes drop to his and the corner of my mouth tugs up. It's all for show. My heart is literally trying to flee from my body at this very moment. "Not a problem at all." I take a step toward him, then another.

Heavy brows dip and he steps back, and I notice he has a pair of shorts on now. "What are you doing?"

We're inches apart when I untie my robe, exposing the nightie beneath it. His gaze falls on my chest and I roll my shoulders, letting the robe fall down them. "Like what you see?"

His eyes lift to mine and they're not lustful or soft like I'd hoped, instead, they're formidable. "Put that thing back on."

He really is repulsed by me. But why?

I don't understand. I don't consider myself a catch, but I'm not hideous. I have curves and perky breasts. Sure, I don't wear makeup but...

"I said put it back on!" His voice deepens, and I jolt at his outburst.

"No," I deadpan.

"Excuse me?"

"I said no." I close the space between us. Reaching out with trembling hands, I rest them on his damp shoulders. "Tell me what it is about me that disgusts you so much."

His eyes steer away, while his body tenses, and it's eye-opening. I've never seen Neo fear anything, but he's scared of my touch.

I lean closer, drawing in his exhale, while my mouth ghosts his. "Am I really that appalling?"

He's frozen. Like a statue. Unsure of whether he should break away or remain still.

Moving my mouth along his sculpted jawline, I slide up to his ear and whisper, "Say something."

I'm caught off guard when he shoves me back, hard. So hard that I stumble and land on my ass.

That heart that was ready to flee my body, it's gone. Or at least, it feels that way. Why does his rejection hurt so damn bad?

A ball lodges in my throat, and I fear I'll break down if I mutter a single word.

"Get out!" He points a stern finger at the door.

Maybe that's what I need to do—break down. Cry for him. Show emotion. It's something Neo has never witnessed from me. At least not since I was a kid.

Let it all out, Scar. Fake it if you have to. But when the tears slide down my cheeks, I'm certain they're not forced. "Why?"

He turns away, unable to look at me. I can't tell if it's his distaste for me, or his inability to deal with emotion.

"Just go." This time, the anger has left his voice. It's low and soft. Tortured almost.

He's so weird. And this time, I mean it as, he's so mysterious. I want to break him. No. *I need to break him.* Then I want to be the one to fix him.

What am I even thinking? I'm not doing this because I have feelings for Neo. I'm doing it to protect myself and my family. I can't forget that.

I push myself up, now completely free of the robe. Slow steps lead me behind him as he stares out the window.

My chest cloaks his back and I bring my arms around him. "I'm not leaving."

In an instant, he spins around with a taut chest and scathing glare. He takes a step into me, then another, but I don't break contact. I keep moving and so does he. "If you stay, you're gonna regret it." His hand reaches out like a claw, and he grabs me by the throat, in a threatening but lax hold.

"Make me regret it then."

The backs of my legs hit the footboard of his bed and he shoves me down on my back. "Say it again."

I press myself up on my elbows. "What?"

"What you just said, say it again."

"Make me regret it?"

"Yeah," he whispers, his voice coarse and gravelly. "That's the one." He shoves me back down, the crease in his forehead depthless and his eyebrows knitted together. "You're about to."

Neo shoves his hand to my chest, sinking me into the mattress. "You better hope like hell this isn't a game, Scar, because if it is, you'll be the one losing."

His hand goes right for my inner thigh, fingers pinching deep into my skin.

I drop my head back on the pillow, relaxing into the mattress. "Why's that, Neo? I thought you liked to play games?"

"I do," he exhales into the crook of my neck. "But keep in mind..." he bypasses my panties, running his fingers between my folds, "...I always win."

His calloused knuckles graze the skin of my inner thigh, and I hate that it arouses me.

"I..." I begin, stuttering on my words and losing my train of thought. "I thought I was poison that you refuse to ingest?"

"You are. You're a drug." His chin runs along my cheek as his words play softly in my ear. "One I don't want, but I have to have." He blows featherlight breaths down my neck and my body breaks out in goosebumps. "Do you want me, Scar?"

I don't know what I'm saying or what I'm doing. I'm under his spell. Neo calls me a drug, but *he's* the drug, and I'm afraid, after this, I'll be addicted. Unable to stop myself. I'll need more and more because this will never be enough.

"No," I say honestly, "I don't want you, either...but I have to have you."

It's inevitable. If I don't have him right fucking now, my body will combust. My insides are on fire. My heart is rattling against my rib cage. Everything tingles and burns with desire.

His eyes beam into mine, making me dizzy. "Once we do this, Scar, there's no going back."

Do this?

Oh my god. This is really happening. Neo and I are seconds away from having sex. Reality slaps me hard in the face. I can't do this. This wasn't the plan.

The handcuffs. I need the handcuffs.

I'll just get him a little more comfortable, then I'll grab them and cuff him to the bed, until he tells me what he knows.

I run my hands down his bare arms, gliding over each muscle. "No going back."

Goosebumps break out beneath my touch, and it's a strange revelation, seeing Neo react to another person this way. Let alone, me.

His head lifts, eyes burning into mine while his palms

sink into the mattress on either side of me. "If I fuck you, Scar, things will never be the same for you and your boys."

My boys. Oh my god, Crew and Jagger.

"Get up." I push his chest, shaking my head. "Get up. Get up. Get up."

He lifts up, giving me space. "What are you doing?"

I crawl out from underneath him, shielding my nipples that are puckered against my nightgown. "I can't do this."

I've never seen Neo speechless, but he is right now. I almost feel bad for him, in a way, because the look on his face is not one of anger, but embarrassment instead.

"I'm sorry, Neo. Things shouldn't have gone this far. I...I lied." I bend down and reach under the bed and grab the handcuffs. "I came in here with the intention of cuffing you to the bed until you told me what you know." I hold the handcuffs up, letting them dangle from my finger.

Neo snatches the handcuffs away from me, that look of rage I see so often returning. "You were fucking playing me?"

"In my defense, haven't we been playing each other for days?" I chuckle humorlessly, trying to lighten the mood. "It's a constant game of cat and mouse with us."

"But I always catch you. You run and I chase, and in the end, I win."

"No. Not this time. This time, there are no winners. I can't do this anymore. I just want things back to the way they were. I want Crew and Jagger back."

"Crew and Jagger?" He scoffs. "That's all you care about, isn't it?" His hands wave in the air as he paces the length of the bed. "Fuck everyone else. Fuck your family. Fuck Maddie. Fuck me."

"You?" I spit out. "The only reason I'm even here right

now is because of you, Neo. You're blackmailing me. Do you seriously think I'm going to fall into your bed and let you have your way with me, while demanding I sleep with no one else?"

Saying it out loud makes it seem that much more ridiculous.

"I love Crew and Jagger. What I feel for you..." I don't know what I feel for Neo. Do I hate him? Maybe I don't. Do I have some sort of hidden feelings for him? Possibly. But what I really feel is sadness for him. I feel... "I feel sorry for you." He's lost so much, and it's no wonder he behaves the way he does. Deep down, I think Neo is just really, really lonely.

He stops walking, his shoulders drop and he squints at me harshly. "You feel sorry for me?" His voice rises and falls. "You fucking feel sorry for me? Why is that, Scar? Because you're out to ruin my goddamn life? You should *be* sorry, instead of feeling sorry. Parading around this house like a little tramp, forcing me to look at every flawless inch of your skin. Enticing me and sucking me in just because you can. I'm not supposed to want you, or crave you, like an addict in need of a fix. But I do, because you fucking made me!"

I take a step toward him, then two steps back, while covering my mouth with my palm. My posture crumples and his words loop in my head like a record. Is Neo saying he wants me, but he's not supposed to. But why?

"Neo," I whisper, but he grumbles and gives me his back. "Is this because of your dad and how much he's always disliked me?"

His head lifts then he abruptly looks over his shoulder. "Why would you ask that?"

"It's no secret that your dad has always hated my friendship with Maddie. I always wondered how my dad was so close with him, when he had such a strong dislike for his daughter. Then I learned about the pacts and oaths. He had to stay loyal to him, and he still does. But I think your dad hates my family and he wants you to hate us, too."

"No. My dad doesn't hate your family. He only hates you."

Those words cut deeper than any he's ever said to me before. Hate is such a strong word; one Neo and I have used many times because we know the intensity of it and we know what it does to one another. He says it to hurt me, and I do the same. Until now, I always believed he did hate me, but now, I don't think he does. I think he just pretends to because it's what his dad wants.

"Why? What did I ever do to your dad to make him hate me so much?"

Neo comes closer, eating the space between us, and each step has my soul crying out louder and louder to him. This whole moment offers so much clarity. Everything suddenly makes sense. Neo's dad turned him against me, and from what he's saying, it sounds like he's fighting to live up to his dad's demands.

"Why does he hate me, Neo?"

His neck rolls, eyes landing on my lips. He's close. Really close. I can hear each breath he draws in and feel each one he blows out.

"He hates you because you exist in his world. And I also think it's because he believes you have the ability to take Maddie and me away from him."

My heart pangs. It feels like I've fallen down this dark hole, and I can't see anything. There's so much uncertainty and so many secrets. I just need to get out of this mess. I need Crew and Jagger to hold me and tell me that everything is going to be okay, while I tell them the same.

"This secret you're holding over my head. Does it have anything to do with why your dad thinks I have the ability to take you and Maddie away?"

Please answer the question. Please, God, let him just answer the question and give me one sliver of hope that the end is near.

"Yes."

I sigh heavily. My head falls back, and I pinch my eyes shut. His dad knows my secret, too, then.

"Okay." I nod, bringing my head forward. "Is your dad and this secret the reason you've treated me so awful all these years."

One more. Just answer this one last question. I need this.

"Yes."

This moment feels surreal. All these years. So many fucking years of Neo tormenting me, and it was all because of his dad and some secret he shared with Neo. I never did anything to either of them. They turned against me because of something they heard that may not even be true. The only way I'll know for sure is if Neo tells me what that secret is.

"Tell me. Tell me the secret."

His hands lift, resting gently on my shoulders, while his fingers teeter with the thin straps of my nightgown. "Okay."

My heart jumps into my throat and I draw in a shaky breath. "Okay?"

"I'll tell you and you can get your life back." *This is it. It's finally happening. Now that we're here, I'm suddenly terrified. What is this secret? And what will happen to me once I know?* "Under one condition."

167

A condition? That's fine. I can handle a condition. I've survived this long. "Anything. I just need to know."

"You're sure?"

I nod rapidly. "Yes. Please just tell me what you need me to do."

He leans closer, his mouth ghosting over mine as he whispers, "I wanna fuck you, Scar."

CHAPTER
EIGHTEEN
NEO

"You want to fuck me?"

I lick my lips, running my fingers down the straps of her nightgown. "Did I stutter?"

"But, Crew and Jagger—"

"Will get over it."

"And you'll tell me everything?"

"I'll tell you everything you need to know."

"No." She shakes her head. "I want you to tell me *everything*."

All she needs to hear is five simple words and she'll be too stunned to speak after that. So I agree. "Okay. I'll tell you everything."

She's the one girl who was off-limits. The one fucking girl who I swore I'd never fall for. All my life, my father has told me to steer clear because she'd sneak up on me and pull me into her dark web. After fighting so hard for all these years, I've lost my own game. I need her, and I need her right fucking now.

I wanted to hate her. I tried. Lord knows I tried. But every time I see her, I question why I have to hate her so much.

Who the hell is my father to tell me who I can and can't fall for? It's not his choice to make. It's not the Elders', or the Blue Bloods'. It's mine. It's my fucking choice, and tonight, I choose her.

"Okay," she whispers, a bite of hesitation in her tone, "I'll have sex with you."

"No." I chuckle. "I don't wanna have sex with you, Scar." I shove her back down on the bed where she belongs. "I wanna fuck you."

Her chest rises and falls rapidly, and it's oddly satisfying, seeing her in this state. So vulnerable. So unsure. And, all mine. Little does she know, once I get something I want, I don't give it back. With Scar's hands bunched in one hand over her head, I grab the handcuffs off the nightstand and unlock one of the cuffs.

Her eyes dance from mine to the cuffs. "What are you doing?"

"Exactly what you planned to do to me." I set it around one of her wrists and close it around the wooden bedpost. The sound of it snapping shut startles her, and when I do the other wrist, she knows what to expect. I smirk, brow raised. "I hope you've got the key because I sure as hell don't."

"This isn't funny, Neo. I mean it, you better not be fucking with me."

"You're right, it isn't funny at all. But I'm gonna fuck you, Scar. I'm gonna shove my cock so far in your cunt, blood will be running down your leg, mixed with my cum.

And when I'm done, you'll remember why you hated me all along."

The panic in her eyes only arouses me further. She asked for this, so I'm gonna give it to her.

My hand runs up her leg, stopping at her cotton panties. Cupping my palm against her crotch, I grind my erection into her thigh. "This is turning you on, isn't it?"

She swallows hard, her throat bobbing. "No."

"Then why are your panties so wet?"

Her cheeks flush, and she doesn't respond, but she doesn't need to. Her expression is telling enough. I've always guessed Scar was a little freak in the bedroom. The pads of my fingers circle her entrance through the damp cotton. "I bet you like it rough, don't you?"

Still nothing. But that's okay. I'll get a sound out of her soon enough.

I lean forward, pressing my mouth to hers as I remove my hand from under her nightgown, then I slide down her body. Peering up at her, I flip the silky nightgown up and drag my tongue along the lining of her panties.

"I bet you taste like a fucking dream."

She rolls her eyes and looks away. She can pretend she hates this, but I see the truth right in front of me. Unless she pissed herself, but I doubt that's the case. No. Scar wants this, even if she won't ever admit it.

Her legs close around me, squeezing my head, so I slide a hand up her thigh and spread her wider, tugging down her panties. Her hips lift and I pull them down the rest of the way, then drop them beside her. "Relax, Scar."

"Easy for you to say. You're not the one with your vagina on display for your enemy."

"Ah. Is that what I am? Your enemy?"

"You're certainly not my friend." She scoffs. "Now stop talking. Continue whatever you plan to do."

A smirk curls my lips. "Whatever I plan to do?" I'm still looking at her, though she has no interest in looking at me. "Feast on your pussy, Scar. That's what I plan to do." Her cheeks flush crimson and she exhales audibly.

Bending down, I ghost her clit with my lips, taking care not to touch her. I'm gonna have a little fun first.

Puckering my mouth, I blow out softly, letting the air hit her. She groans and lifts her hips, but I retract and keep the space between my face and her sex.

"What are you doing?" she asks, her legs squirming as she fights to gain some sort of control.

"Whatever I want." I blow again, watching from the top of my eyes as goosebumps break out on her stomach.

"Dammit, Neo," she raises her hips forcibly, "this isn't funny."

I sweep two fingers up her folds and she groans breathlessly. "Sure it is." I move my hand and fan her with more air.

"Please, I'm..." Her words trail off, but I know exactly what she was going to say.

"You're what?" I grin. "Begging me?"

"Yes! Fuck! Yes! Just stop teasing me and touch me."

I love the way she begs, which is exactly why I want more.

Her ass relaxes into the mattress when I put pressure on her clit, rubbing in circular motions.

Then I stop again.

"You stupid son of a bitch!" she seethes. "If you don't know what the fuck you're doing then uncuff me and let me take care of myself."

"As tempting as that sounds because, fuck, it sounds so tempting...I'm enjoying this far too much."

Her knee bends, and she tucks her leg back and tries to kick me, but I move to the side, laughing. "Oh, Scar. You're making this too fun."

"I hate you! Have I ever told you that? Because I do!" She's speaking out of sexual frustration, but I'm loving her insults.

"Tell me more. Let me *feel* the depth of your hatred, Scar."

She lifts her other foot, trying to kick me again, her wrists straining against the metal cuffs. I dodge her blow again, a menacing laugh ripping through the room. "Nice try."

"Fine!" She huffs then relaxes on the bed. "You want a reaction out of me? Well, I'm not giving you one. Do what you want, Neo. At this point, I don't even want an orgasm from you."

Her words pique my interest because I'm certain she all but admitted to wanting me to give her an orgasm at some point. "Is that so?" I blow on her again, this time getting closer and making the air more forcible. I move my head in circles, making sure to hit every nerve ending.

"Yes," she moans the lie. "Might as well just uncuff me now because you're about to get really bored with me."

Boredom is a state of mind, and with this view, I'm all too intrigued. Grabbing her interest again, I slide my tongue between her folds, proving that I'm the one with all the power.

Her legs quiver, falling open wider, and she raises her hips slightly. Now that I know I have control, I'll give her what she wants.

I slide two fingers inside her then suck her clit between my teeth.

With a twisted expression, she closes her eyes, and while she'll deny it, she knows I'm making her feel good. In fact, I've got no doubt she'd beg for more if I stopped right now.

At this point, my cock is throbbing, so I keep going, not wanting to bust a nut in my pants before she's even had a chance to touch me.

Her trembling legs threaten to cage me in, so I lift one, resting it on my shoulder, then the other. Two fingers dip in and out of her soaked pussy, her arousal coating my digits. I'm only as deep as the first knuckle when she bites her bottom lip. Her breasts rise and fall with each unfilled breath.

My head drops, finally breaking my stare on her, and I'm already wishing I could see her eyes when I replace my fingers with my mouth and suck feverishly on her sensitive nub. Her hips rise slightly, and she whimpers. I do it again, forcing the sound out of her on demand. I love nothing more than control, and right now, I have it all. I'm also surprised at how much I love that sound. I didn't get it in class when I fingered her, though, I tried like hell. I craved her humiliation. But right now, I don't wanna share it with anyone.

"I need to touch you," she cries in desperation. "Free one of my hands."

It could be a trick, but either way, she'll still be restrained by the one cuff, so I remove my face from between her legs and reach my arm up, clicking the lever on the back of one of the cuffs. Her hand falls and she rolls her wrists before grabbing a fistful of my hair.

Teeth bared, she slams my face into her sex. "You wanna play, asshole. I'll play."

Holy fuck that was hot. I'm more turned on than I think I've ever been. I shove my fingers back inside her and feast. With an animalistic growl, I suck one of her folds then lift my head to see her face. Scar whimpers, but doesn't relent as she slams my face back down. "Keep going!"

I repeat the motion of sucking and licking her clean, while riding my fingers in and out of her hastily—not that I've got a choice with her fingers knotted in my hair.

I wish I didn't enjoy this so much. I hate that I'm as hungry for her orgasm as she is. I'm not sure I've ever wanted to satisfy a girl so much in my entire life. Scar had one thing right. It shouldn't have gone this far, but now that it has, there's no going back.

I could pull my fingers out right now and shove them down her dirty throat. Instead, I relish in the way her pussy swallows my fingers while her thighs squeeze my head. And I was right, she does taste like a dream.

She's got the upper hand now, and while I've always craved power, I'll make an exception this time.

Thoughts of my father creep into my mind. There's no going back. I've already tainted myself, so I might as well enjoy it. But if I go down in this damn Society, she'll be right there with me.

My fingers plunge deeper, sending her up an inch on the bed. I add another finger, spreading her apart. Her hips rise and fall, moving with my motions. Each thrust, never enough. She wants more than what I'm giving her. I want more. I'm not sure Scar can ever fully satisfy me because I will *always* want more of her.

Maybe I was wrong for the way I treated her all these years. So what if she's not as pure as the world believes she is. I could continue to keep her secret, and no one needs to know.

But I'll know. I'll always know what she is.

The reality that I can never keep her hits me hard, again. My chest feels heavy. There's a bite in my stomach. A feeling I don't get often. This feeling of dread.

The thing is, if I can't have her, I don't want anyone else to have her either.

"Oh my god, Neo!" Scar cries, snapping me out of my tortured mind. "Holy shit."

It wasn't until she grabbed my attention that I realized I had three fingers buried deep inside her while forcefully sucking her clit. I keep going, taking all my aggression out on her pussy. One I will never touch and taste again after this one night.

The handcuffs around her wrist rattles, and she fights for her other hand. I relent, teasing her a little more, and she warns me with a tight jaw. "Don't you dare fucking stop, Neo."

I resume the motions, and she cries louder, the sound like an unchained melody. A song just for me.

When proof of her orgasm coats my fingers, I pull them out and sweep my tongue up and down her sex, slurping up her mess. "Mmm. Fucking delicious."

Shoving my shorts down in one swift motion, I spring my erect cock free. I don't even steal a glance at her face until I'm met with it. Our noses brush and I slide right inside her, filling her back up with my dick. My mouth moves to her neck and I suck with enough tenacity to leave an impressive bruise. Her free hand grabs my head, using all her strength to try and stop my sucking motions, but this time, she loses. Once I'm certain I've left a mark, I suck harder, doubling it in size.

"Neo," she growls a breathy sound, "don't you dare give me a hickey."

"Too late. You're marked."

For days, I had to watch her parade around with a quarter-size mark on her neck. Proof of what Jagger and Crew did to her. Now, they get to see what I've done.

I come forward and grip the dipped V of her nightgown, then pull, tearing it down the center.

Her feral, blue eyes widen, mouth agape, and I use this opportunity to feed her by shoving two of my fingers in her mouth—the same ones that just swam inside her—pressing down on her tongue. "See how fucking good you taste." She closes her lips around them, sucking, and it's a fucking beautiful sight. I lick my lips, missing the taste of her already.

Grabbing both of her legs, I raise them up, straightening my back with a slight arch as I push myself up on my knees. I power drive myself into her so hard, the base of her head hits the headboard, rattling the handcuffs again. Her breasts bounce with each movement, and my balls fill with an intense need for release.

I look at her, eyes locked—wide and lustful. Her beautiful, ocean blue eyes. I swallow hard, chasing away the emotions rising in my chest.

Just before I reach the height of my orgasm, I pull out and grab my cock, pumping it while aiming it at her face. "Tongue out." When she doesn't, I repeat myself, "Tongue out. Now." Hesitantly, she parts her lips and sticks the tip of her tongue out. I reach up, grabbing her cheeks with one hand, while forcing my thumb and index finger between her teeth, then I release, squirting my cum all over her tongue. A few rhythmic grunts escape me as I slow my strokes. Then I lean forward and whisper, "Swallow," before letting go of her mouth. When I do, she swallows as she was told to do. "Atta girl."

Dropping to the side of her, I steady my breaths.

She peers up at her cuffed wrist. "Unlock this."

"Nah. I think I'll leave it for a while. Keep you as my prized possession for a few days."

"Fuck off, Neo. Just let me go."

"Say please."

"You're an asshole."

"If you want to be freed, ask nicely."

"I'm gonna kill you."

"That wasn't very nice." I love her feistiness far too much. I kind of want to keep her here for a while, just to toy with her.

"Fine," she surrenders. "Please."

With a click of my fingers against the lever, her arm drops. "Was that so hard?"

"It was pure torture." She sits up, rubbing her imprinted wrists for a second, before flinging her legs over the other side of the bed. When she stands up, her torn nightgown slides down her back to the floor. She picks up her robe and scurries to the bathroom.

It's apparent she has regrets, naturally so. I should, too, but for some reason, I don't. In fact, I feel more at ease than I have in months—maybe even years.

I just fucked the enemy, and I liked it. Sort of wanna do it again.

When Scar returns, I fold my arms under my head,

watching her as she scours the room in search of something. "What are you looking for?"

"What's left of my nightgown."

I nod to the floor where it landed. With a scoff, she bends down and snatches it up. Heavy steps bring her back over to me, and she crosses her arms over her chest, clutching the frayed fabric. "Okay. I did what you asked, now spill. What is it that you know?"

This is it. The moment I've been waiting for. The moment where I get to look her in the eyes and tell her a secret that will haunt her and her family for the rest of their lives.

I get out of the bed, still completely naked, while Scar holds my eye contact out of fear of her gaze falling elsewhere.

She looks angry. So fucking angry, and it so happens that angry is my favorite look on her.

"A deal is a deal, Neo."

She's right. A deal is a deal and I never back down when I strike one.

"You sure you wanna know?"

I'm biding time. This doesn't feel as good as it's supposed to. Not even close. Once I tell her, there is no going back. She will know and I will lose all my leverage. After today, both our lives will change forever.

"Hell yes, I wanna know. Now tell me, dammit."

I could keep this secret. No one ever has to know. We can all go on pretending and the rest of the Blue Bloods would be none the wiser. Or I tell her and I shame her for an eternity.

She snaps impatiently, "Now, Neo!"

I draw in a deep breath and rest my lips against her ear.

I'm not even looking at her and that was supposed to be half the gratification, but now, it doesn't feel very gratifying. Still, I say the words, "The reason I have to hate you, and always will have to hate you, is because you're a half-breed, Scar. You're not, nor will you ever be, a true Blue Blood."

This doesn't feel good. It doesn't feel good at all.

CHAPTER
NINETEEN
SCAR

THE FIRST WORDS out of my mouth are, "Liar." The second two —after I shove him back so I can see his face—are, "Shut up."

He doesn't say anything. He heeds my advice and he fucking says nothing! After letting words so hurtful fall from his mouth so carelessly, how dare he not say anything!

I can feel the evident crease in my forehead. In fact, it's so pronounced that I'm certain it will be a permanent fixture on my face. "Why would you say something like that?"

My arousal is still dripping from his cock as he stands there, silently. His chin drops to his chest and I know it's out of fear I'll see the lie written all over his face.

"Tell me!" I slam the nightgown to the floor. "Now, Neo!"

His eyes lift slowly, his head still hung low. "I said it because it's true. Your mom—"

"Shut up!" I scream again. I don't want him to stop talking but I need the lies to stop. "Tell me the truth."

Finally, he levels with me. "It is the truth!"

But he's still lying. He wants to hurt me. That's why he's saying this. Neo can't be trusted and this is proof. I just gave him my body, practically fed him my soul on a silver platter, all for him to feed me lies.

"We had a deal, dammit. Tell me what it is you think you know and tell me the truth, or so help me God..." I skim the room, searching for anything to aid my quest for the truth. My eyes land on a half-empty beer bottle on the nightstand. I snatch it up and dump the contents on the floor. Splatters hit my leg as the liquid makes contact with the hardwood.

"What the hell are you doing?" Neo reaches for the bottle, but I hold it back, before raising it in the air.

"Don't try me, Neo. I will bust this bottle over your head right now, then I'll use the broken glass to slice your dick, if you don't tell me the truth right fucking now!"

He immediately cups his crotch and I'm certain we're getting somewhere. "Put the damn bottle down, Scar." I step forward, and he steps back. His shins bump the bed and he sits back down. "I'll tell you, but don't interrupt. Let me finish. Okay?"

I inhale profusely and speak on the exhale. "Go on."

Neo looks past me. Maybe because he can't bear to look at me anymore. He got what he wanted from me and after this, I'll be invisible to him.

"Your mom's senior year of high school, she committed treason against the Society by having a relationship with an outsider."

"Whoa. Now I know that's a lie. My mom was with my dad her senior year."

He lifts a scowling brow. "Can I finish?"

I wave my hand, telling him to keep going.

"Now I don't know all the details of the relationships

with your dad and this guy, but I know your mom was caught by the Lawless and exposed to the entire school. This guy was set to be brought forward to tell his truth, but before he could, he went missing. In fact, he was said to be dead, but he never was. The case was brought to the local authorities by your mom, but The Elders silenced them, putting everything in a folder and tucking it away, never to be opened again."

My mom went to the local authorities? This doesn't make sense. My mom knows the Blue Bloods don't involve outside law enforcement. "Why didn't she just go to The Elders?"

"She did. She was a high school student, having a forbidden relationship with an outsider. No way in hell did they want this guy found, not to mention—"

My heart gallops at lightning speed. "Not to mention, what?"

"Who he is...or was?"

"Dammit, Neo. Just tell me. Who is this guy you claim my mom had a secret relationship with?" His mouth opens, but the words don't come out. "Just tell me. Come on. Aren't you enjoying this, Neo? It's what you wanted all along. To blow up my world. So tell me. Who the fuck is he?"

"Believe it or not, Scar. I'm not enjoying this in the least. It wasn't on my list of things to do today and now that the time to tell you is here, it's not nearly as satisfying as I thought it would be.

My airways open, and I scream, "Who the hell was it?"

"It was...a Beckett."

I gasp audibly, both hands clutching my chest. "No."

Neo nods, reaffirming what he just said. "Your mom slept with Jeremy Beckett and got pregnant, then she slept with your dad and passed you off as his all these years. You're the product of vengeance, Scar."

"My dad isn't my dad?" I mutter, not even believing it as the words leave my own mouth. "No. That's not true." I look at him again, waiting and hoping he'll start laughing and say he's fucking with me. "Where did you get this information?"

"My father told me when I was twelve. It was the day after I pulled your hair because you came into my room."

"You pulled my hair countless times. You expect me to remember that?"

"No. But does it really matter when he told me? The fact is, he told me. He ingrained in my head that you were the enemy and that any sort of relationship with you would be lethal. So much so, he refers to you as a snake."

I don't understand why Sebastian would tell Neo such a thing. Does he really believe that I'm half Beckett, half Sunder? If he had any reason to believe Kol Sunder was not my dad, he'd tell him. They're friends.

But they're not friends. That's another lie I've been led to believe my entire life.

"I have to go," I blurt out.

Neo springs off the bed, following in my footsteps as I walk to the door. "Where are you going?"

I spin around, hands in the air. "I don't know. I have no fucking clue, Neo. But I have to go somewhere. I need to know the truth."

"Hey, Scar," Neo says, stopping me in my tracks while I grip the door handle. "For what it's worth, I don't wanna hurt you anymore. I'll keep your secret if you want me to."

I draw in a bumpy breath that rattles my chest. "Thanks," I say, before opening the door and leaving.

"CREW!" I holler, pounding both fists on the wooden door of the dorm room they've been staying in. "Jagger! Please. Open up." Draping my hair around my shoulders, I cover the golf ball sized hickey Neo left on my neck. I don't know what the deal is with these guys and hickeys, but it has to be some sort of control thing.

The door rips open, and I throw myself into Crew's arms, sobbing uncontrollably.

His fingers comb through my disheveled hair, while his other arm holds me close. "Baby, what's wrong?"

"I..." I swallow down the saliva pooling in my mouth. "I'm..." I gulp and sputter and fight for breath. "Everything."

Crew pulls back, his hands now cupping my cheeks. His head lowers slightly, so he can see my eyes. "What the hell did he do to you?"

"I think...I think he just ruined my life."

"Come sit down and tell me everything." He takes my hand and leads me to a double-seated couch. The room is nothing like the one Riley and me shared. There's a small kitchenette to the right, a small living room and two doors that lead to, I presume, his and Jagger's bedrooms. It's not a dorm room; it's a small apartment.

"Where's Jagger?" I ask him, my eyes dancing around the small space. I have no idea what I'm looking for because, obviously, Jagger isn't here, but...

When one of the doors opens, my words trail off. At first, I think it's Jagger, but when my eyes drag up a pair of smooth, bare legs and past the white towel, I see that it's Hannah.

My eyes shoot to Crew's. "Why is she here?"

185

"Ignore her," he says, before turning his attention to Hannah. "Give us a minute, please."

"Why. Is. She. Here, Crew?"

He's still holding my hand, so I tear it away from him. "Where is Jagger? Is he in there?" I jump to my feet that beg to fail me as I cross the room to the door, all shaky and off-balance. My heart is beating a million beats a minute as I shove the door open. Once I get a clear view inside the room, I shout, "Jagger?"

Hannah pokes her head out of the adjoined bathroom, steam rolling out with her. She nods toward the bed. "He's sleeping." Then she closes the door again.

I'm gonna fucking kill her. But first, I'm chopping this asshole's dick off.

My thoughts elude me as I storm over to the bed and tear the black comforter off him. Sure enough, lying flat on his stomach, butt-ass naked, is Jagger. I'm trying really hard not to jump to conclusions because I know Jagger always sleeps naked, but it's really hard not to when another girl is here.

I raise my hand, bringing my open palm down on his bare ass.

He shoots up in the bed, his limp dick dangling between his legs. "What the fuck?" he growls, while soothing the handprint on his ass. "Scar? What are you doing?"

My arms cross over my chest, hip raised up as I scowl at him. "You first. What the hell were you doing?"

"Have you been crying?"

On his knees, he moves across the bed to come closer to me, but I hold up a hand. "Don't!"

His hands fly up as he looks around the room. "What did I do?"

Hannah's voice comes over my shoulder. "Thanks for letting me use your shower. See ya tomorrow at school."

My eyebrows cave in, and I glower. "Do you even have to ask?"

He points at the door, where Hannah just walked out into the living room area. "What the hell is she doing here?"

"Don't play dumb with me, Jagger."

Crew comes in the doorway and Jagger grabs his boxers off the floor, stepping one foot in at a time, before snapping the band around his waist. "I was a-fucking-sleep. I didn't know she was here. Do you think...? No, Scar. Hell no. I didn't fuck that girl."

"You didn't?" My question isn't one of naivety. I have no reason not to believe Jagger, and if he says nothing happened with Hannah, I trust that.

"Of course, I didn't."

"Then why is she even here?"

Jagger snatches a pair of jeans off his dresser and puts them on, then fishes for a shirt in an open drawer. "Fuck if I know." He looks at Crew, knowing he has the answer, so I do the same.

"Crew?" I drawl. "Did you know Hannah was here this whole time?"

He shrugs causally, a glint of humor playing on his lips. "Fine. Yes. Just thought it would be funny to watch you beat the shit out of Jagger. Hannah found out Melody is the one who pushed her in the tunnels. I think Riley let it slip when Melody stayed with her the other night. Since that night, everyone knows about the BCA Stalker, they just don't know who it is."

"So you," I say, looking at Crew, "one of the biggest assholes here, did her a solid and let her use the shower?"

"Fuck no." Crew huffs, coming farther into the room. "We took this dorm room from Victor Hammond and his roommate and booted them in with some other guys. Apparently, Victor and Hannah have something going on, so she came here to use *his* shower and found us instead. I agreed, so long as she kept an extra eye on Melody. Just in case she's the one who's still helping Jude."

That makes more sense. Poor Hannah. She has to be hurting, knowing it was her best friend who shoved her head against a wall. That's almost unforgivable. Then again, I've done worse.

Everything I've done hits me at once, knocking the air out of me. I drop down on the bed and the tears begin to fall again. Only this time, they are not over the news Neo just shared with me; they're all because of what I did to get that information. And even if I had nothing to gain from it, I think I would have had sex with Neo anyway.

My face buries into my hands, my cries ringing through the empty space between my fingers. "I messed up, you guys. I really messed up."

When the weight of the mattress shifts, I look to my left and see that Crew has taken a seat on one side of me, while Jagger sits on the other side. "I owe you both a huge apology. I should have never pushed either of you away, but selfishly, I did."

"I always knew there was a reason, baby. Just wanted to give you the time you needed." Crew curls his fingers around mine and holds them in my lap.

"I never wanted Neo. I mean...not a relationship, or really anything for that matter." Saying it aloud makes me realize how untrue that is. Neo has been in my head for days. I chalk it up to being around him so much, but it's more than that. Tonight wasn't just about him holding a secret over my head. I wanted him, and in the worst way, I got him.

"He forced you to end things with us, didn't he?" This time, it's Jagger who speaks, but his voice is not one of sympathy, it's laced with anger, as it should be. With his arms draped at his side, he clenches his tee shirt tightly in one hand. So tightly, the white of his knuckles protrude. It kills me that I've hurt him so badly.

It's time to be honest. I don't expect them to forgive me for what I've done because I'm not even sure I can forgive myself, but I owe them the truth about what I've done and who I am.

I glance at Crew, then Jagger, before saying, "There's something you both need to know."

They don't say anything, just wait impatiently to hear what I have to say. "This is going to come as a shock, and I don't expect you to believe it, but..."

Jagger rolls his hand in the air. "But what? Out with it already."

I swallow hard before saying, "Maddie's awake."

Crew's eyes snap to mine. "What? Maddie's awake? How do you know this?"

"Because she's here, at the Academy. She was never missing." I wipe my dewy eyes and sniffle. "A doctor informed Neo that Maddie was being kept in a medically-induced coma. He got her out of the home, and once she was no longer receiving the sedative through her IV, she woke up."

"Wait." Crew shakes his head, finding this hard to believe, much like I did when I first saw her here. "Maddie's here?"

Jagger pulls his shirt over his head and doesn't say anything. Once it's in place, he just stands with his eyebrows tightly knitted and his hands in the front pocket of his black jeans.

"Yeah. She's here. I've seen her. Talked with her. Laughed. Cried."

Crew paces a few steps, keeping his thoughts to himself, but I wish more than anything I could hear them.

I'm watching Crew intently, when Jagger finally speaks, his tone harsh. "Of course he did. It's fucking Neo." His attention shifts to me. "And you knew all along?"

"I wanted to tell you guys—"

"But you didn't. Instead, you pushed us away, while you and Neo played house with Maddie. Is that right?"

I walk closer to him and reach for his hand, but he jerks it back. "Don't."

"It's not like that Jagger. Neo blackmailed me."

Crew's body movements freeze momentarily. "Blackmailed you with what?"

My heart pangs at the memory of what Neo told me. It's still so raw, and I'm not even sure if there's any truth behind it, but nonetheless, I feel the sting of his words deep inside me.

"Did you fuck him?" Jagger asks, point-blankly.

I'm taken aback by his question, not really expecting it. My mouth falls open, but all that comes out is, "I..."

"Did you fuck him?" he repeats. "It's a simple yes or no question." His hand extends and he flips my hair to the side, exposing the mark on my neck.

Jagger accepts my silence and the hickey as an answer. His lips draw back and he bares his teeth. "Unfucking believable, Scar."

I grab his arm, but he tears it away. "You've got some nerve coming in here and attacking me because you thought I slept with another girl, which I didn't, by the way." With his shoulders drawn back, chest inflated, he barrels for the door and doesn't stop.

"Jagger, wait." I attempt to go after him, but I'm stopped when Crew throws an arm out in front of me.

"Not so fast."

I crumble in that second. "I'm so sorry, Crew. None of this was supposed to happen."

The disappointment in Crew's eyes slices through me with the potency of a knife. "So it's true. You fucked him?" He observes the mark, but still demands an answer. "Yes or no?"

I break eye contact, chin down, and I nod.

Crew tosses my arm away like it's trash. "That son of a bitch." He whips around, giving me his back. His knees bend and he slouches, then comes back up, all the while tugging his hair on both sides of his head. As fast as he let me go, he grabs me again. Both arms this time, while his eyes level with mine. "Did he rape you? Just say the fucking word, Scar, and I'll kill him."

I shake my head, telling him the truth. "No."

"So you wanted it?" He exhales dramatically, jaw ticking as he awaits my response.

A door outside the room slams shut, startling me, and I know it was Jagger leaving. "I had to do it, Crew. He knew things about me that he was going to hold over my head if I didn't—"

He draws in a breath, holding it. "Let me get this straight. Neo knew a secret about you and threatened to expose it if you didn't sleep with him?" My chest feels so tight. I can barely breathe. Let alone think or speak. " I need you to be honest with me, Scar."

If I admit that's what happened, I have no doubt he'll go after Neo. What he won't understand is that, in the end, I wanted it just as much as Neo did.

"Neo made the deal, but I accepted it because it's what I wanted. These last couple days, I've seen humanity trying to claw its way out of Neo. I...I saw him differently."

"You saw him in a different light and decided to jump into bed with him? Jesus, Scar. Do you know how that sounds?"

I drop my head back, eyes closed as I collect my thoughts. It's damn near impossible to explain how I feel because I'm not even sure myself. Ever since I kissed Neo, something awakened inside me. It was a moment of clarity, and after hearing Neo tell me his dad is the one who brainwashed him against me, everything has changed. Neo wasn't lying when he said that my entire life would change once I knew the secret he was holding.

I bring my head back forward and own up to what I did the best I can. "I know it sounds ridiculous."

"Ridiculous?" Crew spits out. "It's unfathomable. What? Do you plan to fuck every guy who cracks a smile or gives you a compliment or shows themselves in a different light?"

On instinct, I slap him across the face. "How dare you judge me!"

"Well, what the hell do you expect?" His nostrils flare while he soothes his cheek, his voice rising with each word. "First Jagger and now Neo. Are you trying to build your own harem, or what?"

"No!" I shout, anger and pain both unleashing at once. "I messed up, Crew! I'm sorry. I...I don't know what else to say.

I guess...go to Maddie. You're better off with her." I storm out of the room, tears falling down my cheeks as I head straight for the door to leave.

Once I'm out, I don't even bother glancing over my shoulder to see if Crew's following, because I know he's not.

I don't even know who I am anymore. When I first got to the Academy, someone told me this place would break me. I had no idea until now how true those words were.

A memory of my first day here pops into my mind. It was something Riley said.

"Hey," Riley whispers, pulling me off to the side of the trail, "wanna hear a secret?"

"You know I do."

"I heard a rumor that a member once had a relationship with an outsider here at BCA, and when the Lawless found out, they killed the guy."

"Come on," I sweep the air with my hand, "you can't believe everything you hear. Sure, all the Lawless, then and now, are pricks, but they aren't actual murderers." Even if it wasn't long ago, I assumed they were all capable. Funny how things change.

Her shoulders rise, and she clicks her tongue. "I dunno. I think you'd be surprised."

Is it possible that the member she was referring to was my mom? Neo said the guy, being Jeremy Beckett, went missing and was presumed dead. It would make sense Riley heard the guy was killed.

There's only one way to find out. I need Riley to tell me everything she knows.

CHAPTER
TWENTY
CREW

GO TO MADDIE. You're better off with her.

Scar's words are on repeat in my head, and no matter how loud "Bother" by Stone Sour is blasting in my ears, they don't drown out the sound of her voice.

How can I be better off with Maddie, if it means being without Scar? There's no way. My mind can't even comprehend the possibility of a life without Scar.

Maddie doesn't have my heart, Scar does.

I need her like I need air.

The music suddenly stops, warranting a glare at Jagger. "What the fuck, dude?"

"I can't think with that shit playing." He pulls out a stool beside me and takes a seat. His elbows press to the center island. "You been up to see her yet?"

My response is a point-blank, "Nope."

"She knows you're here now. So what's up? Not ready to see her?"

Jagger and I came here to find out if it was true. Sure enough, Scar was right. Maddie's here, alive and well.

I pinch my eyes shut, trying hard as hell to remember what Maddie looked like before the fall. I try to bring her smile to life in my head. Grasping at straws for a feeling that doesn't exist. For years, I tried to feel something other than friendship for Maddie. She's got all the qualities any guy would love, but she's not Scar. In the past, I looked at each day as more time to bide while waiting for Scar, but now, I can't do that. I won't pretend anymore.

Neo walks into the kitchen, and Jagger and I share unspoken words with just a look.

"You both look like someone fucking died. This is a celebration. Not a funeral."

I spin around in my chair, glowering hard at Neo. "Should be yours."

His hands clap to his chest as he smirks. "So, you two can share her, but I can't have a turn?"

Jagger shoves his stool back and gets on his feet, and I do the same. Three steps bring Jagger nose to nose with Neo, as I follow, taking his back. Neo curls his fingers, egging Jagger on. "Oh, you wanna fight me for her? I dare ya."

"Fight you for her? I've already got her, dickhead."

"No, you don't. In fact, neither of you do. If I remember right, she dumped your asses before jumping into bed with me. And now that she's had a taste, she'll want more. They always do."

I'm watching Jagger's right fist in slow motion as it meets Neo's left cheek, sending his head snapping to the side. He didn't even see it coming, which makes this all the more satisfying.

Jagger and I are alike in many ways, but I have the ability to keep my cool. Him, on the other hand, he has no chill when it comes to anyone treading on his territory. In this case, that territory being Scar. He's pissed at her, but he's more hurt than anything, and he expresses his pain with rage and violence.

Neo, who usually backs down in an attempt to diffuse any situation like this with me or Jagger, retaliates this time. His arm locks around Jagger's throat as he holds him in place with Jagger's back to his chest. He's got enough pressure around his neck to shoot Jagger's eyes wide. He opens his mouth, fighting to breathe.

I position myself in front of Jagger, grabbing Neo's arm and trying to break his hold. "Let him go, man. You're gonna kill him."

"Why? So he can sucker punch me again?"

I'm not one to fight, or take sides, but it's a long time coming when I cock my fist and land a shot on the same cheek Jagger just did. Neo loses his hold on Jagger, who crouches over, catching his breath.

Neo's jaw clenches as he grazes his cheek with his fingers. "Of course you two would gang up on me. Have for years."

"Gang up on you?" I laugh under my breath, tapping both sides of my head. "Are you fucking delusional? Do you see what you've fucking done?"

"Oh yeah. I'm the asshole for trying to protect my sister?"

"This isn't about Maddie, Neo!"

"Isn't it, though? Isn't Maddie where this all begins and ends?"

"No," I huff. "Not with me. Maddie isn't my endgame. Scar is."

"Well, if you know what's good for you, you won't

mention a damn thing about you and Scar right now. You break my sister's heart, when she's still recovering, and I'll rip yours from your chest with my bare hands."

"The last thing I wanna do is hurt Maddie. You should know that. Just because I'm not in love with her, doesn't mean I don't care about her."

"Well," he simpers, "you tell her about you and Scar and it'll hurt like hell."

"I'm not talking about that right now. Besides, it's really none of your business. Maddie is an adult now and you can't protect her heart forever."

Neo rubs the back of his neck, staring down at the floor. "I can try my damnedest."

"Look. This conversation isn't about Maddie, or even Scar. It's about you and the way you treat the people you care about."

"Care about?" He scoffs. "What makes you think I care about either of you? No one gives a damn about me. Why should I care about any of you?"

"You don't give anyone a chance. You try to steal everyone's happiness, just to give yourself a moment of your own. Well, how's it feel? You happy now?"

He rolls his neck, brows dipped low in a heavy scowl. "No. I'm not fucking happy. I don't even know what happiness feels like anymore, Crew. At least, I didn't, until tonight."

Jagger straightens his back, and it's clear he's fighting the urge to deck him again. "There it is. Trying to rub this shit in our faces again."

"You think that's what I'm doing right now? Rubbing it in your face that I just destroyed your girl's heart? That's not what I'm doing." Neo walks over to the entryway into the living room and stops, both hands pressed to the frame, and he drops his head. "I didn't know what happiness felt like anymore, until tonight, because I found out exactly what it *doesn't* feel like. And it sure as hell wasn't happiness I felt when I blew her world apart."

His hands fall to his sides and he walks sluggishly through the doorway, disappearing into the living room.

I look at Jagger, who's just as stunned as I am. "Correct me if I'm wrong, but was that almost...sincere?"

Jagger scratches his head, and his shoulders rise. "I've got no idea what to think when it comes to that guy."

My stomach is in a ball of tightly-knitted knots. The weight of the guilt I've carried all these months is suddenly unbearable. I raise my hand to knock, but my movements freeze. Then I drop my hand back down.

I've done a lot of people wrong in my life, and it's usually no problem for me to keep walking with my head held high. There are a select few who I take my walls down for and Maddie is one of them, along with Jagger, Neo, and of course, Scar. It doesn't matter that Maddie and I will never be, what matters is that she's always been one of my best friends. Part of me thinks I stayed with her so long out of fear of losing that friendship, along with Neo's. But I can't live in fear anymore. Life's too short to settle with someone who doesn't light a fire inside you. Scar lit that fire years ago, and while the flame may have flickered from time to time, it never went out.

You've gotta do this, Crew. Just go in. You're not going in there to see a girlfriend or an ex. You're going to see one of your best friends.

I knock my knuckles softly on the door.

"Come in."

The sound of her voice hitting my ears is like music—reminding me of a song she loved to listen to, "Drops of Jupiter" by Train. And when I push the door open and I see her sitting there, it's affirmed that she's returned from her stay on the moon. "Hey, gorgeous."

She smiles, and I find myself doing the same. "Hi, Crew."

The weight slowly lifts as I cross the room to an empty chair beside the wheeled one she's currently sitting in.

I nod toward the chair before sitting down. "Do you mind?"

Her arms spread wide. "Do I get a hug first?"

"Yeah. Of course." I lean down, wrapping her up in a hug. She feels so fragile in my arms, but she looks the same. Her hair is longer, and her cheekbones are more pronounced, which I assume is from being tube-fed nutrients for so long. But, other than that, she's the same Maddie I've always known.

I pull back and grab the chair, spinning it around in front of her and sitting on it backward. My arms lay on the back-rest. "How have you been feeling?"

"Bored." She snorts. "So damn bored. What I wouldn't give to be on my feet and play a childish game of hide-and-seek right about now."

I laugh. "Those were the days."

"How about you? How are you doing?"

How am I doing? That's a good question. "Would you believe me if I said I'm doing okay?"

Her lips press into a thin line and she shakes her head. "I know you, Crew. Your eyes don't lie."

"Oh yeah?" I rest my head on my hands. "What are they telling you right now?"

She leans closer, squinting while dissecting my eyes. "You're sad. Lost, maybe."

"I guess you're right." I chuckle. "My eyes don't lie."

Maddie adjusts the white chenille blanket on her lap and sinks back, getting comfortable. "Listen, Crew. I didn't wake up a fool. I'm well aware that while I was asleep, you were awake and living your life. I don't want you to think that I'm not taking that into consideration. The person you were before I fell is not the person you are now. And the same goes for me."

"What are you saying, Mads?"

"I guess what I'm trying to say is, I don't expect us to pick up where we left off...unless you want to."

Averting my gaze, I chew on my bottom lip. Maddie catches the action. "Avoiding eye contact, biting your lip. Are you forgetting I've known you since we were both in diapers?"

"Ya know," I look at her, "I think you probably know me better than anyone. No matter what happens, I don't wanna lose you, Mads."

"A million light years could pass and you'd still have me. What I wanna know is, have I lost you?"

"No," I say honestly, "you'll never lose me. You're my best friend."

Maddie nods, and now she's the one biting her lip and averting her gaze. "Best friend, huh?" I swallow hard, hoping she didn't take it the wrong way. "I can handle that." She snaps her fingers at me, eyes beaming. "But I have to come before Neo. It can be our secret, but I need you to say the words."

I chuckle. "You come before Neo. But it's our secret." Maddie holds out her pinkie finger, and I wrap mine around it. "I'm glad you're back."

"Me, too."

Maddie and I spend a solid hour catching up. She asks a lot of questions about me, the Academy, Jude, and even Scar. It's nice having my friend back. She doesn't know about me and Scar and it might take some time easing her into that, but right now, she's happy and that's all that matters.

At one point in our conversation, she mentioned Neo and Scar being together, and I kept my lips sealed because, hell, maybe they are starting something up. I always knew Neo kept a sliver of his heart open just for her, probably the only part that's not charred black. Throughout their fights and threats, I'd always stand by idly as the sparks flew. But I never let it affect what I had with Scar because I know what we have is real. Her relationships with other people don't take away from her relationship with me.

Neo was raw tonight. Jagger and I saw a part of him we haven't seen in years. Ever since his mom died, he's been unable to express any emotion other than hatred. A couple weeks ago, we were walking to the river to try and catch the stalker—which was a bust—but Neo kept fucking with Scar. He was flipping her hood, flirting with her. That's when I knew he was hiding his feelings. Neo doesn't flirt, and he certainly doesn't let a girl make him laugh, unless it's a sinister one.

I've got no doubt there's something going on, even if

they'll both deny it. Jagger knows it, too. It's the reason he's been so pissy lately. He's worried we're losing her to Neo, and no matter how hard I've drilled it into his head that we're not, he fails to believe it.

So now, we need to talk—all four of us.

CHAPTER
TWENTY-ONE
SCAR

"EVERYTHING. I need you to tell me everything you know about the case," I beg and plead with Riley, all the while knowing she might be limited on what she's allowed to confess. She's already said there isn't much to tell in the case of the student having a forbidden relationship with an outsider, but there has to be more. The guy supposedly died at the hands of the Lawless. Someone has to know something.

She runs her mascara up her lashes, while leaning close to the dormitory bathroom mirror. "Honestly, Scar. There isn't much to tell." She blinks through each swipe, coating her lashes. "Everything I heard was while I was eavesdropping the summer before my junior year here."

I press my palms behind me against the cold vanity, while twisting my head to watch her. "Who were you eavesdropping on? Why did the conversation start? How did it end?"

Moving to the next eye, she watches herself in the mirror while she talks. "It was a Chapter meeting. Probably seven to nine Elders were gathered in the meeting room, while I was playing a game on my phone outside the door. They were talking about a female member having an affair with an outsider. Said he was set to testify against her in front of the student body, so she could be punished, but he died first. Apparently, she had a connection to one of the Lawless members and he helped her or whatever."

Or whatever? The casualness of her tone makes me wish this were just an insignificant conversation. I've got no doubt in my mind that my mom was that female student. And the Lawless member she had a connection with—none other than my dad, or so I thought, Kol Sunder.

Everything Riley is saying matches perfectly with what Neo said.

My heart pangs with unbearable agony. Dread washes over me. I've lost my identity, and I have no idea who I am, or where I belong anymore.

Do I dare confess this to Riley, or anyone, for that matter? Where do I go from here?

"Hey," Riley says, sticking her mascara wand back in the tube. "What's the matter?"

I drop my hands from the sink and turn around to look at myself in the mirror. I'm a mess. A hickey on my neck that reminds me I'm a whore. Dark circles wrap around my tired, red eyes. My hair is still matted from having sex with Neo. In fact, his dried cum is still on my neck. I haven't showered, I haven't eaten. And I won't until I know the truth.

"I've made a mess of things, Ry." I purse my lips tightly, fighting back the urge to break down. "I think I need to go home." As soon as the words leave my mouth, I lose it.

Riley holds me tight, while I sob into the sleeve of her robe. The same robe I just returned to her. "First of all, whatever mess has been made, we can clean up. Second, you're not leaving. You are not a quitter, Scarlett Sunder."

"Maybe I am. Maybe that's why I don't like change or trying new things, because I'm afraid I'll quit when things get hard."

Riley grabs my face so that I'm looking at her. "Listen to me. You are one of the toughest girls I know. If anyone should quit, it's me. I'm the world's worst Guardian. I'm like an elf at Santa's workshop, who doesn't know how to build toys. What kind of elf can't build toys? Better yet, what kind of Guardian can't crack a case?"

We both laugh, and it's a nice moment of comical relief. I step back and wipe the back of my hand up my nose. "You're a great Guardian."

"No, I'm not. I'm a terrible one. But I'm not quitting, and neither are you. Now tell me why you think you made a mess of everything."

I look at myself in the mirror again, hating everything about me with each word that leaves my mouth. "I had sex with Neo."

My eyes meet Riley's wide ones in the reflection of the mirror, and her mouth drops open. "You had sex with him?"

I nod, lips pursed, and tears ready to fall again. The lump in my throat has expanded and my chest shakes with each breath. "I did, and while I don't like myself for why I did it, I don't regret it." That does it. My bottom lip quivers as I sob again, but I don't stop talking. "And I hate myself for liking it. I'm so angry that Neo showed me this other side of him that no one else gets to see."

Riley rubs my back and I drop my head, looking into the empty sink. "Scar, you're not a bad person for seeing the good in someone who wants the world to think he's a monster."

"But to have sex with him? Crew and Jagger's best fucking friend? What does that say about me?"

"It says, you're a girl who knows what she wants and found it in three different guys."

I lift my head and rub my fingers under my tear-soaked eyes. "I don't think Crew and Jagger will see it that way. Besides, I don't want a relationship with Neo. I still can't stand the guy half of the time. He's still a selfish asshole."

"So it was just sex? To get what you wanted from him?"

I nod. "I think so."

"Well," Riley quips, "what was it he was holding over your head? You don't have to tell me if…"

"I'll tell you." I pivot around to face her. "But you can't tell anyone. Not a single soul."

I know I can trust Riley. She's one of the good ones and she's been on my side since the minute I got to the Academy. But I wouldn't fault her for turning me in. After all, I'm a fraud. It might actually make things easier. Get kicked out of the Society. Get on with my life.

"Your secret's safe with me. Promise."

"Apparently, I'm not a Blue Blood," I spit out, no thought process behind it. No time to sugarcoat it and wrap it up with a cute bow. "My mom had an affair with an outsider. A Beckett."

"Oh dear God, Scar. Tell me your mom isn't the girl from the rumors."

My sunken shoulders and bitten lip tell her everything my lack of words do not.

"Okay." She nods, breaking eye contact. "Okay. This is fine." Her gaze shoots back to mine. "Who all knows?"

"Obviously Neo's dad because he's the one who told Neo years ago. Apparently, it's why Neo has always despised me. All this time, he looked at me as an outsider. It's no wonder he was so cruel."

"Don't make excuses for his bad behavior. Neo could have come clean prior to fucking you. But why now? Why is he telling you this all of a sudden?"

I shrug my shoulders because I haven't the slightest clue. "I guess he had his fun and he was done. I think his intentions were to hurt me by telling me the truth, but in the end, I don't think that's what he wanted."

Riley holds up a finger and begins counting them off. "So...Neo's dad, Neo, me, and you. That's it, that we know of?"

"That I know of? Yeah. I haven't told Crew, Jagger, or Maddie yet."

"Don't," she spits out. "Don't tell a single soul until we know for sure."

"But how are we gonna find out the truth?"

Riley quirks a brow, a mischievous grin on her face. "I have my ways."

"Thank you," I gush, giving her a hug. "Thank you for not looking at me like I'm a disgusting Beckett or shunning me for being a half-breed."

"Your mom was born into this Society, Scar. You still have Blue Blood blood in your veins. If anything, it's time to show the Becketts that their attempt to destroy our blood-lines is an epic fail because our kind unites as one, no matter what."

I'm not sure how she did it, but Riley has given me a sliver of optimism. I just hope the guys feel the same way, once they know where I really came from.

RACHEL LEIGH

We break up our hugging session, and I follow Riley back to her room, so she can change and head over to the house with me. She's decided to stay another night because Melody has completely taken over her dorm room.

Once we're inside, I make myself comfortable on Riley's bed while she changes. "Any word on Jude from the guys?" I ask her, knowing that she's been in contact with them about their plan. I've been so busy with everything else, I haven't even thought about what we're going to do with him.

She's between her armoire closet doors, tossing clothes over her shoulder. "Nope. They're still convinced it's him and I'm still convinced it's not."

"I dunno, Ry. It's not looking good for Jude. Either way, he's still a..." My words trail off when a revelation hits me full force.

Riley pokes her head around her closet door. "Still a, what?"

My mouth falls open and all the blood drains from my face. I sit up, feeling dizzy. "Ry." I look at her. "If Jeremy Beckett is my dad, that means—"

"Jude Beckett might be your brother."

I gasp at the realization. The guy we have tied up in the tunnels, could very well have the same blood as mine running through his veins. Half Blue Blood. Half Beckett.

Sickness pools in my stomach. I wanna claw at my skin and peel it off because I feel disgusted with myself for being one of them.

"I can't do this, Ry. I have to know. We have to go to Jude and ask him if his dad has ever mentioned such a thing." Riley's eyes dance away suspiciously. "What? Why are you looking like that?"

"Nothing. We can go, but there's something I need to tell

208

you first." When I motion my hand in the air, moving this conversation along, she pulls something out of her closet and holds it up. "What's in the bag?"

"Jude's dinner."

I scoff. "You've been feeding him, Ry?"

"We can't let him starve," she says somberly. "I may have been bringing him food and water...and feeding it to him."

"You're feeding him too?" My pitch rises. "For how long?"

She lifts a shoulder. "Since last night, after we were all down there. I went to the vending corner and got him some snacks then went back. We talked, Scar. He told me he's done some bad things, but he's not the one in control. And I believe him."

I can't believe what I'm hearing. Not sure why I'm so surprised after today's turn of events. At this point, I'm not sure anything can really shock me to the core.

"He claims he's not in control, but did he say who is?" She shakes her head no, so I go on. "Well, there you go. If he's been doing all this shit, then he'd at least know the person forcing him to do it, and he'd tell us, just to save his own ass."

"Honestly, I don't think he knows."

"You're too trusting, Ry." I shake my head. "Much too trusting."

"There's only one way to find out for sure." She drops the brown paper bag on the bed and goes back to her closet. When she steps back, she's holding a lockbox. "We need to go through the evidence."

"Evidence?"

She sets the box on the bed, then goes to her dresser and

retrieves a key. Once the box is unlocked, she flips the top open. "Like a true Guardian, I've collected things."

After pulling out a stack of papers, she hands them to me. "These are the notes he left. How did you get these?"

"Let's just say I was watching...a lot." She nods toward the papers. "Start reading them. See if there is any familiarity in what's said. Maybe a link to someone you might know. Someone who might have it out for you. Possibly, someone else who knows your secret."

I do as she says, starting with the first one.

IF YOU THINK THIS IS A GAME, YOU'RE DEAD WRONG!

Then another.

BLOOD IS THICKER THAN WATER!

My eyes lift, and I read it again, this time out loud. "*Blood is thicker than water.* Think that's a clue?"

"Oh for sure. This person definitely knows your secret."

I raise a brow, then tell her, once again, why I'm sure it's Jude. "If it were Jude, it would make sense. Because he'd be... my brother. My blood."

Riley's silence is telling. I'm slowly convincing her, so I read more, in hopes of her seeing the truth.

THE GAMES HAVE JUST BEGUN!

Yeah. No kidding, asshole. You've played your fair share of games, but they're coming to an end.

I read through a couple more, then my body goes numb.

I WAS AT EVERY BIRTHDAY. YOU JUST DIDN'T KNOW.

I remember finding this one in my room. It was the night Neo threw a party...

Neo, being the control freak he is, snags the envelope from Jagger's hand before he can see the contents. His finger slides under the lip, and he reaches inside. When he pulls his hand out, he's holding a picture.

It takes me a second, but I come to realize, it's a picture of me.

"That's me...when I was only a child. It looks like one of my birthday parties. Why would this guy have a picture of me as a child?" Panic ensues, and I take it from Neo. It looks like it was taken through a window. Like someone was standing outside of my family home, watching us. I look at the guys, who are all staring at me like they're waiting for me to lose my shit. No one says anything, so I take it upon myself to ask the question that I'm sure we all have. "Where did this come from?" I flip the picture over and there's something written on the back.

I push away the memory and read the note to Riley. "I was at every birthday. You just didn't know."

She snaps her fingers, pleased with herself. "You see. It can't be Jude. Why the hell would Jude take a picture of you at a birthday party as a child? He wouldn't. Unless..."

Chills skate down my spine as I finish her sentence. "Unless his dad did."

"Of course. Because he knew you were his daughter."

Riley thinks long and hard, and I know she's trying like

hell to acquit Jude, but the evidence isn't working in her favor. "But Jeremy Beckett is dead. If I had to guess, Jude took over his game after he killed him."

For the first time all night, I've rendered Riley speechless.

I stuff the notes back in the lockbox and close the lid. "It's late right now, but as soon as class gets out tomorrow, we're going to talk to Jude, so he can tell us everything he knows. Until then, girl talk in Maddie's room."

CHAPTER
TWENTY-TWO

NEO

THIS MORNING I should have woken up feeling relief. Instead, I have a pounding headache from drinking myself into oblivion last night. Haven't heard from Scar. Not that I expect to. She got what she wanted and probably hates me more now than she did before last night.

When all is said and done, there's one person who I know I've always got at my side. I knock on Maddie's door, because she asked me to. Apparently, we're not kids anymore, and I can't just barge in whenever I want. So here I am abiding by her wishes.

"Who is it?" she asks, as if I could be anyone else.

"Your favorite brother. Who else?"

"State your name. I may have more than one."

I open the door and sneer, "Fuck off. Even if you had more than one brother, I'd still be your favorite."

"Debatable." Maddie places her book on her nightstand. She appears comfortable with a blanket pulled up to her waist and folded neatly. I'm certain someone tucked her in, and if I had to bet, my money would be on Scar.

213

Crossing the room, I grab the handle of her wheelchair and roll it over to the side of her bed. "Scar been here to see you lately?"

"She and Riley were here for a couple hours last night. Haven't you talked to her this morning?"

"Nah. She's pissed at me."

Maddie's head tilts slightly to the side. "What'd you do, Neo?"

I bring my hands to my chest, grinning. "Why's it always me?"

"Because you're you. And because Scar doesn't start shit, she ends it."

"True," I say in agreement before ratting myself out. "I gave her a big-ass hickey then told her something that hurt her pretty bad."

"Wow. Okay. Those are two very different things. First of all, why the hell did you give her a hickey? Those things are gross."

"To prove a point."

"And the point is?"

"That she's spoken for."

"For the love of God, Neo. Stop being so damn possessive. You did that shit when we were kids. It's disgusting."

I chuckle. "What did I do when we were kids?"

"Like you don't remember."

"Humor me."

"Remember that time we were at the park when we were, like, twelve or thirteen, and it started snowing and Scar had on short sleeves?"

"Doesn't ring a bell."

"Jagger offered her his coat, but you got pissed and said she should go get her own, knowing that we were miles away from home. So you threw his back at him. Ten minutes later, you gave her yours."

"I'd hardly call that being possessive, Mads. It was a kind gesture." I dust off my shoulder, smirking. "I happen to be a generous guy."

"Bullshit. It was your way of having her wear *your* jacket, without making it obvious you wanted her to. You've always done stuff like that."

"You girls think too much into shit."

"Just calling it like I see it. I always knew you two would end up together. I kept my mouth shut and let fate do its job."

Looking back, there were some things I did that one might look at as me keeping Scar within arm's reach. My father always taught me to keep your friends close and your enemies closer, so I excused it as that. Maybe I wanted to keep her away from Crew and Jagger because I figured, if I couldn't have her, neither could they. Or maybe I didn't want her with anyone at all.

"Speaking of fate," Maddie cuts in, interrupting my moment of self-discovery. "Crew and I aren't getting back together."

I scoot up in the chair, gripping the arm rests. "You're not?"

She shakes her head no. "Too much time has passed. Too much has changed."

"If he said something that—"

"It wasn't him. It was both of us. When I woke up, Crew was the first person that popped in my head, but it wasn't our relationship I desperately needed, it was his friendship. Can I be honest?"

"No. But if you must."

215

"You're such a dipshit. But seriously, I liked Crew. I liked him a lot. But I think part of me only stayed with him for so long because I knew that's what *you* wanted."

Well, I'll be damned. Crew told me the same thing. If I can manipulate two people I care about into staying in a lengthy relationship, then I sure as hell can keep Scar out of one with my two best friends.

"Mads, I wanted you two together because I thought that's what you wanted." It's a partial truth. I also knew how much Crew liked Scar, and vice versa, so it was a good attempt at keeping them apart.

"I did. Don't get me wrong. I was crazy about Crew. But now...I'm ready to move on while keeping him as my friend, before we try too hard and I lose him forever."

I really hate when other people's plans make more sense than the ones I had for them. "You sure you don't wanna give it one more try?"

If Maddie and Crew are done for good, that means he has nothing holding him back from being with Scar. They've got something straight out of a romance novel. Years of desperation to be together but mountains in their way. If Maddie calls it quits, I won't be able to hold them back anymore.

"We gave it our best shot and it's time for Crew and me to both find our own happiness."

Looking at my sister now—in that bed, unable to walk, but able to feel emotion still and make decisions for herself —it's eye-opening. There's a twinge in my chest. An awkward feeling, but it's sort of nice.

"Do what makes you happy, Mads. You can't go wrong there."

Her arms spread wide, and she nods me in. I shake my head no. She knows I don't do hugs.

"Oh, come on. Give your twin sister a hug."

"Do I gotta?"

"No. But I really want you to."

With a heavy sigh, I get up and wrap my arms around her. Maddie has always had a way of bringing out weird emotions inside me, and right now, she's bringing them up to the surface.

"Go talk to Scar. Whatever you said to hurt her feelings. Fix it. And if you can't, just be there for her. Sometimes all anyone needs is someone to tell them it's gonna be okay."

I pull out of the hug and press my hands onto the mattress, still leaning down. "And if that's a lie?"

"Then you stay by her side until it's the truth."

My lips roll together, and I nod, understanding what she's saying. Be there for her. That's all.

Straightening my back, I stand up and head for the door, but I stop with my hand against the wall. I glance over my shoulder at Maddie. "Hey. Everything's gonna be okay. And that's the truth."

Maddie blows me a kiss and says, "Right back at ya."

I sense her presence before she even walks in the door. My head lifts from my phone that's positioned between my legs under the table. Our eyes catch, and she lifts a brow. As she makes her way toward me, we never break our gaze.

She sets her books down on the table in her normal spot. "What are you doing in Jagger's seat?"

"You said you wanted us to switch. So I switched." Crew

and Jagger aren't here yet. Apparently, they went to drill Jude a little before class, which gives me the perfect opportunity to clear the air with Scar. Or at least try to do so.

She squints at me, questioning my motives. "What happened to keeping your enemies close?"

"Oh, I intend to, but you're not one of them anymore." I look down, feeling my cheeks catch fire with my cringe-worthy admission. I fucking hate feelings.

"You don't have to act weird with me after what we did, Neo. It was just sex."

And that announcement has now grabbed the attention of all nine students, who are already in the room.

Her hand claps over her mouth, pupils dilated. "I can't believe I just said that out loud."

Sliding down a seat, I get closer to her. "Listen, Scar," I begin, but I'm cut off when Crew and Jagger walk in the classroom, all broody and broad-shouldered.

"I'm listening," she whispers. "Ignore them. Tell me." The desperation in her tone is apparent, but I can't. Not now.

"Meet me in the courtyard at lunch." I look at the guys, who are now standing behind us. "All of you."

CHAPTER
TWENTY-THREE

SCAR

"Any idea what this is about?" Crew asks. All three of us are confused about why Neo wanted us to meet him here, but I have an idea and I'm certain it's because of me.

He's gonna tell the guys my secret now. Even after he told me he'd keep it. *Dammit!* I'm a fool for believing anything Neo says.

"Isn't it obvious?" Jagger says. "It's about that fucking leech mark on her neck." He flips my hair for the second time, observing the mark. He's still angry with me and I have no idea how I'm going to repair the damage I've done, but I have to try.

"Before he gets here, do you mind if we all talk?"

Jagger drops down on the ground, knees bent, legs spread. "Have at it."

I don't even know where to begin, so I start with. "I'm sorry, you guys. I was scared and confused and those feelings made me do selfish and reckless things. The truth is, I don't wanna lose either of you." I clutch my chest because it hurts so bad. Tears prick the corners of my eyes, but I fight like hell to hold them back.

"Don't cry," Crew says, rubbing his hand down the sleeve of my winter coat. He knows me so well. I don't even have to shed a tear for him to know they're coming. But it's his sentiment that makes them fall, because I don't deserve it. I don't deserve him. He crouches down an inch and pulls me close. With my chin resting on his shoulder, I look down at Jagger, who's now balling some snow in his hands while soaking his ass in it.

"I don't know what to do to fix this, but I wanna try." I choke out the words, while looking at Jagger, hoping for a reaction from him. "Please let me try."

Finally, he looks up, a snowball clutched in one hand. "Tell us the truth. That'd be a good start." He squeezes the ball, crushing it to particles that fall weightlessly from his hand.

I nod, while swallowing down the painful ball in my throat. Crew steps back, observing me while I speak. When I start to choke up again, he takes my hand—his way of telling me he's here for me. "Okay. I told you why I ended things with you guys. Neo was keeping a secret that he threatened to expose."

"Don't care about that," Jagger says. "Why'd you fuck him?"

I'm taken aback by his hostility, but I won't let it stop me from saying everything I need to say.

"I planned to seduce him and cuff him to his bed until he told me the truth."

I scratch the back of my neck, realizing how ridiculous that sounds. "Obviously, it failed." I hold up my wrist, showing them the cuff marks that I received instead.

Jagger jumps to his feet and grabs one of my wrists. "He did that to you?"

"Yes. But I allowed it." Shame, mixed with guilt, stirs in my stomach.

"Why the hell..." Jagger waves his hand between us. "Never mind. Just get on with it."

I take in a deep breath and let it out in one blow. "Things got intense. Almost to an unstoppable point. He was different. Gentle, almost. Then he promised to tell me what he knew if I had sex with him."

"Gentle, my ass," Crew blurts out. "He took advantage of you."

"No," I snap, needing to make myself clear. "I wanted it. I wanted the truth more, but it was consensual." I pause for a beat, eyes dancing between the two of them. "Then he told me."

"So what was it?" Jagger asks. "What was this big secret he used to crawl between your legs?"

"Can we talk about that later? First, I wanna talk about us."

"Not gonna lie, Scar," Jagger begins. "I'm pretty pissed that you lied. If you wanted to sleep with Neo, at least have the courtesy of talking with us about it first."

"I know." I sob. "I'm so damn sorry. There's no excuse. I should have been honest about everything from the beginning." I'm full-on bawling now and no matter how hard I try, I can't stop. "Is there any way you guys can possibly forgive me?"

There's a long bout of silence that has me grasping for any chance they'll give me. Begging, rather. "Please." I drop to my knees in the snow, face in my hands. "I'm so sorry."

The weight of someone's arm wrapping around me has

me looking to my left. When I see that it's Jagger, I throw myself at him and turn into a blubbering mess. "Don't let me lose you," I whisper in his ear.

He cranes his neck, looking at me, and tucks my hair behind my ear. "You won't lose me. But I don't want you to see Neo again."

"Come on, man," Crew cuts in. "That's not possible."

Confident with his decision, Jagger's brow arches. "It's very possible. I want you to stay away from him, unless it's absolutely necessary to be around him."

My posture slumps, right along with my heart that's settling in my stomach. "For how long?"

Jagger licks his lips, an expression of surety on his face. "Forever."

That's impossible. It's Neo. Maddie's brother. Their best friend. My...Neo.

"Fucking Melody and Hannah are going at it in the cafeteria," Neo says, appearing out of nowhere. "I was gonna break it up then I figured, what the hell, let's give the students a show. With any luck, they'll kill..." His words trail off when he looks down at me and the guys. Crew has since joined my other side, and we're all slouched on the ground. "Who fell?"

"No one," Jagger says as he gets up. "Scar was just filling us in on what happened with you two."

"About that," Neo starts, but he's cut off when Jagger holds up his hand, stopping him.

"We don't need another replay. We need you to stay away from our girl, got it?"

Neo looks at me and his expression slices through my chest, parting it in two. "Is that what you want, Scar?"

My head drops and I pinch my eyes closed. *Please don't make me answer. Please don't make me choose.*

Neo presses for a response. "Well, is it?"

Jagger reaches for my hand and I accept his offer. He pulls me up and drapes an arm around my shoulder. "Tell him, baby. Tell him you never wanna see him again."

"I..." I go to speak, but the words get lodged in my throat. "I'm sorry, Neo."

I've seen many different shades of Neo. Mostly black, maybe a little gray, but blue is a new one and it's my least favorite color on him.

Jagger smirks at Neo before walking me around him, Crew following.

"Hey," Crew says, "I'll catch up with you guys in a minute." He kisses my cheek, then pats Jagger on the back before jogging back over to Neo.

One glance over my shoulder is all it takes for my heart to break in three different pieces. One for Crew. One for Jagger. And one for Neo.

"Head up, girl," Riley says. "You got your boys back."

Forcing a smile on my face, I lift my chin. "I know. And I'm happy. I just don't know why I feel so much dread inside me."

She looks at me, while pushing a branch out of our way. "Neo?"

"Why do I even care? I mean. Look at all the nasty shit that guy has done to me. I shouldn't care, right?"

"No one can tell your heart how to feel. Not even you. Neo's the worst, but the worst are usually the most broken."

I nod in agreement. "He is broken and it's his stupid dad's fault. I hate that son of a bitch for turning his son into a robot."

We make it to The Ruins, in what feels like no time. There's a pretty thick layer of snow on the ground, so we trek our way through it in our knee-high Muck boots.

"So, what are you gonna do?" Riley asks.

"Nothing. What can I do?" It's a rhetorical question, so I keep going. "Crew and Jagger are moving back into the house as we speak. Neo says he's not going anywhere. It's about to be really fucking awkward at the Lawless house. Not to mention, Maddie still doesn't know I'm dating her ex."

Riley bends down and lifts the trap door, letting it drop hard against the cement slab. She turns around and takes the first step. "Yeah. Your life's a mess, but all messes get cleaned up eventually." She continues down, and I follow her lead.

We walk through the tunnels, talking about Hannah and Melody's blowup at lunch today. Apparently, Hannah shoved Melody's face into her mashed potatoes and gravy, which led to Melody trying to shove an apple in Hannah's mouth. Then chaos unleashed and a food fight broke out. I'm just sorry I missed it. I'd love nothing more than to see Melody get everything she deserves.

When we reach the door to the room Jude's in, Riley hesitates. "Promise me you'll keep an open mind and hear him out?"

I sigh. "Fine. I'll try my best."

She pushes the door open and we step inside. Really, he doesn't look bad. He's been fed and watered. Looks like he's gotten some sleep. If it weren't for the dried blood all over his face and clothes, and his wet pants, I'd say he's not doing so bad.

I growl at him on instinct. Like an animal seeking out her prey. Then Riley nudges me and whispers, "You promised."

"All right," I throw my hands up, "I really have no interest in beating around the bush here. So un-tape his mouth," I tell Riley. Once she does, I drop to my knees in front of Jude. "Am I your sister?" I say, point-blankly, while holding my composure, even if my heart is ready to burst through my chest cavity.

Jude looks at Riley who says, "Tell her the truth. You have to be honest with us. It's the only way we can help you."

Help him? My ass. I'm not helping this psycho. But I don't tell her that. Instead, I narrow my eyes and ask again. "Am I your sister?"

"I...I think so."

My knees quiver, while all the air is sucked out of my lungs.

There it is. The truth. It would be too much of a coincidence for more than one person to tell me this, so I have no reason not to believe it.

"And our sperm donor is Jeremy Beckett?"

Jude nods, and in this moment, my world comes crashing down.

Kol isn't my dad. The man who gave me piggyback rides and picked me up from school every day. The man who built forts with me when Mom had to work late and made me hot cocoa with extra marshmallows. He's the one who watched out the window, waiting for me to come home at night. He bought me a pearl necklace for my sixteenth birthday and said, "No matter how old you get, you'll always be my little girl."

My chest trembles. My hands. My legs. My lips. Everything trembles. Everything hurts.

I have to pull it together. I have to know everything.

"When did you find out about me?"

"I've always known you were my sister. Jeremy brought me along every time he'd go see you. I think my first memory is when I was like eight. We went to your school. You were playing on the playground and a little boy pushed you. You were wearing a pair of black pants with holes in the knees and a dirty jean jacket."

"He watched me?"

"All the time," Jude says. "Every birthday. Every hol—"

"My birthdays?" I gulp. "So it was him. But how did he leave me this..." I slap the note in Jude's lap, "if he's dead." Jude looks away suspiciously, so I shout, "Tell me, dammit!"

"It was me. I left the note."

"Jude," Riley says softly, "we need you to start from the beginning. Tell us everything. It's your only chance to survive."

Jude's gaze dances around the room. He licks his lips. He wiggles his hands. He does everything he can to buy time, but when time is up, he begins, "Jeremy might be my father, but he was no dad to me. He looked at us both as pawns in his game. He wanted to use us as a wedge between the Blue Bloods and the Becketts. But, deep down, I wanted to be one of you guys. I hated myself for what I was. Still do." He swallows hard, his Adam's apple bobbing. "He killed my mom."

Riley and I share a look, because we already knew that to be true.

"So I killed him."

Now that we didn't expect.

Riley crouches beside me, eyes on Jude. "You killed Jeremy Beckett?"

"I had to. He was working with someone who planned to hurt Scar."

Chills ride down my body. "Hurt me? Who?"

"I don't know," Jude replies. "But I think it's whoever is blackmailing me and who made me do all this horrible stuff. After I killed my dad, I ran away, but somehow, he tracked me down. I've never met him, but he left me notes. More than I left you. Endless notes. Everywhere. Threatened to turn me in for murder if I didn't do exactly what he said, so I did it."

The door flies open and voices come behind me. I whip my head around and see Neo, Crew, and Jagger, all panic-stricken.

"Finally," Crew gasps, throwing himself at me, "we were worried sick. What are you two doing here?"

"We—"

"Doesn't matter," Neo says. "We've all gotta go right fucking now." He grabs my hand and pulls me while I reach for Riley.

"Go where? What happened?"

Jagger grabs a roll of duct tape and rips a piece off then smacks it back on Jude's mouth. I watch as he does it, replaying all my half-brother's words in my head. Riley was right. Jude's not a monster. He's just like me.

"There's a fucking news crew here," Neo says, the tendon on his neck standing tall. "We need to get to Maddie."

"A news crew?" I'm so confused. *What the hell is going on?*

227

Neo pulls me out of the room while I pull Riley.

"Somehow they caught wind of Maddie's disappearance, and they're here to report on it."

"Oh shit," I cry out, while picking up my pace through the tunnels. I look behind me and see Crew and Jagger locking up the room, then my eyes fall to my hand that's being held by Neo. He follows my gaze before his eyes drag up to mine, then like it's no big deal, he says, "I have to call my dad."

CHAPTER
TWENTY-FOUR
NEO

I POP the top off a bottle of beer then slam it in one big gulp. When I lower my hand, I pound the bottle to Maddie's dresser. "We all have to stay here. No one knows anything but us. They won't get a story from anyone else."

"Is your dad coming?" Crew asks, and my response is a nod.

Really don't want him to. He's the last person I wanna deal with, but this is his mess, not mine.

I open another beer.

Then another.

The next thing I know, two hours have passed since we've all been holed up in this room.

"They're still out there," Scar says from where she's hiding behind the curtain.

"This is all my fault," Maddie bellows. "Just tell them I'm here. I can't hide forever."

"It's not your fault," I sputter, pointing a limp finger at Maddie. "It's that fucking Jude Beckett's fault."

Riley's voice comes out of nowhere, like a sneaky mouse.

229

"It is not! Jude didn't do any of this. He's being framed. Sort of."

Scar gives Riley a twisted look, and I can't help but wonder what unspoken words these two are sharing right now.

"What's she talking about?" I ask Scar, unsure if she's the right person to ask. I've probably got a better chance of hearing the truth from Riley at this point.

"Jude was blackmailed, the same way he blackmailed Melody. Someone else is behind this. He's just another pawn in this sicko's game."

I finish my drink of beer then snap my fingers. "I fucking knew he had help."

"Not help!" Riley presses. "It's not him!"

"Oh, yeah? Who the hell is it then?"

"I...I don't know."

I mumble, into the mouth of the bottle pressed to my lips, "That's what I thought."

Scar crosses the room and swats my arm. "Don't be an ass, Neo."

My eyebrows lift, humor playing on my lips. "I thought we were beyond name-calling."

She rolls her eyes as she sits down on the bed with Maddie, ending this conversation before it has a chance to get good.

The effect of all the beer I drank has taken hold, but reality slaps me in the face when my phone buzzes in my pocket. I pull it out and look around at everyone in the room. "It's him."

They all go quiet and I take in a deep breath before answering. "Hey, Dad."

"Get your ass down here and unlock this fucking door

before I break it in."

"Yes, sir."

I don't say anything to anyone before I leave Maddie's room. With hurried steps, I skate down the hall, then take two steps at a time going down. Somehow, I manage to keep my balance, but when I pull open the front door and see my father, my stomach gets queasy.

With a stern look, he steps around me, followed by another guy, who I take to be his security guard. Before I close the door, I glance outside and see the news crew, along with my father's publicist, who is giving them a story—or a lie. Whatever appeases them.

Once the door is closed, Dad curls his lip. "If I find out you know where your sister is..." He raises a stiff hand, snarling. "So help me God, you will feel my wrath."

"How the hell would I know where Maddie is?"

"Don't you take that tone with me." He leans close, drawing in short, wispy breaths. "Have you been drinking?"

My shoulders draw back, chin up. "I had a beer."

Nostrils flared, he squares off. "Your sister is missing and you had a beer?"

"I'm sure she's fine. Maddie's a tough girl."

"Maddie is supposed to be in a coma! She's anything but fine!"

Scar comes down the steps slowly, but stops before reaching the bottom. I shake my head slowly at her, warning her not to come down. But it's too late. My father sees her before she has a chance to go back up.

"I'm sorry," she says softly, "I didn't mean to interrupt. I was just wondering if you've talked to my parents."

"You're sorry," my father huffs, turning his full body to face her. Scar backsteps up two stairs. "You know, you should be sorry. If it weren't for you, none of us would be in this mess." He turns back to look at me, but I'm too focused on Scar, who looks like she's on the verge of tears. "I thought I told you to stay away from that snake."

Scar continues to backstep up the stairs, and her chest rises and falls rapidly.

Once she's gone, I come to her defense. "Don't call her that!"

"Don't call her that?" He laughs. "But that's what she is, Neo. She's a fucking snake. And let me guess, you let that whore wrap herself around you, didn't you?"

"Shut the fuck up! I told Scar the truth, so now you have nothing to hang over their heads. How does that make you feel?" I snap, immediately wishing I could take it back.

I've never stood up to my father. Not once. And when his open palm slides across my face, leaving a sting I'm all too familiar with, I'm reminded of why I don't.

But I don't even flinch. Just hold my arms at my sides, head down. *Don't look him in the eye. It just pisses him off more.*

"Congratulations. You just ruined that girl's life. How does that make you feel?" He tsks, spinning around, unable to look at me because I'm that despicable to him.

My voice drops to a near whisper as the reality of my outburst hits me full force. "Isn't that what you wanted? To hurt the Sunders?"

"In my own time but you…" He growls, now facing me again. "You stole me that gratification. Ya know, it's a shame your sister is the one who's been asleep all this time. This place might not be falling apart if you had been the one who fell off that mountain."

I can hear the grinding of his teeth. Every inhale. Each

exhale. The quiet makes every noise he makes that much louder.

"Go tell your asshole friends their parents are at the community center. Don't let 'em leave the house until my team has the reporters out of here." He points a stern finger at me. "If I lose this election because of you, you're dead to me. Do you hear me, Neo? Dead to me."

I nod and give him a low-toned, "Yes, sir."

CHAPTER
TWENTY-FIVE

SCAR

"YOU GUYS GO AHEAD," I say to Crew, Jagger, and Riley. "I'll catch up."

Jagger gives me a look of disapproval, but I brush it off. He gave me an ultimatum earlier, which was far too gracious, considering what I've done, but right now, we all need each other—Neo included.

"We'll wait here," Crew tells me, positioning himself with his back to the front door, blocking Riley and Jagger's opportunity to leave. "Go take care of what you need to, then we'll all ride together."

I force a smile on my face and say, "Thanks." Then I turn around and go back upstairs.

When I reach Neo's room, I knock on the door, but it must not have been latched because it pushes open. I poke my head in the door and see him sitting on the floor against his bed with a bottle of beer between his legs. "Hey. You okay?"

"Like you care." He doesn't even lift his head. Just runs his finger around the mouth of the half-empty bottle.

"What can I say, I'm an empath at heart."

"Bullshit."

"When it comes to people I..." My words trail off because I was going to say care about. But saying it out loud to Neo makes it too real.

"People you hate. People you'd rather see dead than alive. What is it, Scar?"

"It's nothing." I step inside. "Look, if you wanna talk—"

"I don't." His eyes lift to mine and he picks up the bottle, using it as a pointer toward the door. "Now if you don't mind, I'd prefer to get shit-faced and forget the last eighteen years of my life."

I've never seen Neo so vulnerable. So...sad. It literally breaks my heart to see someone so tough crumble the way he is right now.

"All right, Maddie's got her dinner. I'll lock the front door behind me." I pause for a beat before saying, "I guess I'll see you later."

He takes a long swig of his beer before giving me a growly, "Why?"

"Why, what?"

"Why would you see me later? Didn't you tell your boyfriends you'd stay away from me?"

I lick my lips and fill my lungs with air. "It was a temporary bandage on a big problem."

He finishes off his beer and grips it tightly in one hand. "I'll save you some trouble. Get the fuck out of my room."

"Neo, please don't be like that."

"Like what? Like I've always been? This is me. Take it or leave it. Now get out."

When I don't go, he chucks the bottle at the wall. My body jolts, eyes wide with surprise. "Go!" he seethes. Brown pieces of glass scatter around the hardwood, a wet spot splattered on the wall dribbles down onto the floor.

"Get the fuck out!" he howls, giving me no choice, so I do what he demands. I leave.

"READY TO TALK ABOUT IT?" Crew asks, at the same time he hands me a helmet.

"Not yet. Let's just go see our parents and see what they have to say. We'll talk later. Promise." When we get back from this meeting, I have to tell Crew and Jagger the truth about who I am. It can't wait any longer, now that Neo's dad knows I know. They'll either tell me it changes nothing, or they'll tell me it changes everything.

Content with my decision, Crew pulls down his helmet and flings one leg over the seat before dropping down. I follow suit and get behind him, wrapping my arms around his waist.

The snow hasn't stopped falling since last night, and it looks like we've got a good six inches. With any luck, it'll stop soon because the last thing we need is our parents getting snowed in at the Academy. We need them gone and we need them gone now.

My nerves are at an extreme high when we pull up to the community center. The last time I saw my mom and dad, I was a different person. Now when I look them in the eye, I have to lie. The same way my mom has lied to me for the last eighteen years of my life. I'm not even sure if my dad knows I'm not his biological child. I can't imagine he doesn't if Sebastian knows.

Crew offers me his black gloved hand and helps me off

the sled. Once we've hung our helmets, we meet Jagger and Riley halfway. "Brr." Riley shivers, hugging her arms to her chest.

Jagger scoffs, looking up at the falling flakes. "This snow needs to stop because if I'm forced to stay a night with my dad at this place, I'll lose my shit."

"My thoughts exactly," I tell him.

Jagger lifts a smile on his face, finally. That one simple look offers me a moment of happiness. I was so worried I wouldn't see it directed at me again. When he takes my hand, my stomach floods with warmth.

I curl around his arm, gripping it with my other hand as we all walk up to the community center together. Riley is talking with Crew about her dad, while telling him she's certain he's not here because none of this pertains to them. I'm not expecting him either, since this gathering is about Maddie and the Aima Chapter in the Society, which Riley is not part of.

Regardless, I'm glad she's here for moral support. It'll also make my parents happy to see I've made a friend that's a girl. For the longest time, forever really, Maddie has been my only female friend—or friend at all, for that matter. I've never liked people much, and while I still don't like most, these ones walking up here with me right now are keepers. Especially the cute boys.

I look up at Jagger and find his soft honey eyes already on mine. "Should we break this up before they see us?" I'm referring to his hold on me, or mine on him, rather. But I don't have to say so, because he knows. And when he responds with an assured, "No," it reaffirms everything we have.

For obvious reasons, they can't know about Crew and

me yet. There's always a chance it'll get back to Maddie and I need to be the one to tell her before she hears it from someone else.

Crew opens one of the double doors and holds it open for the rest of us. Once we're inside, we all stomp the snow from our boots and shake the flakes off our coats.

Riley shivers. "Warmth. My old friend."

We're not even three feet down the hall, when our parents spill out of one of the larger rooms on the right.

"Oh, Scarlett," my mom gushes as she attacks me with a hug. Dad stands directly behind her, stern and serious, with his hands in his pockets. He's not always like this, but when he's around these guys, he puts on a tough-guy facade. At home, he's a soft teddy bear.

My first instinct is to push my mom away and demand the truth, but the joy of seeing her overpowers my anger at her lies. We will deal with that, but now isn't the time. This is about Maddie, and me and the guys need to reassure our parents that everyone is safe here and Maddie is not on BCA property.

So, for now, I let her hold me as long as she wants to because she gives the best hugs. Once she steps back and observes me, making sure I'm healthy and safe, she lets my dad step in.

"We've missed ya, baby girl." He wraps one arm around my neck and pulls me close.

"Missed you, too, Dad." My heart is shattered. It's a struggle just to hold it together. How is it possible that this man isn't my dad? It's not. I cannot even fathom the possibility.

"We're gonna find her," Dad says, assuming my emotional state is because of Maddie's disappearance. He hugs me tighter, and when he steps back, I pull him back in, not ready to let go.

After a few moments have passed, I loosen my hold on him and he kisses the top of my head. It doesn't matter what anyone says, or what blood is in my veins, *this* is my dad.

Everyone is chatting and saying hello when I glance at Jagger, who's standing three feet apart from his dad, not saying a word. I've always felt tension between those two, and right now, it's thicker than ever.

"What's this thing going on with you and Cole's son?" Dad asks, catching my stare at Jagger. "Saw you two walking up together. Looked pretty cozy."

"Dad," I drawl, swatting his arm. "Were you spying on me?"

"Always. And now that I know the Cole boy has his eyes on you, I'll be spying on him, too."

Better get those eyes checked, because you're gonna need to watch more than just me and Jagger.

Crew and his parents break up the conversations with a heavy bout of laughter, and it's a nice relief from the dreary days we've had here at the Academy this week. The Vances are very funny, down-to-earth people, much like my family. Jagger's dad, not so much. And his mom, who is a high-fashion photographer, is always traveling, so we rarely even see her, even at meetings. I'm not surprised she's not here.

"And who is this?" Mom asks, referring to Riley.

"Oh yes! I'm so sorry, Ry." I grab her arm and pull her over. "This is my friend, and roommate, Riley Cross." My parents don't know I'm staying at the Lawless house and that's another thing I intend to keep from them.

"As in, Nel Cross and Anna Cross?" Dad says.

"That's right, sir," Riley responds respectfully. It's

strange seeing her engage with adults. It's a new side of her and her composure is extremely professional.

"I thought your dad's name was Samson?" I cut in, wondering who Nel is.

"It is. Samson Nel Cross, Jr. Those who know him personally call him Nel, and others refer to him as Samson."

My eyes glance from my dad to my mom. "So you know Riley's dad?"

They share a look. A really awkward look, then both nod. "Mmmhmm," they say in unison.

Parents are so fucking weird.

"Shall we go inside and get this meeting started?" Crew's mom asks. She's clutching a small black leather purse to her stomach with her unpainted fingernails. When I think of Crew's mom, I think of someone who spends her days baking and crocheting blankets for her future grandkids. She smells like warm banana bread and cinnamon sticks and has a smile that just washes all your worries away.

"We shall," my mom retorts, taking my hand before hesitating a moment. "Riley. Honey. We're so happy for your friendship with our daughter," she speaks for her and my dad, much like she always does, "but this meeting is a personal matter. You understand, right?"

"Absolutely," Riley retorts. "I actually have something to take care of." She looks at me. "I'll catch you later?"

My eyes widen and she presses a hard smile. I know exactly where she's going. She plans to go see Jude. "Okay," I roll my lips at her then smack them together, "see you later."

Mom leads me into the meeting room, but I freeze in the doorway when I see Sebastian Saint sitting at the head of a long table with an open folder in front of him. He lifts his head, eyes landing right on me. His scowl is so prominent that I'm sure he's just given himself three permanent creases on his forehead, simply to prove his point at how much he loathes me. I heard him earlier talking with Neo. He doesn't know, but I heard every word he had to say about the snake, who he thinks is trying to strangle his son. Or bite. I can't remember. I'm pretty sure he's claimed I'm out to do both.

Instead of bowing at his royal highness, I put on a big smile of my own and say, "Hello, Mr. Saint. So good to see you again."

He scoffs and licks the tip of his finger then flips a page in the open folder, without even looking at it.

Mom squeezes my hand, stealing my attention. When I look at her, she's wearing the same smug look I am. I'm so glad my mom shares in my distaste for that fucker.

"Ladies," Dad whispers, leaning close, "show your respect for the governor."

I fake a gag and Dad shoots me a stern look.

Sebastian clears his throat, then slides his chair back while we all gather around like he's a god. He buttons his suit jacket back up then presses both hands to the table and leans forward slightly.

"Thank you all for coming on such short notice. As you know, my sweet Maddie was taken from her home a couple short weeks ago. I've been working quietly with our inside law enforcement to bring her home safely. But with no such luck, we've been forced to resort to the public for help." He looks my dad in the eye. "Thanks to your wife."

Dad steps forward, jaw locked, but Mom pulls him back.

He opens his mouth to speak, but all that comes out is a hoarse grumble.

"With all due respect, Sebastian, while your daughter, a young girl and an innocent member of the Society, has been missing, you were busy traveling and collecting votes. It was painfully obvious you had no interest in her return until after the election. Someone who cares had to step in."

"Mom," I gasp quietly, "are you the one who called the news crew?"

Mom hushes me with a hard glare and waits for a response from a very shaken Sebastian.

"How dare you!" He raises his voice and slams a heavy fist down on the table, rattling it. "My daughter is my business and mine alone. It's high time you worry about your own daughter before she disgraces this Society the same way you have."

"What's he talking about, Mom?"

"Go on, Luna. Tell your daughter exactly what I'm talking about. And while you're at it, how about if you fill your husband in."

My throat tightens, breathing constricted. "Stop!" I shout, before anyone can say another word. The last thing I need is my family's problems blasted to two families they're close with—the Vances and the Coles. "I already know!" I turn to Mom, take her hand, and pull her out of the room, all the while, tears pool in my eyes.

Mom's hand trembles in mine. "Scarlett. What on earth are you talking about? What is it you think you know?"

Dad follows, pulling the door closed behind us. "Everything." My eyes slide back and forth between theirs. "I know what you did at this Academy, Mom. I know I'm not—"

"No," Mom blurts, a shake in her voice. "Stop right

there." She looks at my dad, her own tears threatening to fall. "Kol," she mutters in a sympathetic tone, "I always feared this day would come."

My dad reaches out, grabs my mom's hand, then mine, and squeezes us both. "So did I."

Eyebrows squeezed, I twist my head. "Wait. You know?"

"I know you're my daughter in all the ways that matter. That's all anyone needs to know. And I'll be damned if Sebastian Saint is going to hurt our family."

"But..." I sniffle and croak, "I'm not a Blue Blood. I can't stay."

"Prove it," he deadpans. "That's what I'll say to anyone who tries to tell us otherwise. Prove that I'm not your father. That you're not a Blue Blood. Because they can't. They'd have to run a DNA test on every member of the Society for generations to prove that your blood isn't pure."

"But Jeremy Beckett..."

"Is dead. And he's never coming back."

"What if they're all wrong, though. What if I really am your daughter?"

Dad places his hands on my shoulders and looks me in the eye as he says, "*You are my daughter* and a DNA test is not going to tell me otherwise. It's why I never wanted one. Because, for one, it doesn't matter. And two, there doesn't need to be anything out there that someone can use against us one day."

Mom breaks down, sobbing quietly into the sleeve of her beige down-filled jacket. "I'm so sorry. I never wanted this to see the light of day. I'm so ashamed of what I did back then."

"I'm not," Dad says. "In fact, I'm grateful because it gave us our daughter. If it weren't for that forbidden relationship, we wouldn't have any children at all. So we'll all keep this secret, and I'll make sure Sebastian will as well. Don't you worry about him."

My mom and dad once told me they tried to have more kids, but weren't able to, but it didn't matter because they had me and I completed our circle. I never questioned how I was conceived; yet, they couldn't have another. Just assumed it was because of the time that had passed as I got older.

"So we just go on with our lives like the truth doesn't exist?"

Before either of them can respond, the meeting room door flies open and Sebastian steps out. With a stern finger pointed at me, he hisses, "You don't belong here."

Dad slaps Sebastian's finger away, then he grabs him by the wrist, twisting and bending, until his only option of getting free is to beg for mercy.

"I've put up with your shit for far too long, Sebastian, and that ends now. You leave my family alone or it'll be yours that pays the price because my skeletons might have fallen out, but yours are still hiding and I know exactly where to find them."

"Good luck with that. I run this whole goddamn state, and I have the power, Kol. Not you. Not your wife. And sure as hell not your half-bred snake of a daughter."

Sebastian looks me dead in the eye and hisses like a snake himself. "You stay away from my son, and when Maddie comes home, you stay the hell away from her, too."

I roll my eyes, smirking, my way of telling him *not a chance in hell.*

Dad shoves Sebastian away, then he straightens his jacket when the others join us.

"Well," Mrs. Vance says, "I see we've made little progress. I suggest we all go home and leave the kids be. Crew has ascertained that all the students are safe here. I've made a call to the headmaster, who says there have been no reports of any incidents." She pats Sebastian's shoulder, then curls her lip at her hand, showing her own disgust for the guy. "Luna and I will continue our search for Maddie. Good luck with the election. We all hope you get everything you've ever wanted this term."

Mrs. Vance presses a chaste kiss to my cheek. "See you at Thanksgiving, sweetie." Then my mom's. "Coffee this Sunday?" Mom nods in response.

The Vances leave, along with Crew, who walks them out, followed by Sebastian. Jagger's dad shakes hands with my father, then bids me and my mom goodbye. Jagger, however, stays.

Dad shifts his attention to Jagger. "That's my little girl right there." He points at me, smiling before it drops quickly. "Hurt her and you answer to me."

Jagger swallows hard then nods. "Not a chance."

After a lengthy, tight hug, my parents leave with the notion that we'll talk more about everything when they pick me up for Thanksgiving break in a couple weeks.

It's just Jagger and I when the door opens back up and Crew comes inside. His cheeks are red from the cold and he shakes the snow from his boots. "It's coming down harder."

He closes the door behind him then steps into our circle. "So," he begins, "what the hell was that all about?"

I bite my bottom lip and take Crew's cold hand, then Jagger's warm one. "I have to tell you guys something. And it's going to change everything."

They glance at each other quizzically, before returning their eyes to me. "What is it?"

I nod toward the open meeting room. "Mind if we go in there? You might wanna sit down for this."

Heavy breaths escape them, and I'm certain they're preparing themselves for something that involves Neo. In some ways, this does, but not in the way they think.

Crew pulls out the first chair at the first table in the room and he sits down. Jagger doesn't sit; instead, he presses his hands to the table, taking the same stance Sebastian did at the other end.

"What's this about?" Jagger lifts his head, eyes on me.

"Remember how I told you guys that Neo knew a secret about me?"

"Yeah. That's how he coerced you into bed. Got it." Jagger's sarcasm is thick and laced with contempt.

"Anyways," I continue, "I got the secret out of him, and it's a big one. It's life-changing, if we allow it to be." Crew must notice the tremble in my legs because he slides his chair back and pats his lap.

I sit down on his knee, and he wraps an arm around my waist. "Whatever it is, we've got you." He looks at Jagger. "Don't we?"

Jagger straightens his back and runs his fingers through his hair. "Yeah. Yeah, of course."

When I question him with slitted eyes, his shoulders drop. "Look, I'm pissed about everything, Scar. But nothing's changed. I don't wanna lose you and I intend to keep you at any cost. So yeah, you've got us."

I reach out and grab his hand, as a tear slides down my cheek. It warms my heart to know I have these guys by my side—along with Riley and Maddie.

"Thank you, guys."

I inhale a deep breath, and on the exhale, I tell them the truth the best I can. Through cracked vocal cords, I say, "Kol isn't my dad."

Crew shifts beneath me and Jagger goes to speak, but I hold up a hand.

"My mom had an affair during her senior year here and got pregnant and they passed me off as Kol's because... because she had an affair with Jeremy Beckett. He's my biological father, and Jude Beckett is my brother." I blow all the air out of my lungs, emptying them. My body is far too anxious for their response, so I stand up, shaking my hands at my sides while watching them both.

"Wow," Crew says first. His hand draws back through his hair, eyes down. "I, umm...don't know what to say."

"You're sure?" Jagger asks next. "Neo doesn't have the best record for telling the truth."

"I'm sure." I sniffle, then I use the sleeve of my coat to wipe my eyes. "I overheard Neo and his dad talking about it earlier and that outburst in here today was Sebastian trying to control the situation before his son could reap the benefits. Not that Neo wants to anymore. Then, my parents admitted it. So yeah. It's true."

The room goes silent. Much too silent, and my heart is racing in anticipation for someone to say something. Anything to drown out these thoughts in my head.

Will they ever be able to look at me the same again? Am I Beckett to them now? Will they oust me to the whole Society?

"Who else knows?" Jagger finally asks.

"Just my parents, Sebastian, Neo, Jude, and Riley. I assume. Well, Jeremy Beckett, obviously, but he's dead."

Crew gets up and steps around the table, his hands pushed firmly in his pockets. "And we're sure that bastard is dead?"

"Yeah," I nod, "Jude confessed to killing him."

"What the fuck?" Jagger grumbles. "Where the hell is all this information coming from?"

"Riley and I talked to Jude today, and honestly, guys, I think he's telling us the truth."

"Fuck Jude," Crew hisses. "Doesn't matter what that scumbag says. He's been taunting us long enough. We've finally had some peace here with that son of a bitch tied up. I say we just kill him and go on with our lives."

Stubbornness takes hold and I'm getting really tired of no one listening to what I have to say. "You're not listening to me. If he's telling the truth, that means someone else is in control. So what good will killing him do?"

"Atonement. Revenge. Penance," Jagger says, agreeing with Crew. "I can think of a lot of words and not a single one would hold the meaning of *regret*."

This isn't the path I wanted this conversation to take. "Okay. We're getting ahead of ourselves here. Does my secret—my blood—change anything between us?"

"No," Crew says while Jagger shakes his head. "And I agree with your parents, no one else needs to know about this."

Jagger gets serious, placing his hands on my shoulders, while he slouches down. "You can't tell anyone else because if this gets out to the wrong person, life as you know it will be over."

The reality of his words hit like a sharp knife to the chest. "What about Neo's dad?"

"Something tells me your dad will handle Sebastian just fine."

I nod in response, hoping like hell he's right. "Can we go home now?"

Jagger pulls my head to his chest, cradling it. "Yeah. Let's go home."

TWENTY-SIX

JAGGER

RIGHT NOW SCAR has a lot going on. She's confused about her feelings. Struggling with her identity. And helping us solve the mystery surrounding us all. We've got a guy, who could potentially be her brother, tied up in the tunnels. We've got Maddie hiding in an upstairs bedroom. I don't think things could possibly get worse for any of us. On a good note, Scar agreed to stay away from Neo as much as possible, so Crew and I have that in our favor.

But at what cost? What will we have to pay? Her happiness? I mean, come on. There's no way in hell Scar thinks Neo is anything but a selfish prick. He's my best friend and I'll even admit that. Hell, Neo would admit that himself. After everything the guy has done to Scar, we should hate him. In fact, we should've got rid of his ass a long time ago. We let him stay, though. We keep him in our circle because, one: we made a pact; and two: Crew and I know who Neo was before his life went to hell. He's had a rough go at life and the more people that push him away, the worse off he'll be.

Looking at Scar now as her head is resting on my chest, her legs flung over Crew's while he snores, I can't help but feel bad for making her choose. Who am I to deny her happiness if Neo can give it to her in the same way we do? All three of us guys have always been close. I'm not sure I've ever gone a single day without talking to one of them.

What the hell am I thinking? Scar doesn't even want Neo. And even if she did, it doesn't mean he wants her back.

With my chin to my chest, I look down at her tired wide eyes as she stares off, lost in thought.

"Hey," I say, tipping her chin slightly with my thumb, "whatcha thinking about?"

She gives me a lopsided smile and says, "Everything."

"You wanna talk about it?"

Her head rests back down again, and she curls closer, squeezing me tighter. When her legs move a couple inches, sliding across Crew's who's on the other side of her, he snorts in his sleep. I swear I've never heard anyone snore as loud as this fucker. I'm not sure how Scar deals with this shit a couple nights a week.

Scar chuckles, and suddenly, his snoring isn't so bad. Can't be if it brings her a sliver of happiness.

"Do you really think my secret will be safe? That no one will find out?"

"Babe," I tip her chin again, desperate to look her in her eyes, "is that what you're worried about?"

She blinks away the tear drops on her lashes. "It's a big thing. If this got out to The Elders in other chapters, there's no way I wouldn't be abolished. I'm a product of vengeance."

"Think about it, Scar. If the Becketts had this master plan all these years to break our bloodlines, do you really think they only succeeded with you? There's probably dozens of members who aren't who they think they are, or who they say they are. You're still you. Still Scarlett Sunder."

Scar lifts her head, her chin pressed firmly to my chest. "You're right. I never thought of it that way." I lean forward, pressing my lips to hers, grateful that I could give her some peace of mind.

"Not to mention," I continue, "Sebastian hates the Becketts as much as we all do. He won't share your secret because he doesn't want to give them that power. If anything, he just wants to use it to hurt your family. You don't have to worry. He's had years to out you. If he hasn't done it now, he doesn't intend to."

The partial grin on her face tells me my words have helped calm her down. "I love you," she says softly against my lips.

"I love you, too. And I want you to know, I was never gonna let you go when you pushed me and Crew away."

Her chin moves against my chest with each word she says, her heart beating into my side. "I was never planning to let you guys go either. I can barely breathe without you."

"No more boxing with my heart, though. Okay? That shit hurts."

Her features soften with a frown. "Never again. I promise. I'm so sorry I hurt you."

"None of that matters now. We're back where we belong and I can say for certain, this mess is almost over."

A heavy sigh escapes her. "I hope you're right. So, what's the plan with Jude?"

I shrug my shoulders against the pillow. "If what you say is true, and he's not really the puppet master behind this scheme, then we need him to start at the beginning, so we can trace every move this guy might have made."

"He said he killed his dad. You think he's lying?"

"At this point, anything is possible."

I kiss Scar's forehead, and she slides up farther onto me. Her breasts press into my rib cage and I lift up, letting her feel my erection. She snickers. "Crew's in here sleeping."

I grab her ass cheeks with both hands and squeeze. "So what?"

In just a ribbed white tank top and a pair of black panties, she's looking far too hot not to devour. I pull her face down, bringing her mouth to mine. "It'll be fun. Risky, even."

She smiles against my lips and mutters, "Like a game of 'let's not wake Crew'?"

"Exactly." She wants to make it a game, then a game it is. Whatever it takes for me to feel her walls clench around my cock.

Scar sits up, straightening her back, her legs enveloping my body. With a smirk playing on her lips, she grabs the bottom of her shirt, arms crossed, and lifts. Her perky breasts pop free and I immediately fill my hands with them. "Fuck, baby."

I run my fingers along the hem of her panties then snap the elastic. "These next."

She leans forward, back arched, and her nipples graze the hair on my chest. "Take them off me."

"I'd be honored." With one hand, I grab her cotton panties and give them a swift tug. She maneuvers her way out of them, until they're dangling from her ankle. With a kick, they fly off, landing somewhere on the floor.

Her hand rests on my cock and she gives a subtle

squeeze. My hips rise, and I growl. "See what you do to me, Scar?"

"Your turn," she says, the lust in her eyes turning me on more and more with each passing second. I drink her in. She's so damn beautiful—so alluring. All these years this could have been mine, but I was too much of a fool to realize it.

I grab her hips, grinding her against my erection that's threatening to bust through the fabric of my sweatpants. "What're you gonna do to my cock once I bring it out?"

She nibbles on her bottom lip seductively. "What do you want me to do?"

"Show him how much you've missed him. And make it extra sloppy."

Her mouth gapes and she licks her lips. "What are you gonna do for me?"

I slap her ass, hard, and she jumps. "I'm gonna make you come on my face."

When she tugs at my pants in desperation, I tip her chin with my finger. "Do you want that, baby?"

She nods against my touch, so I sit up, her legs now folded around me like a pretzel. My lips press to hers, and I say, "That's my girl."

Grabbing her by the waist, I lift her light body, before sliding out from beneath her and placing her back down on the bed. She lies down, her head propped with a stack of pillows. Once I'm on my feet, I take off my sweatpants and wrap my hand around my cock, pumping it a few times before straddling her.

She watches intently as I continue to stroke myself, all the while wetting her lips more and more. "You want this?" I ask her, and she nods with a heavy pant. "You like sucking my cock, don't you, Scarlett?"

"Mmmhmm."

I know she does. Just like I know she loves when I call her Scarlett.

Her nails trail featherlike down her chest as she gives herself goosebumps. She stops at her breasts, cupping them both in her hands then massaging them. It's the sexiest thing I've seen in a while, aside from a frontal view of her legs spread. "You want me to come all over your tits?"

She swallows hard, liking the sound of that. "Yes," she whimpers. "Please. Just give it to me." The despair in her tone is highly arousing. I've never met a girl so desperate to suck cock. But Scar likes to please me, just as much as I like to please her.

One finger slides up her slit and her legs part instinctively. Using the pad of my finger, I massage her clit, giving her a little tease. When her hips thrust, I stop then move to her face, dragging my finger along her plump wet lips. Then I do it again, getting more of her juices. "I need those lips nice and wet."

Her tongue darts out, tasting what I'm putting on her, and I use this opportunity to stick the shallow end of my cock in her mouth. She grabs my hips, turning her head slightly to get a better angle.

Still pumping the base, I guide myself in and out of her mouth, nice and slow. My hips rock back and forth, and I use one hand on the back of her head, to brace myself, and the other on her breast. Her tongue circles my head and her feral eyes lift to mine. The look alone is enough to set my soul on fire, not to mention her lying on this bed as my oyster.

"Fuck, Scar." I slow my motions, trying to drag this out as long as possible.

Crew stirs a little bit, but Scar doesn't even take notice, just keeps sucking my cock like it's heaven on a stick. Her lips smear and spread, wrapping beautifully around my girth. My fingers tangle in the mess of hair at the back of her head.

When Crew moves again, this time bumping her side, she lifts her head slightly to look. I fist her hair harder, refocusing her on me. If he wakes up, there's a good chance she'll stop, and I'm about to explode all over her tits like I promised her I would.

Scar pulls back slightly, popping my head out of her mouth, but she doesn't stop. Her tongue runs down my length, and when she comes back to my head, she drags her teeth across it. My body jolts when her tongue laps around my shaft, hitting my nerves.

I grab her hand, that's now resting on her chest, and position it between my legs. "Play with my balls, baby." And she does. Cupping them both in one hand, she flexes her fingers and kneads my sack. "Fuck yeah." She takes my cock in her mouth again, coating it with her saliva, while stroking my lower half and sucking the tip.

My eyes skate from her wide, ponderous ones, down to her mouth, to her breasts, then to her legs that rest wide open. With a slight stretch of my arm, I run my fingers up and down her pussy, getting her nice and wet, so I can lick it all up later.

"You're soaked, Scarlett. What are you gonna do about that?" A jolt of electricity shoots through my body. My stomach fills with heat, and my breath hitches. I pat her pussy then circle my fingers at her entrance, playing with her juices.

I growl a heady sound, and my reaction causes her to suck me harder and faster. My balls tighten and I pull out, pumping myself feverishly as beads of cum shoot all over her breasts, coating her nipples and running down the sides. If I could take a picture, I'd jerk off to it daily because it's a sight that many dream of. My only regret is that I didn't get to watch my arousal drip from her mouth, so I run my fingers down her breasts, dabbing some of my cum then trailing it around her lips. "You look so good with my cum on your lips, baby."

She licks it up, then says, "Kiss me."

I lean forward, while pushing two fingers inside her pussy, and whisper, "I'd rather taste you."

Her response is a heady, "Yes, please."

I pull my fingers out, and I spin her body around so that her ass is hanging off the edge of the bed and the base of her skull is resting next to Crew's leg. I'm still on my feet when I push her legs all the way up until her knees are almost touching her shoulders. She grabs her ankles, holding them in place. She has no shame putting her dripping pussy on display for me. One of the things I've always loved about Scar is her confidence and *I don't give a fuck* personality.

Dropping my head between her legs, I grab a handful of each of her hips, my fingers pinching with enough tenacity to bruise her delicate skin. She whimpers a sound that has me even more hungry for what's in front of me.

When her legs enclose around me, I say, "Relax, baby." I spread her wider. "I'm gonna make you feel so good."

Starting with her clit, I tease a little with the tip of my tongue. Then I push two fingers inside her entrance, while sliding my tongue between her folds. Every once in a while, stopping at her clit again. When she settles a bit, letting her body relax, I pull out my fingers and drag my tongue from her clit to her asshole.

There's a shift on the mattress that has me lifting my eyes, and that's when I see Crew bent over Scar, kissing her with his hand around her neck.

My cheeks flush with a crimson rage. *Fucker better not ruin this for me.*

But when I see that he's got his own cock out, I know his only intention is to join in.

TWENTY-SEVEN

SCAR

EVERY NERVE in my body is heightened when Jagger swirls his tongue at my entrance. Jagger never hesitates to make me feel good. My pleasure is his pleasure. And that's what he's doing. He's making me feel so good. But it's not enough. I need more. I need to feel his fingers inside me. His tongue writhing against my sex. I want the stubble on his chin grating against my inner thighs. My entire body trembles and itches for more.

My eyes close when he sucks on my clit. He pushes my legs higher, flattening me like a pancake.

The sound of Crew clearing his throat has my heart racing. When he comes into view, his tired eyes on mine, panic sets in. It's not until I see the glint of a smile on his face that I'm able to calm down. He's shirtless, and when he comes closer, I'm able to see that he's ridded himself of the boxers he was sleeping in. He leans forward, pressing his lips to mine. "Now this is a sight to wake up to." His hand wraps around my throat with little force, and I pant into his mouth.

Jagger stops what he's doing momentarily, and I know he's seen Crew. When he resumes, I exhale a sigh of relief. I'm so fucking turned on right now. I reach my hand out in search of Crew's dick. When he senses what I'm doing, he lays it in my palm. I rub his silky skin and bulging veins, sweeping a bead of precum from his head, then I wrap my fingers around him from the bottom. He sways his hips in sync with my stroking motions.

After a few pumps, Crew positions the head of his cock in front of my mouth, then drags it across my lips, his hand still wrapped firmly around my throat. My jaw is already sore from Jagger, but I open wide, willing to eat the pain for Crew. I groan around his cock because whatever magic Jagger is working down there has me soaring to new highs.

His fingers work my pussy, while his mouth sucks eagerly on my sensitive nub. He spreads my cheeks wider, burying his face between them.

Electricity courses through me and my body reacts by squeezing Crew's dick harder while sucking on his head. My eyes roll and I'm staring at blackness before they come back down and flutter open. I look at Crew, who's watching my every reaction, with an open mouth and a rapidly moving chest.

He groans. I groan. And Jagger groans. *Fuck me.* I'm going to explode.

The stubble on Jagger's chin chafes my sex and I peer down at him, while Crew's cock is stuffed in the side of my cheek. My walls clench around Jagger's fingers, squeezing and threatening to swallow them whole. "You like that, baby?" Jagger asks, and I reward him with a heady moan.

Crew squeezes my throat tighter, cutting off some of my air supply. My head feels dizzy, but with it comes a rapture

I've never known possible. I cry out around Crew's cock, never once stopping my sucking motions. My entire body is shooting with impalpable pins and needles. My pussy throbs as I combust, proof of my orgasm trailing between my ass cheeks. Jagger moves his tongue up and down swiftly, licking me dry.

Crew loosens his pressure on my throat, then takes himself out of my mouth and replaces his cock with his lips. He strokes himself rapidly. Warm liquid hits my belly, mixing with Jagger's gelled cum from earlier.

Once he pulls back, Jagger removes himself from between my legs and I let them fall together.

I'm in a state of euphoria as I lie there, catching my breath.

Crew drops down on one side of me, Jagger on the other. There's a long beat of silence before I mutter, "Holy shit."

Jagger's face is the first I see as he leans over me and presses a chaste kiss to my forehead. "I think we lost that game."

I laugh, knowing exactly what he's talking about.

Next, I see Crew's face to my side. "What game?" he asks, none the wiser.

"Oh nothing. We were just trying not to wake you up, but I've got no regrets."

We all lie back down, staring at the ceiling in silence for minutes. When I'm certain my legs won't give out, I get up and go to the bathroom to get cleaned up, with the promise that Crew and Jagger will both still be here when I return.

Once I do, I'm happy to see they kept that promise. They're both back in their clothes. Well, Crew in black boxer briefs, and Jagger in his gray sweatpants. There's a wide space between them, just for me.

I settle in, half sitting, half lying down with my head against the headboard, wearing my tank top and panties. Both guys gravitate toward me. Crew's hand rests on my upper thigh and Jagger's on my stomach as he lies on his side.

There's an awkward silence, so I decide to break it. "Well, boys," I smack my lips, "tonight was fun."

"Anything for you, baby," Jagger says, and I know he means it. They both put all their focus on me, all the time, and it makes me feel so special and loved.

"I'm glad this isn't awkward," I tell them, though I know it is. At least, for me. I try my best to separate our relationships, and tonight, I brought them both full circle for the other to see.

"Nah," Crew mumbles, "why would it be awkward?"

"Good." I slap my hands on my legs. "Then it won't be awkward at all for us to all sleep in here together tonight. I feel so content when you're both here."

"Your wish is our command," Jagger says, his eyes slowly closing.

More time passes and Jagger is starting to doze off. I'm staring at the wall, deep in thought about Neo. I shouldn't be thinking of him right now. Especially not when I have my boyfriends here with me. Or at all, for that matter. Yet, I can't seem to get him out of my head. This whole ultimatum with Jagger has been weighing heavy on my heart and I feel like if I don't address it soon, I'll become resentful and angry. The last thing I want is to hurt Jagger, but I can't stay away from Neo. I just can't.

"What's wrong?" Crew asks, sensing my apprehension. While I've been staring at the wall, he's been staring at me.

I roll to my side to face him, letting Jagger's hand fall since he's now sound asleep.

"Can I be honest with you?" I ask Crew, my face pressed firmly against the same pillow his head is resting on. It's a silly question, because I know I can be honest with Crew. He never judges me.

"Always, babe. What's up?"

"I don't want to hurt you and Jagger or piss you off any more than I already have, but I don't think I can stay away from Neo."

"That's what's bothering you?" His pitch tells me he's surprised it's even on my mind. "Don't worry about that, Scar. Jagger was just being pissy. He knows there's no way you can avoid Neo forever."

His words, while reassuring in some ways, still don't settle the ache in my heart. "The thing is, I'm not talking about just avoiding Neo. I'm talking about being around him. Being part of his life, and him being part of ours."

"Neo isn't going anywhere, and neither are we. We've dealt with that fucker for years and will continue to until we're all six feet under. Hell, the way fate plays its cards, we'll probably all make our exit at the same time. We're boys. We fight, and we make up."

"Wouldn't surprise me. You've all been through a lot together, and I'm certain there's more to come."

His fingers glide lightly down my arm, eyes fixated on mine. "Now I need you to be honest with me."

"Okay." I lick my lips. "No more secrets. I'll tell you anything."

"Do you like him?" he quips, his somber expression never faltering.

"I do." There's no thought process behind it. No bullshit.

I tell him the truth. "I pegged him wrong, Crew. I think we all did."

"Look. Jagger and I know better than anyone what an asshat Neo is, but we also know the shit he's been through. And, between us, we're the only ones who have ever seen the guy cry. He's not as heartless as he wants everyone to think he is. It's sort of why we keep him around."

Just the thought of Neo crying raises goosebumps over my skin. It also makes me really sad. I can almost picture it in my head and it's a heartbreaking sight. Sometimes we forget that those who act tough, are really the ones hurting the most inside.

"He's still an asshat, though." Jagger's words hit my ears and my body jolts, head twisting to look at him.

He's got one eye open, on me. "Sometimes we have to hate him, sometimes we have to love him. But he'll always be an asshat."

When Jagger cracks a smile then closes his eye again, I know he's being sympathetic to the situation, and I admire that about him. He's able to put aside his feelings for the sake of my happiness. There are going to be times when I have to do the same, and that's how relationships work. It's all about compromise.

I can only assume he heard the entire conversation and he didn't argue that I couldn't keep up my end of the deal, so now, I'll curl against his chest, while Crew holds me on the other side, and I'll sleep with peace of mind tonight.

CHAPTER
TWENTY-EIGHT

SCAR

LAST NIGHT WAS everything I needed. I woke up feeling hopeful and happy to have my guys back home, and in my bed. For the first time in a while, I see the light at the end of the tunnel.

Maddie's therapist comes today, so I'm skipping school to stay with her. She's excited to show me the progress she's made. I'm so impressed with how far she's come so quickly. I look forward to the day when she's walking, dancing, going to school and parties. All the things she's missed out on.

Today is also the day I begin easing Maddie into the truth that Crew and I are together. It's going to be a slow process. But eventually, I hope she'll find it in her heart to be happy for us. For all of us.

It's time to be honest. Not just with Maddie, but with myself, too.

Maddie is staying in Crew's room. He wasn't super thrilled about it until I told him he could share a bed with me for now. Then he offered to let her stay the rest of the school year.

"Got lunch," I tell her, pushing the bedroom door open with my foot, a tray resting on both of my hands.

"Oh good. I'm starving."

I set the tray down carefully on her bedside table, then settle in at the foot of her bed. With my legs folded like a pretzel, I curl my hands inside my sleeves. "Mind if we talk while you eat?"

She brings a spoon of chili to her mouth and blows on it. "Not at all."

I clear my throat, breaking eye contact. "There's something I need to tell you, Mads."

"This doesn't sound good."

"It's not terrible, but you might not like it."

The sound of her spoon clanking against the ceramic bowl has me lifting my head. "Honestly, Scar. I don't think there is much you can say to upset me right now. I'm just happy to be alive and well. So whatever it is, just tell me."

I've always loved her optimism. Maddie has a way of lifting everyone's moods. She's the life of the party. The goofball who isn't afraid to make a fool of herself. And the one who always speaks her mind. She's basically Riley in a different body.

When I don't say anything, she pushes harder. "Out with it, Scar. It can't be that bad."

"I'm dating Jagger."

That's not at all what I planned to say, but that's also something she needed to know.

Her neck pulls back, eyebrows pinched tightly. "Jagger Cole?"

I chuckle. "Is there another Jagger?"

"But wait. What about Neo?" she grumbles. "Don't tell me you're cheating on him."

"No." I shake my head rapidly. "No, I'm not cheating on him...because Neo and I aren't actually together. Well, not really. I mean, I like him. I think." My palm plants to my forehead. "Fuck, Mads. I don't know. Jagger and I are together. I think I like Neo. And I know I have a crush on Crew."

There, I said it. It's out there and there's no taking it back.

Saying it all out loud makes me sound absolutely ridiculous. Like someone who has no idea what they want. Maybe I don't.

"Crew?" She gasps. "My Crew?"

I bite my bottom lip and scrunch my nose. "Is there another Crew?"

"No. But really, Scar? You like Crew?"

I pinch my eyes shut and nod in response.

"I knew it."

My eyes shoot open. "You knew?"

She picks her spoon back up and takes a bite of her chili before continuing, "Yup. I knew you liked him since we were kids. And even when he and I were dating, I knew it. I also knew he liked you."

"But you said the same thing about Neo—that you always knew he had a thing for me?"

"I did. And I meant it. I also knew you liked Jagger. I pretty much knew you were hot for all three of them for, like, ever."

Her calmness of the situation is very comforting. I had a feeling she wouldn't react hastily toward me. Maddie doesn't get upset easily and she always tries to see the best in every situation.

"Okay, Psychic Maddie. So what do you have to say about all this?"

"What I always say in any situation. Follow your heart."

I drop my head, hiding my red face as I prepare to ask the next question. "And if my heart leads me to all three of them?" I peek one eye up, then the other.

Her tongue clicks and she sets her spoon back down. "I can't help you there. Only you know how you feel."

Again, just like Riley. For once, I just wish someone would tell me exactly what to do because if I'm left to my own devices, I might fuck my life up and all of theirs.

The subject shifts to Riley and Jude, and I fill Maddie in on everything with them, as well as our talk with Jude last night. Maddie doesn't seem to think Jude is telling the truth, and she has the idea that if she sees him, it could possibly jog her memory. Now we just have to see if the guys agree.

I'm walking down the hall, heading back to my room, when it sounds like someone's banging on the wall behind me. I spin around and backtrack, until the sound comes closer and closer. Next thing I know, I'm standing outside Neo's bedroom.

The door is ajar, so I lean close and listen.

"Stupid fucking son of a bitch." Bang. "You call me worthless." Bang. "You created me so what the fuck does that make you?" Bang.

Oh my god. It sounds like Neo is destroying his wall. I poke my head in slightly and, sure enough, he is. There's maybe five, six holes in the drywall. Blood runs down his arms, dropping on the floor, but he doesn't stop.

"I should fucking kill you." Bang. "You call her a snake—"

"Neo!" I gasp, throwing the door wide open. "Stop it." I

grab a tee shirt off his floor and hurry over to him. He looks at me, but his stare is empty, like he's looking right through me. I grab his right hand and wrap the shirt around it. "What are you doing?"

He doesn't say anything, just watches me with stunned, beady eyes.

I hate seeing him like this. So broken. So angry. So hurt.

Leading him over to the bed, while gripping his hand tightly in the shirt, I say, "Sit down."

To my surprise, he doesn't argue or push me away. He sits down and lets me unravel the blood-soaked tee shirt. "Let's hope you didn't break any bones."

Once I've got it uncovered, I use a corner of the shirt to dab at the open wounds on his knuckles. Neo shrieks, and I flinch, hoping I didn't hurt him too bad. "Sorry."

I keep dabbing gently, cleaning up the blood that continues to seep from the multiple cuts. "What did that wall ever do to you anyways?" It's a joke, and I'm hoping he sees the humor in it. I look up at him, smiling, but it quickly fades when I see his watchful stare. "What?"

He still doesn't say anything, and I'm beginning to wonder if he's in some sort of shock right now. It's starting to freak me out.

While he watches me, I look at his hand, continuing to clean it. "Do you have a first-aid kit?" It's a stupid question because why would Neo have a first aid kit. "Stay right here, okay? I'm gonna go get some Band-Aids from Jagger's bathroom." I'm pretty sure I saw some in there once, along with some antibiotic cream.

I wrap his hand back up and rest it in his lap, then go to stand, but he stops me. With his free hand on my upper thigh, he lowers me back down. "Don't go."

"But you need bandages..."

He swallows hard, lifting his healthy hand. His finger-tips graze softly against my cheek, and he watches the action intently. Sliding his fingers behind my ear, he tucks my hair.

"Neo," I whisper, my voice raspy, my heart pounding in my chest, "I don't want to stay away from you. And I don't want to go."

Moments pass. I'm not sure how many, though, because it also feels like time is standing still.

Neo lowers his hand, resting it over mine in my lap. He looks down at his fidgety fingers. "I'm sorry I hurt you."

His words take me by complete surprise. I've never once, in all the years I've known Neo, heard him apologize for anything. That's why I don't take it as a grain of salt. I soak it in, letting the words wrap around my heart like a web of ivy.

But he doesn't stop there. He turns to face me, lifting a bent leg slightly onto the bed. The shirt around his bloody hand falls to the floor, and he raises that same hand to my cheek, cupping it in his palm. "I don't wanna hurt you anymore."

"I...I don't want you to hurt me anymore either."

I'm not sure what this is. What this feeling inside me means. Seeing Neo so raw gives me this overpowering, desperate need to grab ahold of him and never let go. My stomach swims with warmth, my heart pangs with desire. Every inch of my body feels like it's been set on fire and the only way to distinguish it is...

My train of thought is lost when Neo throws his arms around me, our mouths colliding at the same time. We fall to our sides onto the mattress. His feral eyes land on mine, wide and lustful. He pulls back momentarily, mouth agape, before devouring me again—the taste of stale beer on his lips. Our tongues knot, teeth clank, and our hearts pound into one another's chests.

Neo slides his hand up my shirt and I quiver at his touch.

"I don't wanna play these games anymore, Scar." His words come out raspy and thick. "I don't care where you came from or where you're going, I just want to be there. Be with you."

"Neo—" I begin, but he silences me with his lips. He groans into my mouth, and I swallow it down, along with the words I was going to say—*I need you*.

Has anyone ever told Neo that before—that they need him? I want him to know. He needs to realize he's worthwhile, and he's not the scum his dad continues to make him believe he is. I want to kiss every wound, every scar, and show him that he deserves to be loved. That he's worthy.

His body is like a weighted blanket over mine. His erratic heartbeat is a reminder that he's human and not the robot he pretends to be.

One hand cups my breast, while the other edges the hem of my sweatpants. I'm not wearing any panties, which he soon learns when his hand slides downward.

Head lifted, his tired, sore eyes on mine, he says, "You're so warm. So wet. Do you want me, Scar?"

I nod in response, my teeth digging into my bottom lip. "Yes." I need him to believe it. He needs to know I want him.

The tips of his fingers push inside me, and I open up my legs for him. My hand finds his cheek, laying softly against it, and I guide his mouth to mine. It's not hard, not forced, it's gentle and sweet and a side of Neo I've never seen before.

"You're so beautiful, Scar." His words ignite a new flame inside me.

I'm almost certain I'm the first one to get this part of him and the notion stirs warmth inside my stomach. "And you're so beautifully broken."

He kisses me again, our tongues doing laps inside each other's mouths. "Try to fix me. I dare ya," he challenges me, but his words are more a plea than anything else, and it's one that I willingly accept.

My hand slides up his shirt, skating over the raised scars and rigid abs. I keep moving, until I'm pulling his shirt over his head. The edges of his back tattoos run around to his sides and I trail my fingers over them, wondering what each one means. It's an inked story that I want him to read to me. I want all his pain. All his secrets. I want everything he's willing to give me.

Neo slides his hand out of my pants, and he lifts up, before pulling me up by my hand. My eyes dance across his perfect form. He lifts my shirt over my head, now seeing I'm not wearing a bra. He admires my breasts like a priceless work of art, taking in every detail, every curve, every vein.

He licks his lips, and I find myself doing the same.

As he's watching me, I slide my pants down, showing him how serious I am about this. He quirks a curious brow, but then he follows suit and removes his shorts. I halt, taking a nice long look at his engorged cock.

He's back on his side, shoulder lifted off the bed, while I lie flat on my back with my legs spread for him. I take his hand, placing it at my sex. "I need you," I whimper in a breathless state.

Two fingers round my entrance, before sliding in. My breath hitches, back arched. I close my eyes, only to quickly open them again out of fear of missing a single expression on his face.

Never in my wildest dreams did I think we'd be here. All the pushing, shoving, fighting, hating, and years of pent-up sexual tension...and here we are, bringing every emotion to the surface in a non-combative way.

The gentleness of his fingers inside me are such a tease. I'm desperate for more. I grab his hand—his injured hand that's between my legs—and he winces. But I don't stop. I force him deeper inside me, and when his fingers flex, I keep my hand over his.

Neo trails his lips down my collarbone, sucking and kissing, never missing an inch of my skin. When he reaches my breast, his teeth graze my nipple. My back lifts off the bed and I caress the back of his head, running my fingers through his messy, dark hair.

He moves to the other breast, giving it the same attention.

When his fingers curl, delving deeper and deeper, hitting just the right nerves, I cry out, "Oh god."

He keeps going, digging farther inside me, while adding a third finger. My hips buck up, seeking friction, while moans and whimpers slip through my lips. His mouth moves up to mine, our lips ghosting one another's, and I fill my lungs with each of his exhales.

His fingers pump faster, harder, his bloody, injured knuckles grating against my sex.

My body flushes with heat, every cell on fire, and I cry out as I reach the height of my orgasm. Neo silences me with a searing kiss, and even once I come down, body relaxed, he doesn't stop kissing me. Minutes pass, intensifying this moment, and it's now that I realize, there's no way I'm ever letting him go.

Just the thought of him being with another girl stirs jealousy inside me. The idea of anyone else sharing a moment like this with Neo makes my heart plunge into my stomach. I can't imagine him giving himself to another the way he has me. His raw, wounded, open heart is mine for the taking.

Neo slides on top of me, our kissing never breaking, and on a deep inhale, he slides his cock inside me. My legs spread, making room for him as he settles between my thighs.

Just as he does, he pulls his mouth away, and his head lifts. "I want you to be mine, Scar. Let me protect you and your secrets. Only me. No one else."

It's ironic that those words are even leaving his mouth after the thoughts I just had. Was he thinking the same thing? That the idea of me being with another guy is unfathomable.

But just like I couldn't commit to staying away from Neo, I can't make him a promise that I'll be his and his alone.

His body slides up and down mine, his cock filling me up, then leaving me, only to repeat the process again and again.

"I can't," I tell him honestly. His motions slow, and I elaborate on my response. "I want you, Neo, but I want them, too."

His tongue parts his lips, eyes dancing across my mouth. "Tonight, it's only us. No one else."

I nod because, that, I can agree on.

He moves onto his knees and brings my legs over his forearms, holding them in place, then he picks up his speed again. Each second that passes has him moving faster and faster. His mouth falls open and our eyes lock. I watch every expression and listen to every groan that seeps out of his mouth, taking it all in. And when he pulls out and milks himself on my stomach, covering Jagger and Crew's dried cum from last night, I feel content.

There's a slight moment of panic. A feeling of distrust when I come to terms with the possibility that this was a game to him. He could climb off me and kick me out of his room, while laughing at me and my whorish ways. It's something Neo would do. Fear ripples through me, twisting my stomach into tight knots. But when he leans forward, hands pressed to the mattress on either side of me, and a smile lifts his cheeks, I finally let out the long breath I've been holding in.

He kisses my lips softly then says, "I want to be better, and it starts with you."

CHAPTER
TWENTY-NINE
SCAR

Content. That's how I feel leaving Neo's room this morning. Finally, I see everything clearly. For once, I know exactly what I want.

I want all three of them.

Crew: My childhood crush whose hugs feel like home. He's the one who I know will always be there for me no matter what.

Jagger: My first kiss, who makes me feel adored and wanted. He's got a smile that lights up a room and eyes that melt my soul.

Neo: My villain. The bruised and battered guy who hates everyone, but for some reason, decided he doesn't hate me. I want to fix him. Show him what love can feel like. Then I want to keep him, just the way he is. Dark parts, scars, and all.

Yeah. I want all three of them and I'm not sure I can settle for any less. Never in a million years did I think Neo would make a home in my heart, but today, I think he did. I finally saw him for who he truly is. No masks. No bullshit.

No facade. I saw a guy who's been through hell. Who's lived his life trying to please his father, and finally, he said fuck it. If anything, I'm really damn proud of him. Now I just hope he means it when he says he's ready to take back his life. And even more so, I'm grateful that he believes it starts with me. I have no intention of letting him down.

Once I'm all bundled in my winter gear, I head downstairs to meet everyone, including Maddie. When I reach the bottom, I see her seated in her wheelchair, Neo standing behind her holding the handles. His eyes immediately land on mine, and he bites back a smile, rolls his neck and looks down...then steals another glance.

"You look warm," Jagger says, pressing a kiss to my cheek.

"I am now. Not sure I can say I will be once we're out there." I nod toward the sliding glass doors to the porch that's covered in a good two feet of snow.

"No kidding. It's fucking insane. Makes for a good ride on the sleds, though."

"Victor should be here with the shuttle any minute," Neo says. "I'm gonna bring Maddie out there, so we can get her in once he arrives."

The guys made some last-minute calls to arrange for a way to get Maddie to Jude. Crew and Riley have left already, and they're bringing Jude out of the tunnels. We're all hopeful that seeing Jude will jog some sort of memory for Maddie, and we can finally get some closure.

Deep down, I'm hoping like hell he's innocent, but even if he is, I'm not ready to forgive him for all the shit he put me through.

"We'll be right behind you guys," I tell Neo and Maddie.

Neo pushes her through the kitchen and into the living

room, and I give Jagger my full attention. My arms wrap around his big winter coat, and I lift my chin. "Good morning."

"Good morning, beautiful," he says. "I missed you last night."

I bite my lip, averting my gaze. "Yeah. About that."

"I know," he says, catching me off guard.

"But, how..."

"Crew went to check on you last night and you weren't in your room. He came to my room, thinking you might be there, and when he realized you weren't, we both knew where to find you. Sure enough, we opened Neo's door and there you were, sleeping in his bed."

Holding my breath, I ask, "Are you mad?"

His lips press together, and he shakes his head, still peering down at me. "Nah. You were honest with us. That's all we can ask for."

"Look. I know this whole situation is weird—"

"Are you happy?"

"Yeah." I nod. "Yeah, I am."

"Then that's all that matters."

This time, my head shakes no. "No, it's not. You guys always say that, but my happiness isn't all that matters, yours does, too."

The sound of someone laying on the horn of the shuttle interrupts us, and we both crack up laughing.

"Neo?" Jagger says.

"Oh, for sure. It's definitely not Maddie."

Jagger takes my hand and we leave the house together. Once we're outside, we both laugh at Neo, who's cursing us to hurry up from the driver's seat of the shuttle. "We ain't got all day. Get your asses in here," he hollers.

Some things never change.

After a quick stop at the school to drop off Victor—which is a surprise in itself, since Neo would normally make him walk back—we pull up to The Ruins. As instructed, Riley and Crew have Jude tied to a chair above ground. The snow is still coming down pretty heavy, which means we have to make this quick.

Crew and Jagger get Maddie's wheelchair out and I watch Jude's face for an expression of guilt.

"What are they doing?" Jude asks, panic-stricken.

"You'll see," I tell him.

Once it's in place, under the overhang, Neo comes out of the shuttle carrying Maddie.

"Do you know who that is?" Riley asks Jude.

"That's Neo's twin sister, Maddie Saint."

"That's right," I tell him. "And do you know what happened to her?"

Neo comes closer, his smoldering glare pinned on Jude. Once he reaches the chair, he sets Maddie down. She doesn't take her eyes off Jude as she adjusts herself. Crew stands by with a roll of duct tape and Jagger pats a metal rod to his palm.

"Anything?" Neo asks her.

She doesn't say a word, just leans closer, getting a better look at Jude, while trying to jog her memory. "I've seen you before," she says to Jude, and his eyebrows rise. "I don't know where, but your face is so familiar."

"Where has she seen you before, Beckett?" Neo asks sternly.

Jude opens his mouth, sputters and shrugs, but doesn't answer the question.

Neo reaches into the inside pocket of his leather jacket.

When his hand comes back out, holding a gun, I gasp. Crew and Jagger aren't surprised in the least and I can only assume they all had a conversation about this earlier, but I was not made aware of their intentions here.

"What are you doing?" I ask Neo.

He raises the gun slightly, that void expression on his face again. "Answer the question, Beckett."

Jude's bottom lip trembles as he stutters, "I...I don't know. Here at the Academy, maybe? Or maybe she saw me and my dad somewhere in Essex. I really don't know."

Neo raises the gun higher. "You're lying to me, Jude, and I don't like when people lie to me."

My first instinct is to grab the gun from him, but when I reach out, Crew grabs me by the waist, pulling me back.

"You can't shoot him, Neo!"

Neo looks at me, contempt in his eyes. "He pushed Maddie. Tried to kill her. And now it's time to return the favor."

"I don't know if it was him," Maddie says. "Something doesn't seem right. It doesn't feel right."

Riley cuts in with a shout. "That's because he's telling the truth." In desperation, she pleads with Maddie. "Tell them. Please. It's not him."

Before Maddie has a chance to say anything, we're all taken aback by the low headlights coming toward us.

"Sebastian," I mutter. It's the same ORV he was driving the day he came to bring Neo a key for Crew at the Lawless house.

"What the hell is he doing here?" Crew asks.

Neo lowers his gun quickly, and in an attempt to conceal it, it drops to the ground. Jagger helps him out by kicking it behind Jude's chair. "No fucking clue. But everyone stay cool." Neo steps in front of Maddie, and if he's trying to hide her, he's doing a terrible job. Not that there's any point. Sebastian already saw her.

We all watch intently as Sebastian drudges through the snow with his hands in the pockets of his coat, a smile growing on his face with each step.

"My girl," he says, spreading his arms wide. "I'm so glad to see you're safe."

His lack of surprise is astounding. It has me wondering if he saw us before we came here and had enough time to process the whole scenario.

Sebastian leans down and gives Maddie a hug, but strangely enough, she doesn't reciprocate his excitement for this reunion. "What are you doing here, Dad? Isn't the election today?"

"Nothing is more important than making sure my daughter is safe." With that, he stands tall and reaches into his pocket, his expression folds as he pulls out a gun of his own.

I jump back, hitting Crew, who wraps his arms around me. Everyone scatters, moving away from Sebastian, who is now pointing a gun directly at Jude. Riley clings to Jagger, while I cling to Crew.

Neo grabs the handles of Maddie's wheelchair and pulls her until his back hits the tall cement pillar.

"Mr. Saint. Please." Riley cries out while Jagger tries to hush her. "He didn't do it."

Ignoring Riley's plea, Sebastian grills a petrified Jude. His entire body is shaking while tears, blood, and dirt roll carelessly down his face. "Did you try to kill my daughter?"

"No. No, I swear to God, it wasn't me."

My eyes dance from Sebastian to Neo, then to Maddie.

While Sebastian is glowering at Jude, I see Maddie and Neo engaging in a hushed conversation. I'm not sure what they're saying, but whatever it is has Maddie's chin trembling.

"You're lying." Still holding the gun out, he calls out to Neo, "Neo, bring Maddie over here."

"No," Neo says, "you wanna talk to her, be a man and turn around."

Sebastian, dumbfounded by the response, tilts his head slightly. "Excuse me?"

"You heard me. Be a man and turn around if you wanna talk to her."

Slowly, he lowers the gun, then turns to face Maddie. Once he's facing her, Maddie lets out a whimper, "It was you."

Sebastian chuckles. "You don't know what you're talking about, honey. You're ill."

"No." Her breath catches in her throat. "I remember. Scar had just gone down the mountain and I was angry. Angry with Scar and Crew for kissing." She looks at me. "I remember it all." Her attention returns to her dad. "I was planning to go down and give them both a piece of my mind when I heard someone come up behind me. Just as I turned my head and saw you, you shoved me."

"No!" Sebastian shouts, returning his gun to Jude. "He shoved you!"

"No!" Maddie screams hysterically. "It was you." Tears slide recklessly down her cheeks. "Why did you want to hurt me, Daddy?"

While they're hashing this out, I survey the ground for Neo's gun. My entire body is shaking, and I fear something really bad is going to happen, if one of us doesn't take control of this situation fast.

"I never wanted to hurt you, honey."

Sebastian's admission stuns us all. I cover my mouth with my glove, eyes wide in surprise.

"I thought it was her."

He turns to face me, holding the gun at his side now. My body freezes up. Everything is numb.

He thought it was me?

"She doesn't belong here," he goes on. "This disgraceful, little wench tried to corrupt you and your brother. She was going to hurt you." He's speaking to Maddie, all the while looking at me. "She and Crew were going to hurt you."

"Dad," Neo says, tone low, "Scar isn't the enemy."

Neo's words go right through him as he chokes up. "I never wanted to hurt Maddie. She was at the wrong place at the wrong time. When I saw Crew and Scarlett kiss, I thought it was her in that jacket. I should've known it was this whore."

"Dad," Neo saunters toward him, each step slow and cautious, while his eyes are laser-focused on the gun, "has it been you this whole time? Did you leave the notes?"

"No. That was Jude."

I don't even look at Jude for a reaction. I can't take my eyes off Sebastian and that gun in his hand. There's no telling what he might do.

"I knew he was the perfect person to help me destroy Scarlett. After all, he's her brother. And the son of a bitch who ruined all my plans. Ya know, had you not killed your father, he was going to handle all this mess for me. Years of working with him on a plan to bring down the Sunders and get back his daughter, Scarlett, and you blew it all to hell with one bullet. I know you always wanted to be one of us and never wanted to be one of them. But that'll never happen. You're a half-bred dog, just like Scarlett is."

Jude was right all along.

"That was just one of the hiccups in the road. Don't get me started on your piece-of-shit mother. That bitch was always breathing down my neck."

"What are you saying?" Maddie cries. "What does Mom have to do with this?"

"She overheard something she shouldn't have and I did what I had to do. Just like I did what I had to with Maddie. I just needed to keep her asleep until this was all over. Now I'm sorry she has to see this." He raises the gun and I stare straight into the barrel. My mind goes blank. I freeze under the immense pressure of what I'm supposed to do. If I move, he'll shoot me.

"So now, my game is over, but I'm not going out alone. I'm taking her with me." His words are directed at me, followed by the barrel of the gun pointed right at my chest.

It all plays out like a slow-motion movie, one I never want to rewind and watch again. The sound of the safety going off is deafening, and one I'll never forget. I close my eyes, knowing exactly what's coming, when I hear Neo shout, "Like hell you are!" Then I'm being tackled to the ground, while shrilling screams fill the air.

The gun goes off and I'm not sure where the bullet hits me, but I keep my eyes closed, hoping I leave this earth peacefully. I'm just sorry the people I love had to watch me go.

Seconds pass, and when there's no pain, I open my eyes, wondering if I'm already gone.

The weight on top of me is immense, and when the

voices of others hit my ears, I open my eyes and realize Neo is lying on top of me.

"No." I roll him off, tears welling in my eyes. My breath hitches. "No."

There's blood. Lots of blood. Too much.

I look up and see Sebastian standing over me. Everyone freezes as he presses the gun to my forehead. "You made me hurt another one of my kids."

Then another gun goes off. Only, it's not his. And it's not me that gets hit. Sebastian's eyes go wide, staring blankly at me, then he falls to the ground. Standing directly behind where he stood, is Riley. Her entire body is shaking as she holds the gun out. Her head quivers as tears fall from her shocked eyes.

Jagger hurries over to her and lowers the gun, letting it drop to the ground.

Everyone is hysterically shouting and moving around, but I have no idea what they're saying or where they're going. All I can focus on is Neo.

"Someone call an ambulance," I shout, hugging Neo tightly. "He's bleeding!" I sit up slightly and grab his face. "Look at me, Neo. Keep your eyes open. Don't you dare close them. Don't you dare leave me."

I can't lose him. I just got him. I can't. God, please. Don't take him away from us.

"I'm here," Neo chokes out, cracking a smile, "I'm not leaving you."

Jagger lets Jude go, and he tries to comfort Riley, who's far too shaken up. I should be there for her, and Maddie too, but I can't right now. I can't leave Neo's side until I know for sure he's going to be okay.

The guys concoct a plan to tell the officers, and everyone

else outside of this circle, that Sebastian committed suicide after shooting his son, and leave it at that. They don't need to know any other details. The Elders will do everything in their power to seal this, much like they do for any case that involves a Society member. But if worse comes to worst, Jagger got the whole thing on video. Let's hope it never comes to that.

Minutes pass. Way too many minutes. Flashing lights come into view, but I still don't leave Neo's side. I stay with him until they take him and Maddie away.

A medical examiner comes to the scene, along with a couple officers, and when we don't give enough details about the situation, they demand we go to the station and wait for our parents and our attorneys.

"He's going to be okay," Jagger assures me in the back seat of one of the cruisers. "Neo's the toughest guy I've ever known."

The officers are still talking outside of the vehicle. Riley's beside me, still sobbing and shaking uncontrollably. I'm not sure how she's going to cope with what she had to do, but she saved my life today—Neo, too. I'm forever grateful, and forever in their debt.

Crew reaches his hand back from the front seat and takes mine. "We're all going to be okay. This nightmare is finally over."

CHAPTER
THIRTY
NEO

"You're here," I say to Scar, when her face is the first I see.

"Of course, I'm here. We all are." I lift my head and look at Crew and Jagger, who are at the foot of my bed, and Maddie, who's asleep in the other bed in the room.

"Maddie's here, too," Scar says. "We were able to get you an adjoined room. And Riley. She's in the chair, sleeping beside the window."

I turn my head slightly to the left and see Maddie on her back in the bed, sleeping, and Riley curled in a ball in a chair with a white blanket wrapped around her.

"Well," I say, lifting my feet and my arms, "glad to see I didn't lose any limbs. So where'd it hit me?"

"Shoulder," Crew says. "Just missed the brachial artery. You got lucky. They were able to remove the bullet pretty easily. But you've gotta stay in this hellhole for a couple nights."

I'd hardly call myself lucky, but when that gun was pointed at Scar, I reacted. There's no way I was going to let him hurt her again. My memory is still sketchy, but I remember another gunshot and I remember hoping it was directed at him.

"My father?"

Crew shakes his head no.

"How'd it happen?"

"We'll fill you in on the details later," Scar says, squeezing my hand. "Right now, you need rest."

I drop my head back on the pillow. "Still can't believe this bullshit. Was it really him this whole time?"

"Yeah, I think we're all pretty shocked," Jagger says. "Especially Maddie."

"She came with me in the ambulance. I remember holding her hand."

"Yeah," Jagger begins, "Maddie was brought in because of the missing person's case. The cops questioned her and she told them she woke up and left the home on her own free will. It's far-fetched, but she dared them to try and prove otherwise."

I smile. "Sounds like Maddie."

My eyes start to feel heavy, and when I open them again, time has passed.

"Hey, you," Scar says, still in the same spot she was when I must have dozed off.

I try to sit up, but I'm restrained by all the cords and wires. "Where'd everyone go?"

"Crew and Jagger took Riley back to the house. She's still pretty shaken up. Maddie's still here."

"Hey, loser," she hollers from her bed. "Glad to know you're still alive."

"Can't get rid of me that easily, sis."

"Good. Because you're all I've got now. We need to stick together."

"Bullshit," Scar says. "We're all family now. Me, you, Crew, Jagger, Riley," then she looks at me, "and Neo."

I'm not sure what to say. The asshole in me wants to make a joke or ignore these emotions. The heart inside me, that almost didn't make it, tells me this is a second chance to make things right.

"Yeah," I say, "we're all family." I grab Scar's hand and hold it up, running my fingers over her knuckles. "I'm glad you're here. I've got a lot of apologizing to do and you know damn well I don't like dragging out emotional shit, so I'm just gonna say I'm sorry and then let's move on from—"

She shuts me up with her mouth. Her delicious, beautiful mouth.

When she pulls back with a grin on her face, I say, "Glad we can both agree on that."

"I forgive you."

"You shouldn't, but I'll take it."

IT'S BEEN TWO DAYS, and Scar hasn't left my side. Well, she's used the bathroom, showered here, and gone to the cafeteria a couple times, but only because I've made her. Me, her, and Maddie have played our fair share of UNO and almost every game ended with me throwing the cards because I swear to fucking God, Maddie cheats.

They're releasing Maddie today, and I get to go home tomorrow. After a few phone calls, I got round-the-clock care set up for Maddie back in Essex. I'm going home to recover until after Thanksgiving break, and while I hate to leave when everything is so new with Scar, I know it's best to be with Maddie right now. We're both still dealing with the loss of our dad and while I still hate the bastard, it's still a loss. There's a lot we need to handle back home, so my priorities lie there for the time being. We decided not to honor our father with a memorial service. He doesn't deserve it after all he's done.

Besides, it's only a couple weeks, then Scar and the guys will be back in our hometown, too. Things are going to be different from here on out. I mean, me and my best friends are all dating the same girl, so we sort of have to get along now.

But more than that, I feel different. This really is a second chance, and I have no intention of fucking it up this time around.

"I'm gonna miss you," Scar says, with her head resting on my chest.

"It'll go fast, and once we're together again, nothing is going to break us apart."

Her chest rises and falls against mine, and I savor the sound of each bated breath she takes. I cannot even fathom that I almost lost this girl. She's thanked me dozens of times for saving her life, and Riley, too, but I don't look at it like that. I did what I had to do, and I'd do it again in a heartbeat.

She lifts her head, chin pressed to my chest. "Neo," she whispers. "This is going to sound insane, after everything we've been through, and all the hurt I've felt, but...I think I love you. I think maybe, I always have."

"Not crazy at all, babe. When I woke up in this bed and your face was the first one I saw, I knew I didn't want to go a day without looking at it again." I tuck her hair behind her ears. "I feel different. I feel new. And it's because of you. All these wasted years, I fought against my feelings for you because *he* made me, but now, I think I was just scared because I knew I loved you and I wasn't sure what that love would cost me. But now, I'll pay that price with my life if necessary."

She smiles and it's the most beautiful smile. A very kissable smile. One that's all for me. I lean forward and press my lips to hers. "I love you, too."

CHAPTER
THIRTY-ONE
SCAR

I⊤'s BEEN two weeks since Neo and Maddie left to go back to their home in Essex. Before Neo left, he gave me his phone number with the promise that we'd talk every day. I've definitely held true to that, on top of multiple text and sext messages daily.

To say I'm anxious to see him is an understatement. Crew and Jagger have settled into the idea of me being in a relationship with all of them. They say as long as I'm happy, so are they, and I can't argue with that. Things with each of them is going great. This dynamic, while unconventional, works for us. Never in a million years did I think these three would be my boyfriends—yet here we are. I love all three of them, and without one, I'm not whole.

My parents don't really understand what's going on, but that's fine. They don't need to. No one does. Before these guys came back into my life, I was a shrinking violet, barely getting by. From one day to the next, my petals dropped. They broke me down, just so they could pick me up and make me stronger than ever. And here I am, unbreakable.

I played their games, and I won. My prize: them.

"Two more miles." Crew squeezes my leg. "You excited?"

"Very excited. I'm glad we'll all be together again. It's just a shame Riley had to go back home to her family.

"We'll see her next week when we all go back to the Academy. Besides, she's got Jude."

Oh yes. Jude Beckett, soon to be known as Jude Mitchell. He was able to get in touch with his mom's family and they made the decision to ignore the fact that he's not a full Blue Blood. Kenna's family is from the same town as Riley's, so Jude will be staying in Verdemont with his grandparents before re-enrolling at BCA under his real name. Jude's acceptance is the first step in making some changes within the Society. The guys and I have discussed enacting a new rule that we plan to bring to The Elders. No more blood ties necessary. I doubt it'll pass, but we have to try.

My phone pings with a text, and I drop my head to read it, a smile drawn on my face.

Neo: Hurry your hot ass up.

Me: One more mile.

Neo: Feels like an eternity without you.

Me: Is Neo Saint being…sweet?

Neo: What can I say, you wrecked me in the best possible way.

Me: You're welcome

Neo: Thanks, baby. But seriously. I can't wait to squeeze that tight ass and suck on your big titties.

> Me: Stop it. You're making me blush. But remember, Crew and Jagger are staying at your house, too.

> Neo: Fuck it. I don't even care at this point. Bring them in the room, too. I need you so bad.

> Me: Did I ever tell you that's a fantasy of mine? Don't laugh. And don't say things you don't mean.

> Neo: Who says I don't mean it?

> Me: Promise?

> Neo: I promise I'll do anything to make you happy.

If he doesn't stop talking like that, I'm gonna take him up on his offer. I spent many nights dreaming of being with these guys individually and at the same time. I've had them all on their own, now there's just one more dream to fulfill.

AFTER A LENGTHY REUNION that involved lots of hugs and laughter, I've excused myself to my room because the long day really took it out of me. We're all staying at Neo and Maddie's house during break and joining all our families for dinner tomorrow night. One big, fucked-up family and I honestly wouldn't have it any other way.

As I'm undressing, there's a knock at the door.

"Come in," I say, slipping on one of Crew's old football tee shirts. In the past, saying those words would make me nervous, but everyone in this house is welcome in my room anytime.

I'm a bit surprised, and my expression shows it, when Crew, Jagger, and Neo all step into the room. "What's this?" I wave a hand among them.

"This is me keeping a promise," Neo says, grinning. "I told the guys about your fantasy, and well, we agreed to make it come true."

"Stop it." I blush. "This is insane."

Jagger slides up to me, one hand on my waist. "That's a new look. Is Scarlett Sunder being shy?" he teases.

"I don't know if shy is the word, a bit surprised is more like it. Isn't it too soon for this? We're all still adjusting."

Crew rips off his shirt and tosses it to the floor, before plopping down on my bed and stuffing his hand down his gray sweatpants. "The only thing I'm adjusting is my cock because *you* are smoking hot in my tee shirt."

I bite down hard on my bottom lip. Is this real life? Because if it is, I'm about to have the best sex of my life. In fact, if they're fucking with me right now, they're in for a surprise because there's no way I'm letting any of them leave this room until I've orgasmed.

"All right. I'm not shy. Let's do this." In a swift motion, I peel off the shirt I just put back on. My breasts fall free and all I've got on is a pair of white silk panties.

"Mmm," Jagger hums into my neck, cupping my left breast. "Our girl is in for a treat."

Neo, who's been quiet this whole time, crosses the room and steps behind me. Parting my hair to one side, he kisses the back of my neck, while his fingers run down my back. I draw in a deep breath, inhaling them both. If this is a dream, I want to live in it.

Jagger leans down and takes the bud of my nipple between his teeth, and my breasts perk up on impact. I arch my back and lean my head back slightly, while Neo trails his fingers delicately down my spine.

Working his way down my stomach, peppering me with kisses, Jagger drops to his knees. His hungry eyes peer up at me, while his fingers rim the hem of my panties. A guttural growl climbs up his throat as he tugs them down. He keeps going until they rest around my ankles, and I step out of them, one leg at a time.

My eyes slide to Crew's who's now lying naked in the bed with his hand around his erect cock. He doesn't pump it, just holds it like he's waiting for me. When he winks, butterflies free-fly through my stomach.

Neo is still kissing my neck, leaving no skin untouched. His hands run down my arms, and I lay my head back, feeling his face against mine. He grabs my cheeks and tugs my head back farther, pressing his warm mouth to mine. I take his tongue hostage, tangling it in a web of desire with mine, before he sucks it into his mouth like a piece of sweet candy.

Jagger slides his hand up my thigh, and I part my legs instinctively. His fingers sweep between my folds, and I moan.

I look at Crew again, worried that he feels neglected, and when he pats the side of the mattress, calling me over, I'm certain he does.

I take one step forward, hoping Jagger will heed my cue, but when his lips press to my sex and he sucks the same way he kisses my mouth, I freeze. My breath hitches and I cry out, grabbing a fistful of his hair. He sucks harder, taking my leg and resting it over his shoulder until I'm standing on one foot. Neo holds me from behind, keeping me upright. I lean back into him and he devours my mouth again.

I feel the pressure of Jagger's fingers inside me and my walls clench around them. He hums onto my clit repeatedly, the vibrations arousing me further.

I have to get to Crew, but I succumb to desire when Neo rubs his fingers against my asshole, hitting nerves I didn't know existed. Jagger works his fingers inside me, every few seconds flicking his tongue against my clit.

I lift my head, breaking the kiss with Neo, and my eyes find Crew's again. I raise my hand, curling my fingers, and call him over. He crawls across the bed like an animal, then flings his legs over the side and rolls off. Eating the space between us, he comes up to my side. "Thought you'd never invite me."

He cups my cheeks in his hands and pulls my mouth to his. The sound of Neo spitting grabs my attention, then I feel his wet fingers glide between my ass cheeks again. Using his spit as lube, he circles my asshole, then does it again.

"Get her nice and wet for me," Jagger grumbles into my sex. "I'm taking her from behind."

I'm reminded of my first time with Jagger. His exact words after he asked if I'd been fucked in the ass were, *save that for me. I'm taking it next time.* He never did, but the thought of him taking it now turns me on. I've never done this before, so I have no idea how it will work, but I have no doubt my guys will take the lead.

Each thrust of Jagger's fingers sends me soaring higher and higher, and I fear I'll come before I have a chance to entertain all three of them. I want their orgasms, just as much as they want mine. I want to make all my guys feel good.

Reaching down, I tip up Jagger's chin that's coated in my arousal. He licks his lips, cleaning up the mess I made on him. His fingers draw around his mouth, lustful eyes peering up at mine. "Tell me what you want, baby."

Crew and Neo stop what they're doing, taking a couple steps until they're all in front of me, waiting for me to issue demands.

"Let's move to the bed."

Neo takes my hips from behind and walks me forward, while Crew lies back down on the bed; only this time, his feet are dangling off the end. He reaches for my hand and I give it to him, then he pulls me down on top of him. All the while, Neo and Jagger are taking off their clothes and I have to steal a glance because I'm still in a state of euphoria, having all three of these guys as mine.

It's gratifying to know they don't have any unease with the situation, which is a reminder they've all done this before. I shake away the raging jealousy that picturing them all with another girl stirs inside my stomach.

Crew pulls my head down and whispers seductively in my ear, "We're gonna make you feel so good, babe."

His words send a rush of heat through my core and I tuck my knees, straddling his lap while his dick stands tall against my stomach.

With a lift of my hips, I rise, and when he sets me back down, his cock slides inside me. I draw in a ragged breath, a moan parting my lips on the exhale.

My hands rest on his chest, while he kneads my breasts. "Still so tight and warm, and still mine."

"Easy," Neo hisses a warning, and Crew smirks.

Warm fingers pinch my waist from behind, and I know those fingers—it's Jagger. A glance over my shoulder proves it to be true. He leans forward and presses a soft kiss to my lips. When I notice the tube of lube in his other hand, I know it's for me. My heart jumps, and while I'm a little nervous, I'm more anxious than anything.

Neo crawls on his knees beside me, and when he's at my side, still on his knees, he takes his cock in his hand, that's still covered in cuts from his attack on the wall. I run my fingers down the cut of his poised abdominal muscles. When he starts pumping himself, I gulp. I want to lock the image in my memory forever. Bluish purple veins threaten to burst through his silky-smooth skin. An engorged mushroom head with a bead of precum seeps out, and I want to lick it up. "Mmm," I whimper, just looking at it.

"You want this?" he asks, all growly and confident.

I press my lips together and nod before saying, "Yes, please."

I'm regarded with a smirk as he climbs to his feet, a slight bend to his legs. "Open wide."

My tongue sweeps across my lips, and I do as I'm told. His head circles my mouth, saltiness trickling on my tongue.

He eases his way in and I wrap my hand around his lower half, then drag my tongue up and down his length, before taking him to the back of my throat.

Sliding back and forth on Crew, his cock fills me up, and I feel his head bobbing inside my stomach. Strong hands caress my breasts while Neo gets a firm grip on my hair. He tugs my head back slightly, coercing my eyes on his while I suck him off.

"I'm gonna lube you up now." Jagger's voice comes from behind me.

He gives my back a gentle push forward, and Neo

accommodates him by crouching down farther, his cock never leaving my mouth.

Once Jagger has me at a good angle, warm gel dribbles between my ass cheeks, and he massages around it, prepping me.

My heart hammers in my chest, but I try not to focus on how huge his dick is or the small space it's about to squeeze into. Instead, I put all my attention up front, where Crew is riding me from underneath and Neo is watching me work my mouth around him.

"You ready?" Jagger asks, and my only response is a nod.

My eyes widen, and I take Neo out of my mouth and stroke him with my hand.

"Look at me, babe," Crew says, turning my cheek, "just watch me."

I do as I'm told and focus on his eyes and the gentleness of his motions beneath me. We're taking it slow, which is nice because, any faster, and I might come before they do—which I'm sure is their goal.

Jagger pushes my back again, forcing an arch while he puts pressure on my hole with one of his fingers. He slides it in slowly, and I wince. There's a sting of pain at first, but nothing unbearable. In fact, once he pushes deeper, the sting is replaced with a hint of pleasure.

I keep watching, all the while sliding my hand up and down Neo's erection.

Jagger takes his finger out and lines the head of his cock up, and I take in a deep breath as he enters me. "You okay?" Neo asks, and I nod. He turns my head slightly and tips my chin before pressing his mouth to mine. As Jagger slides in more, I pant into Neo's mouth with each thrust I'm given.

Once his head is in, I relax, and Neo returns his cock to my mouth.

Crew picks up his pace, his hips rising and falling underneath me.

Jagger also picks up his movements, giving me just the tip of cock, which is enough for me. He grabs my hips from behind, bracing himself as he guides himself in and out. "So fucking tight, baby. I'm gonna fill your asshole with my cum, okay?"

I don't respond. I can't. I can barely think as my hormones take control.

Every nerve in my body is heightened. Any pain I felt before has been replaced with immense pleasure. My eyes shift to Crew, whose chest is rising and falling rapidly as he thrusts into me. His mouth gapes open and the tip of his tongue darts out.

My only regret right now is that I can't look at Jagger. He's so far away, yet so close as he pinches my hips and delves deeper and deeper inside me.

With three holes full of the men I love, I reach a point of contentment. Everyone picks up their pace at the same time, ramming at each entrance, and I take everything they're giving to me.

"Oh god," I moan around Neo's cock. I take one hand off Crew's chest and position it between Neo's legs, cupping his balls.

Neo gets a firmer grip on my hair, tugging my head back just enough so he can see my face. "Our girl knows how to suck a cock, boys."

"Hell yeah, she does," Crew retorts.

"If you could see the view from back here," Jagger grumbles, then slaps my cheek hard. "Fuck. She's tight." My body jolts and the moan that slips out of my mouth entices the guys to fuck me harder.

Neo's balls tighten in my palm. I put my other hand on the bottom half of his cock and stroke as he drives it in and out of my mouth. "I'm gonna come down your throat, Scar. That okay?" he asks, and I nod.

His head hits my tonsils, and I hold my breath as warm liquid shoots down the back of my throat. Neo keeps moving, grunting as he continues to release. "Ah fuck. You suck so good." He pumps his cock a few more times, giving me every last drop, and I swallow it down before exhaling. Once I do, he pulls out and immediately covers my mouth with his.

He kisses me hard, putting pressure on the back of my head. He doesn't stop as Jagger rams into me faster from behind, and Crew takes me from underneath. I whimper into Neo's mouth, using it to muffle my sounds as I cry out. He inhales each heady breath, swallowing down my moans. I'm on the brink of explosion. To the point where I'm not sure I can take any more because the feeling is so over-whelming.

Tingles scatter through my body. My core tightens and I draw in a deep breath. I clench my walls, squeezing Crew's cock, and my ass flexes, needing more of everything they're giving to me. My eyes roll into the back of my head from the immense pleasure.

"Ugh. Oh god. I'm gonna..."

"Come for us, Scarlett." Jagger's words hit my ears at the same time Crew's do.

"Fuck, I'm coming." He lifts up, holding my waist as he pounds into me. Jagger moves to the same rhythmic motion as Crew, filling me up from both ends.

My hands clutch both sides of Neo's head, and I squeeze. We're no longer kissing, just holding our mouths together.

Jagger grunts behind me, and I reach back, needing to feel him. He puts his hand in mine and squeezes as he comes. He thrusts a few more times before slowing his motions.

Crew relaxes back on the bed, steadying his breaths, and I drop my head back.

"You did amazing," Neo says, kissing my lips one more time. I never in a million years thought Neo would praise me for anything, and now that he has, I'm desperate to hear it again.

"Fuck yeah, she did," Crew says.

"Hold your breath, babe," Jagger instructs me as he slides himself out of me.

I immediately fall forward on Crew, cloaking his body with mine. "Don't ask me to get up for at least ten minutes."

Jagger rubs my back softly, and Neo drops down on his back about a foot from where I'm lying on Crew.

Nothing about tonight has felt awkward, and it gives me hope that this thing we have going on really can work. No. It *will* work, because I can't imagine my life without all three of these guys in it. They have my heart now.

"Good morning," Neo whispers against my hair.

A glance to my left shows that Crew is the one holding me on the other side. "Where's Jagger?"

"He dipped out in the middle of the night and Crew took his spot. A schedule might be needed in the future."

I chuckle under my breath. "That's not a bad idea."

"You still tired?" he asks, and I shake my head no. "Maddie's cooking breakfast."

My forehead creases. "Maddie's cooking?"

"She's got help in the kitchen, but yeah. Want me to bring some up to you?"

"That's okay. Why don't we all go down and eat?"

He kisses my forehead. "If that's what you want."

I adore these guys for always putting me first, but at some point, they have to realize that they come first, too. Until then, I'll soak up all the spoiling.

Neo has been the most attentive person ever. It still blows my mind. Everything I need, or want, he's there. When I just want to talk, he listens. The thing that really warms my heart is knowing that it's only for me. A leopard can't erase his spots, but that doesn't mean I can't bring him home and make him my pet. I know Neo will still be an asshole on many levels, and I don't want him to change who he is, but he's got a soft spot now, and it's saved just for me.

It makes me so sad to think that this could have all been our reality years ago, had Sebastian not tried to ruin it for us. But that's okay. He's gone, and now we have all the time in the world.

Crew stretches beside me and a few minutes later, Jagger comes barging in the door, taking no care to keep quiet. "Wake up. Breakfast is ready."

"We're up, shithead," Crew grumbles, rubbing his tired eyes as he sits up.

I run my fingers down the scratches I left on his back last night. I had no idea I dug into him that bad. He winces, and I say, "Sorry."

Turning around, the corner of his mouth tugs up and he

leans forward. "Don't be. I'm not." He kisses my lips and my body relaxes.

The guys disperse and I get dressed and brush my teeth then meet them in the dining room.

"Smells delicious," I say to Maddie.

But it's Jagger who responds with, "Thanks."

"Wait," I side-eye him, "you're the one who was helping her cook?"

He brings his hands to his chest. "Is that surprising? I can cook."

I pinch my fingers together. "Little bit."

Jagger pulls out a chair for me and gestures for me to sit down, so I do, and he takes the seat beside me while Crew sits to my right.

"This is nice," I tell them all, when Neo and Maddie join us on the other side of the table.

Neo reaches for a pancake, and when he drops it on his plate and begins pouring syrup on it, we all stop what we're doing. I know why I stopped, but I thought for sure I was the only one who ever noticed that Neo doesn't eat in front of others.

His fork presses down as he cuts a triangular piece then he pops it in his mouth. When he lifts his head, he realizes we're all looking at him, so we resume filling our plates.

"What?" He huffs. "You all act like you've never seen a guy eat before." He stuffs another piece in his mouth.

Of course, it's Crew who responds. "Uh. Yeah. Because you never eat in front of anyone. Even us."

Neo shrugs his shoulders. "That was before."

"Before what?" Jagger asks. "The gunshot?"

"No," he retorts, pointing his fork at me with a lopsided grin. "Before her." He winks and my heart swells.

We eat breakfast, talking about anything and everything with full mouths, and when we're done, we clean the table together.

I'm setting a stack of plates in the sink when Neo comes up behind me. His hands rest on my hips, and he whispers in my ear, "Leave that for the housekeeper. I wanna show you something."

I pivot around to face him, giddiness in the pit of my stomach. "Like a surprise?"

"Something like that." He takes my hand, leading the way. We stop at the garage door, and he tells me to bundle up, so I put on my winter coat and boots. Then we step out into the garage, where all the Saint family 'toys' are, and also where Crew and Jagger are sitting in the back seat of a Gator. "What's going on?" I ask them, suspiciously.

Neo jumps in the driver's seat and says, "Hop on."

I'm feeling really confused as we pull out of the garage. It's snowing like crazy, and I'm freezing my ass off, but the adrenaline pumping through me has me sweating bullets.

Fifteen minutes, and three dozen questions later with no answers, and we're driving through Jagger's family property.

I don't bother asking because it'll get me nowhere. Instead, I keep my mouth shut and enjoy the ride.

That is, until I realize we're heading onto my property. "Wait, this isn't Jagger's property anymore."

Jagger leans forward, his chin pressed to my shoulder. "I beg to differ, but we won't start that argument again."

The memories flood me all at once.

"What in the world, Scar?" A guy's voice rings into the small space.

I gasp. "Jagger?"

"*Yeah. It's me.*" He pushes himself up, and I reclaim my spot against the far wall.

"*How'd you know I was here? Better yet,* why *are you here? Shouldn't you be at the movies with 'everyone who's anyone'?*" I air-quote the words used by Neo earlier, when he was pleading his case to Maddie on why she should go with them instead of roller skating with me.

"*Gimme a minute.*" He drops down against the opening and rubs his forehead, babying the spot where I kicked him, if you'd even call it that.

"*Oh, come on. Don't act like I hurt you. I was merely tapping your forehead. Didn't even put any force behind it.*"

"*It didn't hurt at all.*" He picks at his forehead and I'm unsure why. "*But you had gum on the bottom of your shoe.*"

I fight back laughter. "*Oh. Well, it serves you right for invading my space.*"

"*Your space?*" He squints. "*Since when?*"

"*Seriously?*" I glare. "*Since my dad had it built for me on our property.*"

Jagger laughs, running his sticky fingers on a floorboard while trying to wipe the gum off. "*What are you talking about? This is my family's property.*"

"*Shut up.*" I snort, though it's not the least bit funny. Sure, the Coles' family property butts up to ours, but we've got over twenty acres, and there's no way my dad would build my tree-house on the wrong property.

"*You're wrong, baby Scar.*" He tips his chin confidently. "*Last year I walked our property lines with my dad and my uncle and this treehouse is, in fact, on Cole land.*"

I run my hand down my face, watching him carefully to see if he's joking, but he looks dead serious.

Finally, he laughs. "*I'm just messing with you. It's on your property, but you haven't been out here in ages, so I sort of took over it."*

"You can't do that," I spit out. "This is private property."

He drops down, legs bent and hands dangling over his knees. "Oh yeah? You gonna tell your daddy on me?"

"Maybe I will."

I never did tell on him. Never planned to. Not long after that day, my treehouse was gone. All the memories, up in smoke. Neo destroyed it in an attempt to ease his pain, and now, I really hope it helped him in some way.

Neo brings the Gator to a slow roll before coming to a stop. He reaches over and grabs a bandana sitting in the slit of the dash. Holding it up, he says, "Turn your head."

I do as he says but peg him with questions while he covers my eyes with the old, musty cloth. "Why are you blindfolding me? Where are we going? What's this about?"

Someone helps me out, who I think is Crew, based on the soft hand touching my skin.

We walk a few steps, the guys keeping quiet the entire time. Snow rides up my pant leg and I don't even bother to shake it free because I'm too curious as to where we're going.

Finally, we stop. Gloved hands come up behind me, and I know it's Neo, because he's the only one wearing any. Then the blindfold drops. "Surprise," Neo says.

My mouth falls open when I see the biggest, most beautiful, most spectacular treehouse I've ever laid eyes on. Two stories with an arch as high as the trees surrounding it. There's a staircase with lights strung around the banister, and even a small balcony. It's any treehouse lover's dream. It's my dream.

"Oh my god. This is..." I turn to face Neo, then look at Jagger and Crew. "You guys did this for me?"

Jagger slaps a hand to Neo's shoulder. "It was his idea."

"No big deal." Neo shrugs. "I was home for two weeks and needed something to do, and I had a little help from some builders, but I did a lot of the leg work myself."

Without thinking, I throw myself into Neo's arms and sob like a baby. "Thank you."

It might not mean much to a lot of people, but these guys know how much my old treehouse meant to me. It was my sanctuary. It holds so many of my firsts, and now I get to start new ones with my guys. Granted, we're older now and probably won't be here much, but it symbolizes a new start, for all of us, together.

EPILOGUE
SCAR

WHEN I FIRST ARRIVED AT BCA, I was pissed at the world. I hated these boys for luring me to this place. My fists were locked, and I was ready to fight, but each and every time I fought back, I watched as I slowly lowered the walls each one of these guys built around themselves. In doing so, I realized mine were coming down, too.

It's been a very long nine months, but now that it's over, I wish I could go back and do it all over again. Okay, maybe not all of it. Or any of it for that matter.

No. I'm glad it's over, and I'm ready for us to get the hell out of here and begin the next chapter of our story.

"Scarlett. Honey," Mom says, inserting herself into my arms. "I'm so proud of you." She steps back and looks at my friends—Riley, Maddie, Crew, Jagger, and Neo. "I'm so proud of all of you."

"Thanks, Mom." I look at my dad, who's got his arms spread wide, and I run into them. "I love you, Dad."

He kisses the top of my head and says, "I love you, too."

Crew's talking with his parents about his plans to play

football at BCU, and they're overjoyed, laughing and chatting. I'm watching him smile, feeling like my heart could burst at the seams when he turns his head, catching my stare. He winks, sending a swarm of butterflies through my stomach, then resumes conversing with his mom and dad.

Jagger's dad approaches us, all stern and serious, and he clears his throat upon his arrival. "Congratulations, son." He pats his hand on Jagger's shoulder. "Still holding a 4.0 after everything you've been through is pretty remarkable. It's not a 5.0, but we take what we can get."

Any moment of happiness Jagger had quickly diminishes from his face. I step forward, putting a hand on Jagger's arm. "Jagger is actually the class valedictorian, which means he's the best in his class. I'd say it's more than remarkable."

"Valedictorian, huh?" His dad huffs. "You never mentioned it."

"Didn't think you'd care."

"Of course I care. Your education is my top priority."

Jagger sighs heavily. "Yes, Dad. I know. It's the most important thing in the world to you. I get it."

The tension thickens around all of us, and while everyone else excuses themselves from this conversation, I stay at Jagger's side for moral support. His dad is so hard on him and I know it takes a toll on Jagger's mental state.

"Close second." Mr. Cole continues, "You, my son, are the most important thing in the world to me."

Jagger's head draws back, surprised at his dad's admission. "I am?"

His dad throws an arm around Jagger's neck and rubs the top of his head, chuckling. "Of course you are. I'm only hard on you because I know what you're capable of. So," he steps back, looking at his son, "what are your plans after this?"

Jagger looks at me, then his dad, and he shares with him the same plan he shared with me. "Think I'm gonna give law school a shot after my four years at BCU."

We all go silent, awaiting Mr. Cole's response. He's always had big dreams for Jagger to work with him at his company.

After a lengthy bout of anxiety-riddled tension, he says, "I think that's a great plan."

When Jagger smiles, I take it as my cue to give them their moment. Jagger really needed this and I couldn't be happier for him—for all of us.

That is, until Neo and Maddie are standing off to the side, watching while our families reunite and congratulate us on our graduation. My heart splinters in two. I wave my hand at them. "Get over here, you two."

Neo strolls leisurely with his hands in his front pockets, while Maddie walks briskly ahead of him.

My mom and dad gather around us, my dad with his arm wrapped lovingly around my mom. "Neo and Maddie," Mom says, "I wanted to invite you both over for dinner tomorrow night to celebrate graduation. What do you say?"

"Absolutely," Maddie beams with excitement, while Neo shrugs his shoulders and gives a less than enthusiastic, "Sure."

It's so Neo. He might have softened a little, but it's only for me. He's still the same person, and I wouldn't change a single thing about him.

"So, what's next for you two?" Dad asks Neo and Maddie. "Planning to go to BCU with Scar and your friends?"

"Yes, sir," Maddie responds coyly.

"That's the plan," Neo says, while sharing a look with his sister. "Getting our degrees then using every cent of our dad's money to invest in our future PI firm."

Neo, Maddie, and Riley had the grand idea of starting their own PI firm one day. I actually think it's a great idea. They've got the investigative skills and the money from Sebastian's estate to do it, plus enough to live comfortably for a very long time.

I, on the other hand, plan to be their business manager. These are all hopes and dreams, and plans can change, but I have no doubt wherever life takes us, we'll be there together.

Once we've all broken apart from our families and we're gathered in front of the bleachers on the football field, Crew takes his cap off and holds it out, gesturing for us to do the same.

I follow, then Riley, then Maddie, then Jagger, and finally, Neo.

"Get over here." Riley waves Jude over to our circle. He's been hanging around again since his name has been cleared. The guys are still hesitant to trust him, but he and Riley have gotten close, though she's made it clear she only wants to be friends.

"On the count of three," Crew says, "Boulder Cove University, here we come."

We all count together. "One. Two. Three." Then we shout louder, "Boulder Cove University, here we come."

Neo steps back and puts his cap back on. "Here's to hoping next year's Lawless members aren't as big of dicks as we are."

"Bring on the new and older boys." Riley claps her hands excitedly. "I'm so ready."

The End.

If you liked this series, check out the Wicked Boys of BCU!
That's right! We're going back to Boulder Cove!
Book one. We Will Reign, is coming March 10th!
Preorder Now!

Also by Rachel Leigh

Bastards of Boulder Cove

Book One: Savage Games

Book Two: Vicious Lies

Book Three: Twisted Secrets

Wicked Boys of BCU (Coming March 2023)

Book One: We Will Reign

Book Two: You Will Bow

Book Three: They Will Fall

Redwood Rebels Series

Book One: Striker

Book Two: Heathen

Book Three: Vandal

Book Four: Reaper

Redwood High Series

Book One: Like Gravity

Book Two: Like You

Book Three: Like Hate

Fallen Kingdom Duet

His Hollow Heart & Her Broken Pieces

Black Heart Duet

Four & Five

Standalones

Guarded

Ruthless Rookie

Devil Heir

All The Little Things

Acknowledgments

Readers: Thank you so much for reading Vicious Lies!

I want to give a big thank you to everyone who helped me along the way. My alpha reader, Amanda and my beta readers, Erica and Amanda. To my amazing PA, Carolina, thank you for all you do. Thanks to Rebecca at Rebecca's Fairest Reviews and Editing for another amazing edit and proofread, as well as Rumi for proofreading. To my street team, the Rebel Readers, I love you all so much and I'm so grateful for all you do. Thanks to The Pretty Little Design Co. for this amazing cover! And to all my Ramblers, thanks for being on this journey with me.

xoxo-Rachel

ABOUT THE AUTHOR

Rachel Leigh is a USA Today bestselling author of new adult and contemporary romance with a twist. You can expect bad boys, strong heroines, and an HEA.

Rachel lives in leggings, overuses emojis, and survives on books and coffee. Writing is her passion. Her goal is to take readers on an adventure with her words, while showing them that even on the darkest days, love conquers all.

www.rachelleighauthor.com
Rachel's Ramblers Readers Group

Printed in Great Britain
by Amazon

19316861R00192